RETURN TO THE BLACK FARM

ELIAS WITHEROW

THOUGHT CATALOG Books

THOUGHTCATALOG.COM
NEW YORK • LOS ANGELES

Published by Thought Catalog Books, an imprint of the digital magazine Thought Catalog, which is owned and operated by The Thought & Expression Company LLC, an independent media organization based in Brooklyn, New York and Los Angeles, California.

This book was produced by Thought Catalog Books. Cover by Rebecca Coverrs.
Visit us on the web at thoughtcatalog.com and shopcatalog.com.

Made in the USA.

ISBN 978-1-949759-11-2

Return To The Black Farm

ELIAS WITHEROW

This book is dedicated to Gene Witherow
For your endless kindness.
Thank you for showing me how to be a good man.
I miss you, papa.

Chapter 1

The Black Farm lay in ruin. Smoldering earth exhaled wafts of smoke that curled up toward an empty gray sky. Rock tumbled from what remained of the great mountain. The forest shuddered and shook clouds of ash from its swaying canopy. The ocean gasped and the poisonous waters rippled with darkness. Rain cooled the island, but it did not put out the fire that had been started. That had been put into motion.

"Nick."

I didn't move, my body aching with all the pains of hell. My clothes were filthy and stuck to my skin. My head thundered. Water ran down my face, pulling at the dark bags beneath my eyes.

"What have you done?"

I stared up at the sky, skull splitting in agony. The dead sun had been detonated. The island had been fractured. The heavens had been silenced. The world at my back tensed at my presence—a rage building.

I had done this. I had set this in motion. I covered my hands with my face. I closed my eyes. The Pig Born roared around me, great howls of anger and disbelief. They closed in. They pressed tight. I could smell them. Mud. Filth. Evil.

"The Pig," I whispered, refusing to open my eyes. The growls around me grew.

"The Pig did this."

Something grabbed my shoulder.

"The Pig did this," I hissed again, darkness clouding my head.

Sharp teeth snapped closed, spraying warm spittle across my face.

My fists shook at my sides, teeth clenched. "Leave me alone."

Hooves and mangled hands grasped at my beaten body, the mob growing hungry.

"Leave me alone!" I screamed.

Silence. All the silence in the world. It bled into my ears and pressed everything out. The darkness behind my eyelids seeped into the void, and I felt myself falling. Falling into a hole so deep I knew I would never reach the bottom.

A voice. A voice calling down to me from high, high above.

"Did you really think you could just walk away from all this, Nick?"

I snapped my eyes open, gasping, sweat coating my forehead. I blinked in a panic trying to get my bearings.

"Hey, take it easy."

I looked across at my psychiatrist, her eyes large and worried behind her thick glasses. She leaned forward in her chair, one hand outstretched as if to catch me. I closed my eyes and leaned back on the couch I was on, dragging my hands down my face.

"Are you OK? Should we stop?" Noelle asked, concerned.

I shook my head slowly. "No. No, I'm OK."

"What did you see?"

I looked down at my hands and saw they were shaking. I said nothing and felt my stomach roll. I clutched it and felt sick.

Noelle leaned back and scribbled something in her notebook. After a moment, she looked up at me again, the wrinkles around her eyes bunching with curious worry.

"You don't have to talk about it right now, but it would help a lot if you could tell me something, anything. This is the third time you've come here. I want you to know this is a safe place. It's just you and me. I'm here to help you. I *want* to help you."

I nodded without looking at her. "I know you do. I know."

"Do you want to try something new?"

"Sure."

She closed her notebook and set it aside. Folding her hands, she lowered her voice. "You don't have to tell me what happened. What the source of all this is. If you're not ready for that, that's OK. We're going to try some word association to help hone in on what's really bothering you. Is that all right?"

I nodded, holding my stomach.

"Good. Close your eyes. That's right. Take a deep breath, Nick. In and out. Wonderful. Remember, whatever hurt you or whatever you've done... it's not here in this room with us. It's just you and me. Remember that. I'm going to say a word and I want you to say the first thing that pops into your head. Don't even think about it. You ready?"

"Yeah..."

Her voice was gentle. "Family."

"Life."

Noelle pressed forward without pause. "Parents."

"Irrelevant."

"Love."

"Jess."

"Marriage."

"Pain."

Noelle paused and I almost opened my eyes, but she continued before I could.

"Death."

"Meaningless."

"Violence."

"Axe."

"Farm."

I snapped my head up, eyes alight. My heart raced with a sudden surge of adrenaline. My voice came out slow and cold. "What did you say?"

Her face remained completely neutral. "The next word was 'farm.'"

I held her gaze. "Why would you say that?"

"Is that word upsetting to you?"

"*Why* did you say that?"

Noelle patiently reached for her notebook and flipped through the pages. "It was something you said in our first session. Ah, yes, here it is." She cleared her throat. "I asked where you lived and you said outside the city in the country. I asked if you worked on a farm and you said..." her finger traced down the page, "never in a million years."

My throat tightened. "So what?"

She shrugged. "It seemed like you had a pretty strong opinion on the matter. That interested me."

"I think I'm done for today, Noelle," I said, starting to stand, but she motioned for me to stop.

"Hold on, hold on. Please. Sit back down...please."

Hesitantly, I did so.

She smiled at me, a warm expression that eased some of the tension in my shoulders. "You came to me for a reason, right?"

I forced myself to relax. "Yeah...I did."

"Can you tell me what that is? What you hoped to achieve by coming here?"

I shook my head, guts still squirming. "I don't know what I expected, honestly."

"Something's troubling you, isn't it?"

In my mind's eye, I saw myself standing before the Pig, its creaking maw opening to reveal a cavern of darkness.

"Yeah," I said softly. "there's a couple things."

"You have a family, right? A wife and little boy?"

"Mhmm."

"How old is your son?"

"Just turned one."

"What's his name?"

A small smile found my lips. "Theo."

Noelle crossed her arms. "Do you have a picture of him? Do you mind if I see?"

"Yeah, sure," I said, digging for my phone. I pulled it out and brought up a photo from last week when I took Jess and Theo to the park. Jess was beaming, her beautiful blue eyes gleaming with life. She held our son in her arms, his chubby face turned to greet the camera with a wide, innocent smile. A tuft of blond curls fell into his eyes.

"He's adorable," Noelle grinned.

"He's a handful," I responded fondly, putting my phone away.

"Do you worry about being a good father?"

I stared past her, at the wall. "Sure. Doesn't every dad?"

"Some don't."

"Yeah, well…"

"It's good that you do," Noelle pressed. "The fact that you're here, confronting whatever it is that's bothering you, it means you're *trying*. Probably for him, right? You want to be the best you can be for your son? I haven't known you long, but I can tell you're a good person. That's better than most."

I looked down at my hands. "I'm not sure I'd describe myself as a good person."

Noelle stared at me intently. "What makes you say that?"

A flash from the back of my mind. Blood. Screaming. An image of myself at the top of a mountain, covered in dripping red and smiling like a madman.

"I've done...things. Things I'd rather not remember."

Noelle picked her notebook back up. "And why did you do those things?"

Another flash. Jess in the basement of a stone temple, chained and bruised, our eyes meeting.

"To protect someone I loved," I whispered.

Noelle's tone softened. "Let me ask you something."

"OK."

"Say someone broke into your house and had your wife at gunpoint. Or your child. Imagine the intruder standing over him. Over Theo. Your baby is crying. He's scared. He needs his dad and you know the only way to save him is to kill the assailant. What would you do?"

I felt a twist of something long-buried rise in the back of my throat. "I'd rip his throat out." I paused and blinked, surprised by my own words. I looked away and pressed the sensation back down into the pit I had buried it.

Noelle tapped the end of her pen against her lips, her eyes exploring my face. "Why did you turn away?" she asked quietly. "I would expect any father to give me that exact answer."

I didn't respond.

"Are you afraid of violence, Nick?"

My lips compressed into a thin white line. “No.” I closed my eyes. “I don’t know…”

Noelle scribbled something down and then closed her notes. “I think we should probably stop here for now. Whether you know it or not, you’ve made some big steps today.”

I snorted. “Oh yeah?”

She nodded. “I’m proud of you. Don’t give up on yourself or on this. I can help you. I want to help you.”

“Right...right…” I muttered, standing. “Same time next week, then?”

“I’ll mark you down.”

“Thanks, Noelle.”

She surprised me then by embracing me in a hug, her voice gentle “Remember what I said, Nick. You’re one of the good guys. Don’t forget that.”

Awkwardly, I hugged her back. “Uh, sure. I won’t. Thanks.”

I left her office and went to my car, my mind a cluster of conflicte thought. The evening air was cool across my face as I walked across the park- ing lot, hands jammed into my pockets. An array of looming buildings ros around me and reflected the setting sun, turning the world orange. I got m keys out and slid into my car, closing the door behind me. I placed my hand on the steering wheel but couldn’t bring myself to start the engine. I lean back against the headrest and exhaled wearily.

You’re one of the good guys.

“Right,” I whispered to no one.

I collected myself enough to pull out of the lot and point my car in th direction I knew Jess and Theo were. Home. Just the three of us, nestle into our cozy country house, surrounded by an ocean of swaying fields an peaceful quiet.

As I crept through the city traffic toward the suburbs, I tried to silenc my thoughts. They trickled with uncertainty and worry, an anxious jumb of doubt and responsibility. A horn blared behind me and my knuckles we white around the wheel. I eased the car along with the rest of the rush-ho parade and knew I couldn’t go home like this. Not yet. I checked my mirro and then banked left down a side road. I needed a drink. Just one to cal my nerves. Digging up the past, confronting it once again, sifting throug the mental wreckage...

I tried my best not to think about what happened back then. Back when all I could see and feel was the suffocating hell I had gone through with Jess. The impossible trials we had overcome. The shadow of that *place*.

It hadn't been easy. Nothing about coming back had been easy. There were stains and scars that would never leave us. The things we had done, the shock of making it through, the toll it had taken...it was a mountain the two of us had to climb together. Pretending like everything was going to be OK wasn't enough. We needed help. We needed each other, now more than ever. We were the only ones who could possibly understand what the other had endured.

Almost immediately after our return, I had married Jess. It had been a small wedding, but it didn't matter. I loved her with everything in me. I couldn't imagine ever being away from her again. She was my anchor in this second life. This new opportunity to do it all again, without all the misery.

And we were doing it. Despite the odds, we had managed to crawl far enough away from the past that we found happiness once more. Contentment. Peace. We got new jobs, threw some fresh paint on the walls, and gritted our teeth when the memories resurfaced. And they did. We couldn't escape them. We couldn't avoid the shocking horror of our escape.

We could never forget the Black Farm.

There were nights I'd wake up in a cold sweat, curled into myself, sobbing and shaking uncontrollably. Jess was always there to hold me, stroke my hair, and tell me it was OK. That we were safe. That we weren't there anymore. I so badly wanted to put it all behind me, to recover, to be better, but the trenches of darkness ran deep along the surface of my mind.

Jess healed in her own way. I was careful around her. Observant. She didn't suffer the nightmares like I did. She took pills for that. She would just go perfectly still. We could be doing anything and I'd see her slow to a stop and just stare out at nothing. Her face would go pale and I knew she was remembering. When she did this, I would hug her tightly against me and whisper soothingly into her ear. I told her no one would ever take her away or hurt her again. That I'd die first.

I shut down the memories and tried to think about nothing. My head clouded with gray and I let it soak through me. Ten minutes later, I found myself sitting on a bar stool with a drink in hand.

The establishment was quiet, a fact for which I was thankful. A few young couples were nestled in booths, eating dinner, conversing in muted tones. I scanned their faces and my eyes traveled to the corner where a lone man sat smoking a pipe, our eyes locking. He smiled and I looked away. At the counter, I raised my glass to my lips and listened to the ice cubes clink loudly against one another. The alcohol was cold and it dampened the wildfire in my mind.

Jess. Theo. My family. The reality was jarring. Even before our plummet into the Black Farm, I had never really considered myself a family man. It was just something that had happened. Jess and I both knew we needed to try again. We needed something to channel our energy into. We needed something to love, together. Something to strip away the hardship and torture we had endured in the afterlife.

I had been a nervous wreck during the pregnancy. The echoes of the past constantly jabbing at me. The memories of our first attempt, back before, and how it had failed—how it had served as the spark, the catalyst, in our descent to suicide.

My mind wandered into darker waters. The night of our death. How Jess had been crying and crying and crying and then we had done it. Taken those pills and embraced one another, waiting for the peace and silence we sought.

But death had other plans for us.

The rain. Always with the rain.

I shook myself and clawed out of the hole I found myself in. I sipped my drink and stared down into the clear liquid. We weren't there anymore. We were OK. Jess had given birth to Theo with no complications and now our little boy was a year old. He was the sunshine we so desperately needed to clear away the clouds of our own choices. And despite my anxiety and fears, I knew I would always be there for him no matter what. I'd give him the happiness Jess and I had gone so long without.

You killed and ate the raw flesh of another person.

I gripped my glass hard.

Stop it.

"You look like you're working through some problems."

I turned and saw a woman sitting in the stool next to me. I hadn't even noticed her arrival. She was a little older than me, somewhere in her late thirties, early forties, and looked like she had just gotten out of work. Her dark hair draped around her shoulders and her brown eyes met mine with a curious gaze.

"It's been a day," I muttered, draining the rest of my drink.

"That makes two of us," she said, waving the bartender over. She ordered and I watched out of the corner of my eye.

"Headed home for the day?" the woman asked.

"Yep."

She leaned on the bar, staring at me, hand cupped under her chin. "Not looking forward to it?"

"I just needed a drink," I said evenly.

She nodded sympathetically. "I get it. Problems?"

Her drink came and I didn't answer. She took a tentative sip and then smacked her lips, smiling. "That's better."

"Happy for you."

She nodded toward my empty glass. "If you get another one, I'll keep you company."

I pushed my empty glass between my hands, leaving traces of moisture across the bar top. "I shouldn't. I gotta get home."

She smiled with a few too many sparks. "No you don't."

I looked up at her, realizing she was flirting with me. I cleared my throat. "No, I really do."

"Why don't you stick around and I'll let you buy me the next round?" She pressed, a grin curling her lips.

I flashed her my wedding ring. "When I'm not wearing this, I'll take you up on that."

She chuckled. "Boy you're a serious one, aren't you? It's just a drink."

I stood up. "Everything starts with a choice. Have a good night."

She smiled. "Yeah, you too."

I threw some cash on the counter and headed home. I needed to see my family.

Chapter 2

The sun blossomed purple across a darkening sky. I pulled into my driveway, staring up at the fading day through the windshield. The wind ustled through the distant trees and chuckled across the swaying fields that urrounded the house. I got out, letting the evening air brush across my worn ace. I realized I felt slightly better, the drink and drive evaporating some of he haze that had plagued my day.

I walked up the driveway, each step easing the tension in my shoulders. flock of birds echoed over the growing night. Fireflies winked silently ver the high grass. The moon hung like a sugar cookie in a sugar-dusted ky, the first stars making their grand debut. Everything was calm and evrything was beautiful, the peace of the land seeping into my head like a entle whisper.

I got to the front door and pushed my way inside. As I closed and cked it behind me, I heard Jess from the kitchen. She had music on and as singing along to the tune. I smiled and felt warmth spread across my hest. Silently, I walked down the hall and into the dining room. I grinned penly as I spotted my wife, spinning and belting out lyrics as the beat layed loudly through her phone.

I leaned against the wall and crossed my arms, content to watch. Theo as in his high chair and was the first to spot me. His shining brown eyes lit p, and he bounced at the sight of me, his chubby hands outstretched.

I waved quietly to him and then put a finger to my lips, waiting for Je to notice my arrival. She got through half of the next verse before she final did. She let out a little yelp and clutched a hand to her chest, jumping bac I chuckled as she fumbled with her phone, turning off the song she had be jamming to.

"Quite a set of pipes you got there," I teased, remaining where I was.

"You scared me half to death!" she said, calming herself.

"I didn't want to stop the show," I shrugged. "Sounded like you we really putting your heart and soul into that."

Jess snorted and came to me. "Yeah, well, hopefully Theo gets my sin ing voice, not yours."

I embraced her in a hug, laughing. "You hear that, Theo!? Your mo thinks I can't sing!"

"Prove me otherwise!" Jess challenged, waving her phone up at me. "I even let you pick the song!"

I waved her off. "Ah, another time, I don't want to embarrass you front of the kid."

"Uh-huh, that's what I thought," Jess said, shaking her head. She walk back to the stove where an assembly of pots sat stewing. "You hungry?"

"Starved."

"You didn't sneak some fast food in on the way home?"

I waved a hand at her. "I did, but I threw it all up in the driveway. I hungry again."

She eyed me. "I bet you did."

I took two long steps over to her and smacked her butt, grinning.

Jess jumped and spun around. "Could you *not* while I'm stirring t boiling sauce, please?!" She sounded serious, but her eyes twinkled and smile curled the corner of her mouth.

I held up my hand to her. "That was just a warning shot. Next tim won't mess around."

"I'm going to dunk your dumb head into this," Jess giggled, wavin spatula at the pot.

Smiling, I turned to Theo who was still bouncing excitedly in his chai walked over to him and rubbed the top of his head. "Hey there, buddy! D you have a good day?"

Theo gurgled around his rosy cheeks and then let out a happy salutation. "Da! Da! Da!"

I leaned down and scooped him up into my arms, planting a kiss on his cheek. "You keep an eye on Mom today? She have any hotties over to the house while I was away?"

Theo grabbed both my cheeks and continued to try and speak to me, a jumble of half formed words and exclamations.

My eyes widened. "She did!? Why didn't you stop them!? I was counting on you, man!"

Jess looked at the two of us and just shook her head. "Unbelievable. I told you not to snitch on me, Theo."

I leaned forward and whispered into my son's ear. "There's a gun in my nightstand. Next time, just shoot the bastards."

Theo squealed and laughed, rolling his head back like he knew exactly what was going on.

"Hey, I heard that," Jess said, turning off the stove.

"Gotta protect what's mine," I said, bumping noses with Theo, who seemed delighted by the action.

"Damn right you do," Jess said.

I hefted Theo in my arms. "This little nugget eat yet?"

"No, you can put him back in his chair. Dinner is almost ready."

"What are we having?"

"Spaghetti, garlic bread, spicy Italian sausages, and carrot coleslaw," Jess answered over her shoulder as she started to plate everything.

"Oh, GROSS!" I yelled, throwing a hand up.

Jess turned on her heel, a look of shock on her face.

I winked. "Just kidding, love."

"If you're done being hilarious, could you grab some silverware?" she asked, now making a plate for Theo. I sat Theo back down in his chair and did as I was told, inhaling the delicious aroma that filled the kitchen.

"God, that smells good," I said, digging out a couple of forks.

"Been slaving away all day at it," Jess said.

"You're so full of it," I snickered. "How was your actual day?"

Jess finished with Theo's plate and walked it over to him. "It was good. Got a lot of work done while this little guy took his nap."

"Oh yeah?"

"Mhmmm. I'm almost done with the project," Jess said, placing Theo's food down on his tray. Immediately, his little hands shot out and began grabbing handfuls of the saucy noodles.

"Easy, ya little piglet!" Jess exclaimed, diving for a bib and throwing it around his neck.

"Glad you had a good one," I said, filling some glasses with ice water.

Jess went back to the stove and gathered our plates and began to pile them high. "Yeah, it was fine. Oh, someone stopped by earlier. They said they wanted to talk to you?"

I cocked an eyebrow at her. "Yeah? I wasn't expecting anyone. Who was it?"

She shrugged. "I don't know. He didn't leave his name, just said he'd try again later. He was nice enough, it was just kind of random."

"Was he trying to sell you something?"

"Nope, just asked if you were home."

"What'd he look like?"

"He was older, probably in his fifties. Dark hair with some gray. Very polite."

"Huh," I said, racking my brain. "Beats me. If he comes back while I'm gone, just tell him I don't want whatever he's pitching."

Jess set our steaming plates down on the kitchen table and threw me a mock salute. "Yes, sir. I live to serve."

I snorted. "Let's eat, cutie."

We fell upon dinner with enthusiasm, the array of food warming our stomachs and filling the air around us. Theo needed a second helping before I had even worked through half my plate and so I slid some more spaghetti onto his tray. He clapped his hands and his saucy fingers detonated red across my face. I blinked, wiped my eyes, and then laughed, poking one of his cheeks.

"I know it's good, little man, but take it easy!"

When we had finished eating, Jess took Theo out of his chair and cleaned him up while I cleared the table and did the dishes. Once the dishwasher was going, I went into the living room where Jess was donning our son in his PJs.

"He going to bed soon?" I asked, plopping down on the couch.

"Yeah, it's a little after eight already," Jess informed me, struggling to get Theo's flailing arms into the sleeves. "Hold still, ya wild animal!" she begged, finally guiding his hand through the hole.

I slid down onto the floor where they were and grabbed Theo from her right as she finished buttoning his gown.

"Come here, buddy," I said, rolling onto my back and holding him up over me. Theo giggled and waved his hands in the air, his eyes alight.

"Careful, you're going to make him sick," Jess warned, content to lean back against the couch.

"Ah, let him throw up," I said, dive-bombing my son toward the floor and then zooming him back up. "Don't want him to get too fat."

"He's perfect just as he is," Jess smiled. She got down on her elbows and crawled over to me. "Just like his dad."

Still on my back, I leaned forward and stole a kiss. Theo squealed and burped loudly.

"Please don't actually throw up," I laughed, "but if you do, do it on Mom!" I lowered Theo and brought him gently into Jess. "Watch out! Here he comes!"

Jess laughed and took our son in her arms and brushed her nose against his. "He wouldn't do that to Mommy, would you, sweetie? No, of course not! Because Mommy loves her little man!"

Theo smiled as Jess assaulted his face with a flurry of soft kisses. Still on the floor, I put my hands behind my head and watched them, tired, full, and content.

After a little while, it came time to put Theo to bed. Jess volunteered and I lovingly planted a kiss on my son's cheek before he was carried off to his crib. As Jess took him down the hall, I rolled up onto the couch and grabbed the remote. I switched on the TV and idly watched the news until Jess returned ten minutes later, sighing heavily.

"I love that boy," she said, plopping herself down next to me, "but it's always such a relief when he goes down for the night."

I threw an arm around her and brought her in close. "I love him, too, but it's hard not to get jealous of all those kisses you give him."

Jess looked up at me, her blue eyes glowing softly. "You want some kisses?"

"Mhmm."

Without hesitation, she did, our lips meeting, my hands going for her shoulders, then gently up her face and along her cheek. We pulled away and I held her like that, her face cupped between my hands.

"You're pretty great, you know that?" I said quietly.

"You're not so bad yourself."

I paused and really looked at her, my eyes locking with hers. "Hey...." I said gently. "How have you been?"

Jess slowly pulled away, her eyes dropping, knowing what I was really asking about. She stayed nestled against my shoulder, her voice low.

"I've been good. I've been so busy lately...it kind of numbs all that out. So...yeah...I've been good."

"We just haven't talked about it in a while...I wanted to make sure you weren't trying to hide it or something."

"I wouldn't do that to you."

"I know. I just care about you."

Jess slumped further down into me. "What about you, mister? How was therapy today?"

I shrugged and stared at the noiseless TV. "It was fine. It's hard to talk to her. To really open up. I mean, how can I?"

"I know."

"It's just...I don't even know what I'm supposed to say."

"Have you had any more bad dreams?"

"They come and go. You know. The worst of them wake you up, too."

Her hand found my leg. "It's OK."

I sighed, suddenly feeling very drained. "I just want to put all that behind me. Behind us. For good. It frustrates me that I still think about that place."

"It's impossible not to, Nick," Jess said softly.

"I guess you're right."

"What is it that's been bothering you the most lately?" Jess ventured, keeping her eyes trained on the ground.

I rolled the question around in my head like a piece of rotten fruit. "I think I'm worried about how it's going to affect Theo."

"What do you mean?"

I ran my teeth over my bottom lip. "I just want to make sure he grows up to be a good person. I want to be a good example for him."

"And you're worried you won't be?" Jess asked, finally looking up at me.

I avoided her eyes. "I don't know. Yeah."

Jess stroked my face, her fingers tracing my jaw. "Nick, you're an incredible person. You've been everything I need. I know you will be for him as well. You have to believe that."

I just stared straight ahead, letting her words sink through me.

"Nick?"

"Yeah?"

"You're a good person."

I licked my lips, my throat suddenly dry. "Yeah..." the word dripped down into my chest and I felt something stir there. Something long gone cold, but not dead.

"You want to watch a movie?" Jess finally asked, breaking the growing silence.

I nodded. "Sounds wonderful. Something funny?"

Jess sat up and kissed me on the cheek. "Please."

I pulled up Netflix and found us a movie. Jess went and dimmed the lights and soon we were basking in the soft glow of the movie I had picked. The darkness outside the windows filtered into the house and soon I found myself growing sleepy. Jess remained curled up next to me and halfway through the movie, I heard her snoring softly at my side. I rubbed my eyes and blinked, deciding to just turn in for the night. I shut the TV off and scooped Jess into my arms. She murmured something into my shoulder and then draped her hands around my neck. I carried us both into the bedroom and gently slid her into bed after helping her groggily take off her clothes. I did the same and went around to the other side, finally crawling between the sheets with all the relief in the world. I fell asleep in a matter of seconds.

I don't know how long I was out before the dream came.

I was standing along a beach, staring out at an ocean of black. Ebony waves curled silently in the rippling waters. The sky was gray and heavy rain beat down across my body. The air smelled of ash and I could taste it on my tongue. In the distance, something huge lumbered across the horizon, but it was too misty to make out exactly what.

At my back, something bellowed, a massive, earth-shaking gust of wind and rage. It rocked the ground beneath me and shuddered between my ears. I shut my eyes and gritted my teeth against it.

"You did this..." a voice hissed on the wind, so faint I almost missed it.

My eyes snapped open and I was suddenly standing before a great stone temple, its gray walls backed by the remains of a ruined mountain. Wide steps led up to a pair of great doors that were thrust open, exposing a cavern of darkness. Above the doors, an intricate pig head had been carved, its mouth gushing and pouring a viscous red liquid down over the steps.

I shut my eyes against the disturbing sight and when I opened them again, I was dwarfed by a colossal barn that towered before me. Its doors were smashed off its hinges and something was scrawled across the dirty red exterior.

YOU DID THIS.

I stared at the words, felt them sear into my eyes like they were on fire. From the belly of the barn, something moaned, an animalistic exhale of pain and agony. At my back, something moved and I spun, heart leaping into my throat.

My eyes swept across the rain-soaked land and they went wide. An army of mutated, twisted men and women stared back at me, their numbers too great to count. Their faces and limbs and flesh were contorted and misshapen, birthing hideous snouts and open, exposed wounds that bled a thick black pus. Hands contorted into hooves, fingers and bone jutting out in places they weren't supposed to be.

Pig Born, my mind hissed urgently.

One of them stepped out from the densely packed rows, a gnarled finger pointed in my direction from twenty yards away. I swallowed hard, rain mixing with the sweat now standing out on my brow.

As one, the rest of the Pig Born raised their arms and pointed directly a me, completely silent save for the drumming of rain against the dirt. I took a step back, shaking my head.

"Leave me alone," I whispered.

Behind them, from the distant forest, something roared. It shook th trees and split the sky, a wailing exhale of raw fury.

"Leave me alone!" I screamed.

At my back, from the darkness of the open barn, something answered.

"We can't."

I sat up in bed, gasping, the nightmare ringing violently in my head. I panted in the darkness, my face coated in sweat. I scrubbed my eyes and steadied my breathing, a hand going to my chest. Jess was awake and propped up next to me, perfectly still in the dim darkness.

"Sorry," I muttered, gasping still. "Bad dream."

But she wasn't paying attention to me. She raised a finger to her lips. "Shhhhh."

I realized her eyes were wide and she was staring at the bedroom door which remained open, just a crack. I looked at it, at that sliver of black, and felt my stomach sink slowly.

"What is it?" I whispered.

Jess didn't move. She just stared at the door, at the small slice of darkness that led out into the hall. Her face was pale and she gripped the comforter in her fist.

"Jess, what's wrong?" I asked a little more urgently.

Jess didn't look at me, her voice soft and scared. "I think something's in the house."

My guts squirmed beneath her words and I wiped sweat from my forehead. "What do you mean? Did you hear something?"

She nodded. "In the kitchen."

I pulled the covers away and stood, heart hammering. "Go to Theo's room. Stay with him until I come get you."

"Nick—"

I went to the bedroom door and listened. Nothing. Not even the creak of a floorboard. I pulled the door open a little and stepped out into the hallway. My pulse thundered in my ears, my bare feet padding silently across the wood floors. At my back, Jess slid out next to me and skittered down to Theo's room. I heard his door open and then close quickly behind her.

As I crept down the empty hall, I attuned my senses as best I could to pick up any indication of an intruder. My eyes melted into the night and every shadow seemed to sprout limbs that grasped for me. I reached the kitchen and stopped. My throat tightened and I felt my adrenaline spike.

Someone was standing by the sink, their back to me, their gaze trained out the window above the faucet, and into the blanket of night.

I took a step forward, sliding along the counter toward where I knew the knives were. My nerves bunched in my stomach and I felt my ears drum beneath my pulse.

"Hello, Nick."

I froze, the voice shattering the stillness like broken glass. The man didn't turn around, his figure silhouetted by the dim moon outside.

"I came by earlier, looking for you," the man said again, his voice calm and ageless.

Every sense on high alert, my fingers found the knife rack and I pulled one out, brandishing it before me.

"You won't need that," the man said quietly. "I'm not here to hurt you or your family."

I finally found my voice, a weak croak dribbling over my lips. "Who are you? What do you want?"

The man turned around but stayed where he was. He braced his hand along the sink and leaned back, his head turning toward me.

"My name is Ramiel. You can turn on a light if you'd like."

Keeping the knife between us, I reached behind me and fumbled for the switch. My fingers found it and I flicked it on. I steeled myself, not sure what to expect.

Standing before me was a man at least twenty years my senior. His salted hair was swept over to one side of his face, curling down past his gree eyes. Hard lines plagued his cheeks, making him appear even older. Whe our eyes met, he smiled, but it was an empty expression that did nothing t ease the knot between my shoulder blades.

"What are you doing in my house?" I asked, the question coming ou bolder than I felt.

The man, Ramiel, continued to smile. "I just told you. I was lookin for you."

"Why? Who are you?"

Ramiel sighed then, a fatigued release. "Why don't you put down tha knife so we can talk? I promise I'm not here to hurt anyone."

"I'll be the judge of that," I responded, standing my ground.

Ramiel sighed again. "Fine. I suppose it was foolish of me to think your violent ways have changed in a year."

My eyes narrowed, heart sputtering. "What are you talking about? I don't know you."

"Ah. But I know you." He crossed his arms and his smile dropped. "I know what you've done."

"I'm calling the police," I said suddenly, the worms in my stomach growing fatter.

He waved a hand at me. "Don't bother. I'd be gone by the time they got here. It wouldn't matter, anyway. There's nothing they can do to me. And there's nothing they could do to help you."

I kept the knife raised. "I'm going to ask you one more time: What are you doing in my house?"

Ramiel's eyes turned dark. "I'm here to bring you back."

My jaw locked and something twisted in my gut. "Bring me back?"

"You've done a lot of terrible things, Nick," the man said, his voice a low hiss, "and it's time you set them right." He took a sudden step forward, his eyes growing into a bottomless shadow. "It's time to go back to the Black Farm."

I stumbled away from him, the words striking like a hammer's blow. My grip around the knife tightened as my eyes widened. "W-what did you just say?"

Ramiel's hands balled into fists at his sides. "You've disrupted a very delicate balance we all exist in, Nick. It's time to set things right again."

"I-I'm calling the police," I sputtered, backing away, dread springing from the recesses of my mind.

Ramiel shook his head. "I told you they can't help you. They have no hold over me. None of you do. Not here."

My face went slack. "You're..."

Blue light suddenly flared around the intruder's body, a brief flash of hovering ribbons that wavered like lazy flame around his form. In the same instant they appeared, they were gone, leaving my mind spinning.

"You've seen our kind before, haven't you?" Ramiel asked quietly. "In that place. Up on the mountain. Right before you killed him in cold blood. Right before you *ate his flesh*."

Panic exploded through me like dynamite.

No. No, no, no. Not this.

"See...you haven't forgotten. How could you?"

"Leave me alone," I choked vainly.

Ramiel stepped around the kitchen toward me. "Leave you alone? No..
no, I can't do that, Nick. I have a job to do and I intend on seeing it through
You may have escaped that place, but you left hell in your wake."

"That's not my problem," I said, swallowing hard. "I freed myself fron
the Farm. I fed the Pig."

Ramiel raised a finger. "Ah, yes. Yes, you did. And that's exactly it. That'
the root of all this."

"I don't understand..."

"You fed the Pig, but you did it with a gut full of angel flesh. Pure, hol
flesh. And that flesh acted as a poison. When The Pig ate you...when yo
crawled down its throat...you changed *everything*."

"I did what I had to," I whispered, throat dry.

Ramiel spread his arms. "Sure you did. Sure. But you also turned your
self into a toxin. You tainted the Pig. You infected it." He took another ste
toward me. "You made it violently, *horribly* sick."

"Good," I hissed, voice shaking.

"No, Nick. Not good," Ramiel said quietly, "because you see...as bad a
you think that place was...things can always get worse. And I'm here to te
you—*things are about to get worse*."

"Again, that's not my problem," I choked. "You need to leave me and m
family alone. Whatever's going on, I want no part in it."

Ramiel stared directly at me. "The Pig is gone, Nick."

I felt the air leave my lungs in a rush. "What?"

"It's not in the Barn. It's not on the island. It's *gone*."

I blinked, trying to control my rising panic. "I don't understand...how i
that possible? Where did it go?"

Ramiel jabbed a finger at me. "This is all because you poisoned it. Yo
sent it into a frenzy. When you left, it went insane. It wasn't immediate. I
took time for the sickness to really set in. But when it did, the Black Farr
erupted in chaos. The Pig broke out of the Barn where it dwelled and too
off. It's gone, Nick. Gone. And you need to bring it back."

"Bring it back?!" I sputtered, unable to believe what I was hearing. "Why would I want to do that? What good could possibly come of that!?"

Ramiel shook his head, disgusted. "Because we all live in that balance I spoke of. You, me, and everything else that's alive. heaven, hell, the Farm, Earth. If the Pig is allowed free rein, or somehow manages to escape its realm entirely...I don't even want to think about what that could mean for the rest of us. A being with that magnitude of power? It could easily change the fate of existence, if given the chance. If it really *wanted* to."

I leaned back against the counter, his words like weights against my chest. "Shit…"

"Don't think you're exempt from its reach, either. If it's really gone, then imagine what would happen if you woke up one morning and turned on the news. What if it came here? What if it came looking for you? For your family?"

"Why the hell would it do that?" I stuttered.

"Because you're the one that ruined it."

My mind spun, the overload of information overwhelming me. I tried to hold it all in, tried to make sense of the madness. I felt dizzy. I felt sick. I felt like I was slowly being backed into a corner with no way out.

"You have to go back," Ramiel said quietly. "You have to find a way to fix this. If you don't, then everything you know could be destroyed. Or worse."

I closed my eyes. "You're crazy if you think I can somehow make this right."

"Yeah, well, you made it *wrong*, didn't you?"

My eyes snapped open. "Why don't you fix this? I didn't create that place. I didn't make the rules. I didn't put the Pig in charge. Your people did. If you're really an angel, then why don't you fly back to heaven and ask God to do something about this disaster, huh?"

"I can't."

"Why not?"

"Because neither heaven nor hell can interfere with what happens on the Farm. We can only observe and report. If we try to influence the outcome, no matter what the need, then we too will upset the balance that was established long ago."

I pointed the knife at him. "Even if that means risking everything Even if the Pig really has fled the Farm? Even if we're all screwed?"

"We don't think we've reached that point quite yet," Ramiel sai patiently.

"But you just said—"

"I said that so you would understand the urgency of the situation Ramiel interrupted. "But the Pig is sick. It's weakened. If it wanted to brea free from the Farm, it would have to find some way to heal itself. It woul need to recover. Its mind may be lost to madness, but physically it can't es cape yet. It couldn't. The toxins you infected it with would need to be purge first. And that's exactly what we think it's trying to do now."

I pressed a fist to my temple. "Jesus Christ…"

"Are you starting to understand?" Ramiel rumbled. "There's a clock tic ing. If that clock runs out and the Pig is not back where it belongs, its mir rebuilt, then things could get very, very bad."

I said nothing for a moment. My head was pounding and I felt nauseo

"Nick."

I remained silent.

"*Nick.*"

"Shut up," I whispered. "Shut up and get out of my house."

Ramiel snorted. "Have you been listening to anything I've been sayin

I gripped the knife. "I'm not going to help you. Your god created th not mine. Tell him to clean up his own fucking mess."

"You don't want to go down this road," Ramiel warned dangerously.

"I'm not going back to that place," I said quietly, embers cracking b hind my voice.

"You have to."

"I don't have to do anything," I said. "Get your boss to do it."

Ramiel pursed his lips, his eyes narrowing. "I don't think you understa exactly what he is."

"He's lazy," I spat, "and he sent you here to do his bidding. So that I'd *his* bidding. I'm not going to tell you again—get out of my house."

Ramiel stepped toward me, hands raised. "He is not all-powerful. needs your help."

"Why would I do anything for him?" I growled. "After he sent me and the woman I love to a place like that? What kind of a delusional lunatic is he? If he's worried about the Pig, then he can fix it himself. I'm not going back."

Ramiel glared at me, his face pale. "You're *going* to go back. I can't make you, but I can come close."

"What the hell is that supposed to mean?"

Ramiel pointed toward the hall. "You love them, don't you? Jess? Your little boy, Theo? Wouldn't it be terrible if something happened to them?"

I stepped aggressively toward him, voice rising. "You leave them out of this."

"Then go back. Don't make me hurt them. Don't make me use them."

"What kind of fucking angel are you," I snarled, bringing the knife up once more, "threatening a man's family like that?"

Ramiel sniffed. "When did I ever say we were the good guys?"

"Get the *fuck* out of my house," I hissed through gritted teeth.

"If I go, I can't promise your family will be safe. I'm giving you one last chance to stop that."

I brought the knife up under his chin. "*Out.*"

Ramiel sighed suddenly and stepped back. "Very well. I wish it didn't have to be this way. I'll see you soon, Nick."

Chapter 3

I was sitting on the couch in the living room when Jess found me. My hands covered my face, eyes staring out into the darkness between my fingers. She came in slowly, cautiously, bouncing Theo on her hip. He cooed and reached for me.

"Nick?"

I sat up and looked at them. I had a hard time focusing. Everything felt backwards. Upside down. Jess stepped toward me, her face ignited with alarm. I cleared my throat and tried to speak, but the words gurgled uselessly back down my throat.

How long have I been sitting here? What time is it?

"Nick, what happened? Who was that?" Jess asked, sitting down next to me, shifting Theo in her arms.

I looked at my son, looked into his wide, innocent eyes and felt my heart melt with fear. I pulled him from Jess and pressed him against me, planting a kiss on the top of his head.

"It's OK, buddy," I whispered, "Daddy's got you. Daddy's got you…"

"*Nick.*"

The urgency in Jess's voice pulled my attention back to her shimmering face. She was scared. She knew something was seriously wrong.

"I don't even know where to begin," I croaked.

"Who was that?" she demanded.

I stared at her, dreading the words I was about to say. "Jess…"

"Tell me!"

I drew in a shaky breath. "They want me to go back."

She blinked and Theo reached up and grabbed my cheek. His little fingers bunched and trailed across my skin.

"Go back...where?" Jess asked slowly.

I let out a trembling exhale of nerves. "The Black Farm. The man...the man here—the one who came earlier—he told me I have to go back."

All the blood drained from Jess's face, her lips parting. "No...no, we got out. We got out, Nick."

"I know…"

"Why? Why the *hell*?"

I rubbed Theo's cheek. "I don't exactly know. We did something to the Pig when we left. We made it sick. It's gone crazy. They don't know where it is. They want me to go back and fix things."

Jess took Theo back despite his protests. "I don't believe you. Please tell me this is a nightmare you just haven't shaken yourself from. This can't be true."

I spread my hands. "I don't know what to tell you…"

"The man here?"

"Some angel named Ramiel."

"Jesus Christ. Jesus Christ, Nick."

"I know."

"What did you tell him? How did you get him to leave?"

I stared at the floor. "I told him I wouldn't do it, obviously. I waved a knife in his face and told him to get out my house."

"And he just...left?"

I nodded. "Yeah. I don't think he's going to go away though. I'm afraid he'll come back."

"What do they expect you to do? How the hell can they ask this of you? This is insane!"

"I know it is," I whispered, exhausted. "I don't know what they think I can do. I mean, my god, I'm one guy. What chance do I possibly have against a place like that a second time?"

Jess began to bounce Theo on her knee, her voice grave. "We need to et some help. Call the police. Something. That man can't be allowed back n this house."

I sniffed dejectedly. "What do you expect them to do? How can anyone top someone like him? He's not of this world. What could we possibly do?"

"We have to do something!"

"No, we don't," I said, curling my hands into fists, "we don't have to do nything at all. We've paid our toll. We got out. They can't make me go back."

"But—"

"Let them sort out their own mess," I continued, "it has nothing to do ith us. If he comes back...well...I'll think of something."

Jess said nothing for a long while, Theo's broken speech patching the ilence. We both looked at him. Focused on him.

"What time is it?" I finally muttered.

"I don't know. A little after five, I think."

"I'm going to stay home today," I said, staring out the dark bay window.

"It's Saturday, hon."

I ran a hand over my face. "Right. Of course."

Jess placed a hand on my back. "Hey."

I turned to her.

"We're going to be OK. Nothing is going to happen. We got out. They an't touch us. They can't make us do anything. We're safe."

I tried to smile, a sloping incline at the corner of my mouth. "Sure. eah."

You don't believe that, do you?

I pulled myself off the couch. "I'm going to take a shower. I feel disgusting."

The day passed with cautious unease. The sun crawled across the ex- anse of the sky with lazy disinterest. Morning came and went, fading into fternoon, then evening. I spent the hours playing with Theo while Jess got me things checked off her to-do list. It felt fake, like we were just going rough the motions and refusing to confront what had happened earlier. ut despite that, I didn't know what else to do. What else could we do but about like nothing had happened? This was a place we had been before— lowing through time when hell hung around our heads. It's how we had

spent the majority of those first months after we escaped the Farm. We wer
no stranger to shadows.

When it came time for bed, Jess finally relieved me of Theo and mad
sure he went down without much of a fuss. It was only nine, but I felt abso
lutely drained, my shoulders aching from the constant state of paranoia th
had clung to me throughout the day. I went into the bedroom and undresse
collapsing on top of the comforter. After a little bit, Jess joined me. She le
the door open and turned off the lights. I heard her walk to her side of th
bed, a ghost in the night. Gently, she curled up next to me and laid her hea
across my chest.

"How are you doing, big guy?"

I put an arm around her shoulders. "I'm tired. It was one of those days

"It was, wasn't it? But you know what?"

"What?"

She propped her chin up on my chest and looked at me in the darknes
"We're still here, aren't we?"

I smiled at her optimism and felt myself melt a little. "We are. Ho
are you?"

"I'm shit," Jess exhaled, "but I'll be fine. I just need to sleep. Put som
time between this terrible memory and us, you know?"

"I do. I love you."

"I love you, too."

"Theo OK?"

"The little butter ball is out like a light."

I felt my eyes start to droop. "Don't think I'm far behind."

Sleep didn't come easy. I heard Jess fade away long before my own min
allowed me some shallow respite. I felt myself toss and turn as the ear
night hours deepened into deadened silence. Dreams fluttered across m
mind like flickering film, burnt edges and fleeing pictures that I couldr
focus on. Beyond the dreams, I felt myself growing thirsty and the pillo
beneath my head heated.

At some point, something thudded hard into my nerves and I jolte
awake. I sat up in a rush, gasping, my hair hanging in sweaty strands acro
my face. I pushed them up my forehead and pressed my fingers into my eye

My heart was racing. A nightmare sat smoking in the back of my head, the stench of its presence burned into my memory.

I opened my eyes and noticed that the bedroom door was closed. Brow furrowed, I turned to Jess at my side. She was gone.

I swung my legs off the bed and stood, the back of my throat feeling like a desert. I walked to the closed door and pulled it open. The house was dark and silent, the night an ominous coat of paint across my vision.

I looked down the hall toward Theo's room. His door was wide open, an empty cavern of space that held the thick silence to its chest.

Slowly, I walked toward it, my heart still racing. I poked my head inside. Jess was nowhere to be found. Fighting off a growing sense of panic, I hurried to Theo's crib and looked down. My son was gone, the blankets pushed away into the corner.

No, no, no, please, god, no…

I spun around, my breath rapid, and walked back out into the hall. Sweat ran down my eyes and I smeared it away with a distracted hand. Where the hell was my family? I was about to storm into the living room but paused, a sound catching my attention. It was low and guttural, a soft exhale that came from the kitchen.

Trying to suppress my mounting anxiety, I raced toward the noise, my bare feet thumping loudly across the wood floors. I reached the corner and turned to stare into the kitchen. When I did, all the air left my lungs and my eyes bulged in their sockets, a silent scream roaring up my throat.

Jess sat naked at the kitchen table, her arms splayed out before her. Two crude spikes had been rammed into her hands, pinning her to the table. Blood dripped from the gored flesh, her eyes half-lidded with pain, her face beaten and bloody. Her mouth hung open, drool dripping from the corners and across her chest. Her hair was strewn in sweaty clumps around her swollen, blackened cheeks.

Standing next to her, with one slender hand on her shoulder, was a creature that ripped the fear straight from my mind with all the horror of hell behind it. It stood at least seven feet tall, its humanoid body stripped of flesh to expose raw muscle that bled and oozed a viscous red pus. Its arms were long and covered with protruding, squirming fingers that wriggled and pointed and rolled in their sockets. Its head sat upon its shoulders, a massive thing of bone and sprawling black hair. It looked like a horse, except it had horns that curled back behind its head and almost touched the ground at its back. It was bone-white, contrasted by two green eyes that pulsed and glowed and dripped from their sockets like mucus before slithering back into their hollow orifices.

But all of that wasn't what erupted the deepest horror in me. It was what was on the table, laying before my wife, between her impaled arms.

It was Theo. He had been stripped of his pajamas and placed on his back. Protruding from his chest was another spike, a long, thin thing that looked like carved bone. It had been rammed directly into his heart and through the wooden table, holding him in place.

The scream finally found my lips, my body shaking, terror rippling through me like a hurricane. Before I could do anything, something approached me from behind and wrapped its long, powerful arms around my chest, squeezing the air from my lungs. I gasped and felt my ribs compress beneath the overwhelming pressure. Wildly, I looked behind me and saw a second creature, similar to the one before me, its long horse head leering down, its eyes rolling wildly in their sockets. The sprouting fingers across its slimy arms poked and prodded at me like mindless growths, causing me to reel in disgust and fear. But no matter how much I struggled, I could not break free and I couldn't find the air to scream.

The horse headed monster in front of me leaned down across the table and stared down at my dead son. Theo's face was pale and bloodless, his eyes wide open and horribly empty. Tears erupted down my cheeks and I coughed and wrestled, a hoarse plea rumbling through my tightened chest.

The creature reached out and stroked Theo's motionless body, its fingers finding purchase around his small leg. Jess just stared up at the monster, her breath heavy, tears running down her face, taking all the energy in the world just to stay conscious beneath her apparent beating.

In one violent motion, the horse head tore my son's leg away from his body. It happened in a flash of blood and bone, a sick pop filling my head. Jess screamed, trembling, her eyes bloodshot and red.

As she did, the creature holding the leg grabbed her by the throat and shoved our son's severed limb down her throat. Immediately, Jess gagged and coughed, her eyes bulging with shock and revulsion. The horse head tightened its grip around her throat and pushed the leg deeper, its arm entering Jess's mouth and traveling down her throat to deposit the meat into her stomach.

Jess vomited around the creature's arm, her jaw cracking, the sides of her cheeks splitting open. Puke gurgled from the new holes and splashed down onto the floor. She arched her back, gasping for air, her mouth forced open at an unnatural angle.

The horse head pulled its arm out and stared down at her. Its long horns draped over its shoulders like curved blades, a mane of black hair mangled with the white bone. Jess's broken jaw hung uselessly, a ruined expression of horror now permanently pulling her face apart. Her tongue lolled out across her bloodied teeth and she shook beneath an onslaught of chest heaving sobs.

The monster leaned down across our child and ripped his tiny head from his shoulders. Blood splashed across my wife's face as she came back to life in a wave of new anguish. I was screaming, somewhere, somehow, I was screaming and crying and fighting and blind with my own terror.

The horse head grabbed Jess by the hair and lifted her head up, her jaw crooked and gaping. In one merciless gesture, the creature rammed Theo's head down my wife's throat with enough force to break her teeth. She screamed and thrashed, her howls deafened as the monster pushed the head down her throat. Her throat bulged and expanded, her air flow cut off.

"Stop it!" I finally screamed, my throat so raw I thought it would tear. "Jesus Christ PLEASE!"

The horse head holding me leaned down, its teeth clacking in my ear. It spoke, its voice so deep I almost couldn't understand it.

"Go outside, Nick."

Jess's face was beginning to turn blue, the creature continuing to force Theo's head deeper and deeper down her throat.

"STOP IT!" I sobbed, buckling, kicking, spitting.

The voice in my ear came once more. "Go outside."

I squeezed my eyes shut, lost in hell, drool and snot running down my face.

And then, in an instant, the pressure around my body vanished. Gasping, I stumbled forward and collapsed onto the kitchen floor, clutching my chest. Coughing, head pounding, I scrambled to my feet, blinded by tears.

Everything was gone. Jess, Theo, the two horse heads...everything. There was no blood, no death, no sound. It was as if nothing had ever happened. Wiping my eyes, confused, I spun around, chest rising and falling rapidly.

"What the fuck?" I rasped, trying to pull myself together, my whole body shaking uncontrollably. Chest rattling, I tried to piece myself back together, one confused fragment at a time. My hands shook at my sides and my knees threatened to give out.

And the kitchen remained empty.

Finally, still trying to recover, I hurried back down the hall, a prayer on my lips. I stuck my head into the bedroom and all the relief in world flooded through me. Jess lay curled up in bed, sleeping peacefully. I leaned my head against the doorframe, squeezing my eyes shut and allowing myself the first steady breath since waking.

What the hell just happened?

Theo. Check on Theo.

Leaving my sleeping wife, I rushed down the hall and into my son's room. I hurried to the crib and stared down inside. Theo lay bundled into himself, unharmed, and sleepily sucking his thumb.

I knelt down by his crib, relief sweeping through me, and pressed my face against the plastic bars. I felt tears roll down my face as I gazed upon my little boy.

They're OK, Nick. Everyone is OK. It was just a bad dream.

But it hadn't felt like a dream. It felt real. My throat was raw and I could still feel pressure around my chest from where I had been restrained. I got up off my knees and pushed my son's blanket up higher on his small body. Feeling the tension and panic begin to ebb away, I walked back out into the hallway. I gazed down it, into the stretch of darkness, and felt my veins turn to ice. Something flickered by the front door, a single flash, like the afterburn of an image.

It was the horse head.

It's your imagination. There's nothing there.

Hesitantly, I crept toward the door, every nerve climbing back to full alert. The floorboards creaked underfoot as I passed my bedroom once again, throwing a quick look inside to make sure Jess was still asleep.

I reached the front door and released the breath I had been holding. There was nothing there. Only sparks from my own horrible nightmare. Desperately needing some air, I wrapped my hand around the doorknob, but stopped before I could pull it open.

A noise. A clatter. Like something had just run across the roof.

Jesus, pull yourself together.

I opened the door and let the night in, a wash of cool air that dried the sweat across my brow. I breathed it in and stepped out onto the front stoop. Stars winked down at me and a gentle breeze stirred the distance trees. Crickets chirped idly in the stillness and distant fireflies hovered over the grass.

I scanned the land, the calming air billowing earthy aromas—like a storm wasn't far off, despite the clear skies. I stepped down into the grass of my front lawn, my bare feet dampening as I stirred the dew clinging to the trimmed blades. I looked down the driveway, releasing the clinging nightmare from my mind.

There was a man standing in the middle of the road.

When am I going to wake up?

He began to walk toward me.

Wake up, Nick.

But the man kept coming. He reached the grass and continued on his way toward me. I stood like a lawn ornament, willing myself to dissipate the illusion.

When the man reached me, the bottom of my stomach dropped out.

"Hello Nick," Ramiel said quietly, his voice edged with the night.

I stared at him, begging my eyes to lie. "You…"

"I warned you."

I pointed behind me. "That? Did you do that?"

He nodded.

"What the hell did I just see? What was that?" I choked.

Ramiel stood his ground. "That's what happens in twenty-four hours unless you do what I tell you."

I shook my head, cold coils of iron wrapping themselves around m body. "I told you I'm *not* doing it!"

He shrugged. "And I told you I couldn't make you. Do whatev you want."

"You son of a bitch."

"You have a choice to make," Ramiel said, ignoring me. "Go back to th Farm or don't. You now know what happens if you stay."

"You can't do this to me," I hissed.

Ramiel stepped toward me, his voice lowering. "I'm not doing anythin to you, Nick. I'm letting you decide."

"This isn't a choice, it's a death sentence."

"I don't think you understand the magnitude of what you did," Rami growled, his eyes as dark as the sky.

I shook my head. "I don't care. I told you once—fix your own problem Leave my family alone."

"I'm not going to touch your family," Ramiel said softly, "but they wil He pointed behind me, toward the roof.

I turned and felt my jaw lock, my limbs turning to stone. Standing o the roof were the two horse heads, their slender, skinned bodies silhouett by the night. They didn't move, didn't make a sound. They just waited.

"Tomorrow night," Ramiel said, "and they will be allowed access your family."

I couldn't take my eyes off the creatures. My heart raced and I felt m anger drain. It was replaced by cold fear, the premonition blazing in n memory. The horse heads watched me, their long horns curling down the bone-white heads.

"Don't do this," I finally whispered.

"You need to make things right," Ramiel said firmly.

I turned back to him, my eyes searching his face for any sign of symp thy. "They haven't done anything to you. They're innocent. I was the one wh poisoned the Pig. I drove it mad. I'm responsible, not them."

"I don't care, Nick."

I reached for him, hands grasping his shirt. "Please, I'm asking you- don't make me do this."

"It's not up to me. I'm just doing my job."

I felt panic well up inside me like a rising tide, like I was being backed into a corner with no way out as the waters rose. "I can't go back there," I begged. "I won't make it. Not a second time."

"You have to."

I sunk to my knees before him, feeling myself begin to lose control. "No! There's got to be another way! There has to be something else I can do!" I clawed at him, hands shaking. "Don't make me go back! *Please*! That place will destroy what's left of me! I have to be here for my son. He needs me!"

Ramiel looked down at me, his eyes unreadable. "If you set things right, then I will return you to your family myself."

I squeezed my eyes shut, knees sinking into the earth. "There won't be anything left of me to bring back. You don't understand...that place broke me and I just barely managed to crawl back from it. If I return to the Farm…"

"I'm sorry, Nick. This is just the way it has to be."

My hands dropped to my sides, chest rising and falling rapidly. "God... oh *god…*"

Ramiel pulled me up and looked at me hard. "Just get it done."

"How?" I asked pitifully, feeling my eyes begin to swell with tears. The weight in my chest was almost too much to bear. The fear, the impending horror of what I'd have to face if I wanted to spare my family the violence I had witnessed, was overwhelming.

Ramiel took me by the shoulders. "The Pig Born have been whispering...muttering about someone called the Mud Man."

"What does that mean? Who is that?"

"I don't know," Ramiel said, "but he must be important because they keep repeating that name over and over again. Find the Mud Man. I have no doubt he plays some crucial role with whatever is happening to the Pig."

"Jesus Christ, I can't do this…"

"Enough," Ramiel said gravely, "you know you must. You know you have to. Get it done and when things are back in balance, I will return to the Farm and bring you home. I will be watching from the heavens."

"I don't know how you expect me to pull off something like this," I whispered miserably.

"Seek out Danny. He will help you."

I blinked. "Danny? The guy at the Barn? The one who does the orientations? He's with the Pig Born! He *hates* us!"

Ramiel shook his head. "Not anymore. They turned on him once the Pig disappeared. He is their captive now. Free him and I'm sure he'll repay the debt. He knows far more about the Black Farm than I do. You'll need him."

"This is insane."

Ramiel looked to the sky. "I'm done talking about this. You know what you need to do. If you don't," he pointed to the horse heads still standing on the roof, "you know what'll happen."

"Don't say that," I pleaded. "Don't leave me here like this."

"I have to go."

"I'm begging you…"

"Goodbye, Nick. Clock's ticking."

Before I could respond, the air crackled with blue light and suddenly I was alone. I blinked in the night, the world suddenly very quiet. I turned back to my house, feeling sick, and looked to the roof. The horse heads were gone as well.

They'll be back. You know they'll be back.

I bunched my hands over my eyes, feeling helpless and impossibly cut off. My mind tumbled over itself, fear gurgling from every pore. What the hell was I supposed to do? How the hell could I possibly escape this with my family still intact? The recent vision played relentlessly through my troubled head, the shocking violence, the threat of what would happen if I didn't return.

Can you really do this?

The thought caught me off guard.

What choice do you have?

"No," I whispered. "No, I won't. I can't."

Do you think he's lying? Do you really believe he'll just leave your family alone?

"I *cannot* do this."

Then pick a coffin you think Theo would look good in.

"Jesus Christ," I cried. "Oh, god…"

You can't tell Jess. She'd never let you go. She wouldn't understand. She hasn't seen what you've seen. Do it now. Before she wakes.

"No! I have to tell her!"

Why? Why make it any harder than you have to? You know you have to do this. Get it over with. Cross over. Save her the suffering. Don't make her watch. Don't try to make her understand.

"I can't hide something like this from her! She has to know!"

Then write a letter.

I waited for another argument to come, but I was left biting my tongue in hopeless frustration.

Don't drag this out, Nick. Don't agonize over it any more than you need to. You're going to do this.

"But…"

Do it. Write her a letter and get it over with.

I closed my eyes, begging for someone to save me.

They are going to rip your child apart.

Sinking now…

They are going to mutilate Jess.

"Stop it…"

There is no way out.

"Please…"

You are helpless. Do what they want or spend the rest of your life wishing you did.

I pulled my eyes open. It wasn't easy. I felt something seep into my head and trickle down into my chest. It was cold and horrible, and it consumed me. I breathed in the night air and felt sick. A breeze stirred the grass and I felt like the world was laughing at me.

I was terribly, miserably without options.

I trudged back into the house, each step feeling like the last I would ever take. Memories of the Farm sprang up around me, twisted flashes of violence and horror.

The Barn. The Pig Born. The rain.

Always with the rain.

I walked into my living room, surrounded by shadow.

The Needle Fields. The ocean. The Keepers. I shuddered at that. I could practically hear them, their great, lumbering stone limbs traversing the ocean around the island. Keeping us all trapped.

I thought about the temple. The Cult. The Hooves of the Pig. What were they doing now? Now that I had burned down their place of worship? Where were they? Where was Peter, the one who had ushered me in—the one I had murdered trying to free Jess?

They're all waiting for you.

I tried to catch my breath, sitting down hard on the couch.

Every evil you left behind, every wrong, every act of violence...it's all waiting for you, Nick.

In the darkness, I opened the coffee-table drawer next to the couch and dug out a piece of paper and a pen. With shaking hands, I began to write. And as I did so, I began to cry.

I realized I was more terrified than I had ever been before. The pen scratched across the surface of the page as I struggled to put down the words I knew I needed to say. As I did so, I began to hate myself. I began to realize something as the words poured out of me.

You're not doing this to save her the heartache. You're doing this to save yourself from it.

I wiped my eyes and continued to scratch away.

You're a coward, Nick.

"I'm doing this to save them," I hissed, vision blurred.

Jess is stronger than this. You're leaving this way because you're afraid of how she's going to look at you. You're afraid you won't be able to say goodbye.

"Stop..."

Your hands are shaking. You're terrified.

I continued to write, forcing the words out.

You're not coming back this time, you know that, right?

"He promised," I argued, heart sinking into despair.

Sure, he did. Of course he did.

I finished the letter in silence and then folded it. I wrote my wife's name across the front and placed it on the coffee table where I knew she'd see. I wiped my eyes and stood, dreading what came next. I tried to just move without thinking, but fear whispered around the edges of my mind.

I went to the bathroom and pulled open the medicine cabinets. I stared at the array of sleeping pills before me. The pills Jess needed to sleep without screaming. Forcing myself in motion, I grabbed all of them and went back into the living room. I sat back down on the couch and popped them open, spilling them gingerly onto the table before me.

This looks familiar, doesn't it?

Every part of me screamed to go kiss Jess goodbye. Every fiber of my being told me to go and take one last look at my sleeping son and tell him I loved him. But I knew that if I did that, I wouldn't be able to go through with it.

"Goddamn it," I choked, wiping my eyes. "*Goddamn*it."

I stared down at the pills and finally scooped them up. I looked down at them and clenched my teeth.

This is the only way.

"I know."

Make things right on the Farm. Save your family.

I closed my eyes, tears trailing down my face.

And then do whatever is necessary to get back to them.

I threw the pills into my mouth and swallowed. I laid down on the couch and felt terror close in around me.

I was going back.

Jesus, I was going back…

Horribly, I began to die.

Chapter 4

Dying was a lot like I remembered. Slow, painful, a void of hopelessness that pulled me in deep and swallowed me down into the darkness. I didn't fight it. I didn't resist. I simply allowed myself to descend beyond my body and into the jaws of the afterlife. I felt my consciousness slip, slide, and then plummet, sending me soaring through a blinking sputter of sensations that rendered me immobile and isolated. My mind was ripped from my flesh and cast into the abyss. Thought spun and whirled and chattered and screamed and dispersed into a million different directions. I came apart before I slowly began to take shape once more.

Awareness trickled back like a dam about to break—one trickle of water at a time, squirting through the tiniest cracks of death. I felt myself begin to breathe again. I sensed blood surging through my veins. My bones creaked beneath muscle.

And then I felt the rain.

Hesitantly, I reached for my face in the gloom, my vision not quite my own again. My fingers brushed across skin, then ran through my hair. I ran my tongue along my teeth. I felt my chest rise and fall. I felt cold.

I tried to open my eyes, failed, and waited another moment before trying again. Gray sky stared down at me along with an endless wash of pouring rain. It drenched through my clothes and clung to my arms, legs, and face, chilling me to the bone. I rubbed my eyes, everything spinning, and I coughed violently.

Once I got myself under control, I sat up, gingerly. My eyes focused on my surroundings, pulling the world in around me. Dread seeped into my mouth and leaked down my throat and pooled in my stomach. Fear came next, a terrible, familiar horror that pulsed with every beat of my heart.

The Black Farm sprawled out before me, a colorless expanse of gloom and ash. The mountain stood, a broken collapse of rock and dirt. It sloped down in on itself, its summit now annihilated from when the Pig had detonated the dead sun. I let my eyes scale the heavens and my jaw locked.

A black hole shivered between the clouds, a massive, gaping thing that bled its darkness across the expanse. Inky cobwebs extended from the epicenter, snaking outward like fragmented cobwebs.

That's where the dead sun used to be, I thought, shock rolling through me. *That's where the explosion was, the one that destroyed half of the Farm.*

The memory rippled through me like the rain streaking across my face. I dropped my eyes to the barren wasteland I sat in. Broken earth jutted out of the dirt like broken teeth, ash and granite littering the entirety around the crumbled mountain. Great rises and canyons now stood where there had been nothing before, the aftermath of the explosion shockingly apparent.

Groaning, I forced myself to stand, suddenly very aware of how exposed I was. I turned and looked behind me, half expecting to see an army of Pig Born charging my way. Instead, I was greeted with a wall of trees, a lush green canopy—the first splash of color I had seen. The forest grew thick and tight, intermittent with a tangle of underbrush that began just beyond the edge of the border.

I ran my gaze along the edge of the woodland, down the line that separated the island in half. In the far distance, I thought I could see the borders of the ocean, but I couldn't be sure. I shuddered at the thought, the memory of my excursion through the nightmare waters striking cold through my mind. The Keepers. Where were the Keepers? I squinted in the cloudy haze, through the torrential rain, but failed to spot an outline along the horizon. I knew the great stone giants were out there, patrolling the seemingly endless sea, but for now they remained hidden and out of sight.

You need to move, Nick. Get out of the open.

I peered into the trees, into the heavy gloom that lay inside. I knew a lot of the Suicidals were probably beyond the thick veil, surviving as best they could, away from the Pig Born that hunted them. How many times had I traversed these woods? How many times would I be spit out of the clouds and down into this terrible place?

I suddenly felt paralyzed as a thought thudded into the back of my head: *You're back. You're really back.*

A wave of dizziness hit me hard and I bent over, placing my hands on my knees. I closed my eyes and tried to steady myself. In the distance, I thought I heard someone scream.

Get into the woods. Hide. You have to hide.

Swallowing my fear and discomfort, I took a shaky step and then another. My feet kicked up ash and clods of broken dirt, soaked through by the endless rain. I stared straight ahead as I marched, trying to rebuild any courage I might still have.

I passed into the trees and entered the forest. My boots crunched through dead leaves and kicked at loose stones. The world dimmed beneath the canopy high overhead, and the rain lessened to a drizzle that leaked between the leaves.

I didn't have a destination in mind, just a singular goal: find Danny. I had no idea where the Pig Born were keeping him, but after a couple minutes, I decided to head toward the Barn. It was the only thing that made sense. Maybe I'd find someone, a fellow Suicidal who could help me.

I kept as quiet as I could, slinking between the trees, staying as vigilant as possible. A horrific sense of surrealism clutched my mind as I traversed through the dense underbrush. I almost expected to wake up, the whole thing some terrifying nightmare my traumatized mind had conjured up. But I kept walking, knowing that this was all very real and I needed to be extremely careful.

At some point as my feet grew sore, I heard something. I stopped, going on full alert, and crouched behind a tree. I trained my ears toward the noise and waited, the sound of my heartbeat thumping in my head. After a couple moments, I realized that something or someone was walking through the woods to my right. I shifted against the tree and braced myself, the crunch and snap of twigs growing louder. It began to sound like there were multiple people headed my way.

I squinted, trying to seek out some sign of movement. Every branch and hanging leaf grew illusions and shape. Then, finally, I saw something. Dark figures through the greenery. Three of them. They stomped through the woods with a carelessness I didn't like, their movements aggressive and confident. As the forms took shape, I felt my breath seize in my throat.

It was Pig Born. A trio of them, their appearance twisted and mutated beyond natural norms. Snouts and crooked jaws jutted from faces not quite human. Their ears hung limply with too much skin, their arms and legs bent at odd angles to sprout long fingers and half-shaped hooves.

As they drew closer, I saw that they would pass in front of me by about ten yards, left to right. I huddled down even further and allowed myself only the slightest of glimpses from around the tree. One of the Pig Born held a thin chain, a snaking trail of iron that it pulled without effort. I followed the chain across the ground and when I reached the end, I felt my eyes widen.

They were dragging a man, his body stripped of clothing and covered in deep lacerations. Mud and leaves clung to his beaten, ruined flesh as he was dragged along, a pattern of growing infection. The chain ended in a rusty hook that had been inserted into his mouth and punctured out from his lower jaw. Blood ran down his neck in thick streams, lost beneath the dirt and forest floor. As the party passed in front of my position, I locked eyes with the man.

He was alive. Mouth agape, teeth shoved aside, all he could do was moan. Whether it was a cry for help or a warning to flee, I couldn't tell. The noise earned him a sharp tug on the hook and his eyes rolled into the back of his head as a spurt of blood ejected from his mouth and jaw. The Pig Born laughed at their victim and continued on their trek, my presence remaining hidden.

I don't know how long I waited until I moved again. The sound of the Pig Born had long since evaporated, but the scene I had witnessed kept me rooted. I sat with my back against the tree, trying to calm myself.

The violence. It reminded me just how much I could *hurt* in this god-damn place.

I began to move again, forcing myself into motion. I tried to push the captured man out of my head, but it wasn't easy. I knew what that was like ow hopeless he felt. How you just hoped someone would kill you and get over with.

The trees expanded around me, spreading out, making it harder to slide etween them, the distance now greater from trunk to trunk. I began to el more and more exposed, acutely aware of every noise I made. I glanced rvently around, eyes snapping in every direction, begging to just make it rough to the other side in one piece.

Time plodded alongside me, each passing minute another victory. As I itered the inner bowels of the forest, I began to hear movement all around e. It was faint, but it was there. It was only a distance rustle or a snapping vig, but it was enough to raise the hairs on the back of my neck. Once or vice I thought I saw movement, passing shadows in the belly of the trees, it it never lasted long enough to be certain.

After some time, I paused and leaned against a tree, catching my breath. wiped sweat from my face and listened to the rain above. I estimated I was out halfway through to the other side. It had probably only been a couple ours, but it was impossible to tell. All I remembered was that the forest vided the island right down the center from beach to beach.

What are you going to do once you pass through?

I scanned the underbrush, biting my lip.

Something crunched loudly behind me and I spun, heart surging. I sup-essed a surprised cry as a party of people approached, at least a dozen.

How did you let them sneak up on you!?

I backed away slowly, hands raised. Their faces were rugged and worn, it they were human. Their clothes were in tatters and mud coated their skin d clung to their boots. They stopped and stared at me, a wall of distant es meeting mine.

"You scared the hell out of me," I sputtered weakly, meeting their un-adable looks.

One of them stepped forward, an older man with gray stubble. "Where'd u come from?" he asked, his voice rasping with a weariness I knew all too ell.

My eyes darted between the small crowd, choosing my words carefully. ist got here. Figured the woods were safer than the open plains."

The man grunted. "Hm. You figured right. You know what this place is?"

I nodded.

The man scratched his stubble. "Do ya now? And how might that be?

I quickly decided that it was a bad idea to tell these people that this wa my second trip to the Farm and so I cleared my throat and lied. "Uh, I ra into someone a little while back. They kind of filled me in."

Stubble nodded. "Mm. I see. And where you headed?"

I just pointed into the woods. "That way. Trying to find some place lay low and stay away from those monsters out there."

"Yeah, they're a nasty bunch, ain't they?"

I swallowed hard. "Yep. But you're not like them, are you? You're huma You're Suicidals."

"That we are," Stubble said, looking around at his companions. Th remained silent, all eyes on me.

"I uh, I heard there was someone I was supposed to see here," I conti ued, trying to get a read on these people. "I think his name was Danny. Yo know him?"

Stubble studied me hard for a moment before answering. "Sure, I kno him. What's it to you?"

I shrugged as casually as I could. "Just heard I was supposed to seek hi out. You wouldn't happen to know where he is, would you?"

The man looked back at his party and some mysterious conversatio seemed to pass unspoken between them.

"I'm not looking for trouble or anything," I assured, not really knowi what was going on with this strange group of Suicidals. "I'm just trying make sense of this place."

Stubble took a slow step toward me, his voice neutral. "You could co with us if you'd like. We're headed the way you're going. Think we mig actually be after the same thing."

"Is that so?" I said carefully, "and what would that be?"

The man stood directly in front of me, so close I could feel his breath my face. "You want to find Danny. We want to find our leader. You see, h been taken by the Pig Born. And we need him back."

I took a second to process what this man was saying. "Hold on.. Danny...is Danny one of you?"

The man smiled, a strange thing in such a dark place. "You might be useful after all."

I suddenly felt incredibly uncomfortable, and I retreated a step. "Uh, look, I think I'll be better off on my own, but thank you.'"

Stubble gripped my shoulder, cementing me where I stood, that smile still plastered to his grizzled face. "Don't be ridiculous. You're new here. You need protection from all the nasty rodents that scurry around this godless island. Don't you want to feel safe?" As he spoke, the rest of the Suicidals closed in, forming a circle around me. My heart raced and my shoulder ached beneath the man's iron hand.

"Who are you people?" I whispered, trying not to panic.

"Just a couple desperate souls looking to make a deal," Stubble said quietly. Before I could say anything else, he grabbed me by the back of the neck and his companions swarmed me.

Terror ignited through me as foreign hands grabbed at my arms and legs, heavy fists swinging into my stomach and chest. I flailed wildly, a cry rising beneath the beating. Something connected hard with the back of my head and I went to my knees, stars exploding.

They're taking you.

Screaming, I surged back to my feet in a rush of panicked adrenaline. Three men, including Stubble, were directly in front of me, clawing for control. I stepped into them and planted a fist into one of their faces. I was rewarded with a howl and I turned to strike the next. Before I could, I was jumped from behind. One, two, three people all pushing me down into the dirt. A foot caught me in the ribs and another across the back of my legs. I felt my energy disperse, replaced by pain, sharp stinging aches that kept coming. My face was shoved into the mud and my arms were roughly jerked behind my back. I sputtered and coughed and tried to buck my captors off, but each time I moved I was awarded another blow to the ribs. Rope coiled around my wrists and bit into my skin and I realized I was being bound. I tried to look behind me, but a rag was wrapped around my mouth like a harness and I was gagged, the knot secured tightly to the back of my skull.

Finally, panting, the assailants stood and angrily pulled me to my feet. Gasping around my gag, I blinked away the blurred pain. My stomach and ribs pulsed with discomfort and I felt nausea swirl in my gut.

Stubble stood in front of me, his face turned down in a scowl. "Didn't expect you to come easy, but shit, you made it hard on yourself."

I just stared at him, twisting my hands in my ropes uselessly.

He nodded to his companions. "He does anything stupid, hit him. Hard." He turned around to the Suicidals at his back. "You can get the others now. Add him to their ranks. And keep an eye on this one. He's new, so he probably still thinks he has a chance."

The dozen odd men and women formed rank while something was retrieved from the bushes a couple yards back. Head still ringing, I watched as two others like me were hauled to their feet, previously hidden by the bushes. It was a man and a woman, both about my age. They were bound and gagged in a similar fashion, their faces purple with bruising. Our eyes met, and I saw something that chilled me to the bone. Absolute hopelessness.

Stubble waved them forward and the two captives joined my side before we were pushed forward deeper into the woods.

"Get a move on," Stubble growled. Three of you should be more than enough to trade."

Dread consumed me as we walked, my two fellow prisoners silently stumbling along at my side. I glanced at them once or twice and saw the man was crying, his eyes streaming with silent tears. The woman's face was stone beneath her black eyes.

Occasionally, one of our captors would shove me in the back, urging me forward, and I had to fight not to fall. Stubble led the way, half the party in front of me, the others trailing from the rear. I fought the constant panic in my chest—the terror of where I was being taken and what was going to happen to me. Memories sprang like monsters in my mind, visions of possibility that I fought against. I knew just how bad this place could be and what it was like to be taken.

What if they're taking you to Muck?

My face paled and I struggled to remain in control of myself. My eyes were wide and I stared at my feet and begged to just wake up from all this.

After some time, Stubble slowed to a stop and held up a hand, demanding silence. I shifted where I stood, unsure what was happening. The others in the party pressed close, the air percolating with tension.

One of the captors went to Stubble and leaned in close, his voice low. "What is it?"

Stubble crouched and placed his palm to the ground, as if feeling for something. After a moment, he stood, his face taut.

"One of them is coming."

The man at his side crouched and pressed his hand to the dirt. As he did so, I felt a tremor run beneath my feet.

"A Keeper," Stubble whispered, turning to the rest of us.

The man at his side looked up at him. "Is it Berserker?"

Another tremor ran through the earth, stronger this time. I looked around at my fellow captives, but their eyes were laden with their own problems.

Stubble waited a moment for the ground to shudder once more before shaking his head. "No. One of the others. It's coming too slowly for it to be Berserker."

"Is it coming this way?" one of the others asked.

Stubble shook his head. "I don't think so. But still, I want everyone to be extra cautious. We all know how unpredictable the Keepers have become. Hopefully it goes back to the ocean and leaves us alone."

"I don't understand why they leave those waters now," a woman to my left muttered. I met her eyes and she spat a wad of phlegm at my feet.

"We all know the rules changed when the Pig blew up the dead sun," Stubble said quietly. "Berserker is the only one we really need to worry about, though. Now come on, we're almost to the other side."

I was pushed forward and I stumbled along, still feeling an occasional shudder beneath my boots. What did he mean, the rules had changed? Were the Keepers now roaming not just the ocean, but the island as well? And what was Berserker? Questions bubbled up my throat and I swallowed them roughly back down. I wasn't sure I even wanted to know the answers.

Just as the last of the tremors faded, we broke through the treeline and out onto the other side of the Farm. The rain greeted us once again and I felt it chill me in seconds. In the gloomy haze, I could make out the Barn to our right, barely visible through the torrential downpour. Our party headed left, across the grasslands, our feet squishing into the mud and ruined earth. I began to shiver as the miles dragged on. All around us, through the sheets of rain, I could hear faint screams and cries, shouts, and snarls as the Farm breathed around us; Pig Born and Suicidals, forever locked in a game of violent cat and mouse, the gears of violence spinning eternal.

At some point, I spotted a large mob of mutations gathered in a circle, their growls and attention directed to the center of whatever lay within. They were far away, across a series of soggy foothills, but I could still hear the wails of pain from whatever sport was being conducted. Stubble steered us clear of them, their attention trained on hidden tortures.

"That's going to be us soon."

I looked over my shoulder at the bound woman behind me. Her eyes were empty and her tone was hollow. She said it so matter-of-factly that I could only turn away without response.

"Keep your mouths shut," someone growled. "And someone get her gag back in her mouth."

The land stretched out before us, a rolling wash of wet hills and scattered patches of dead trees. We continued to catch glimpses of life, both human and otherwise. They scurried away upon seeing us, our numbers too great for confrontation.

After an unknown amount of time, I began to make out structures ahead. They were crude and broken, shoddy constructs made of wood and twine. A large milling of Pig Born surrounded them, their hunched, twisted figures giving them away. Their numbers were in the dozens and I felt my heart begin to race, my blood heating beneath the cold rain. They looked up at our approach and began to form a line in front of the leaning ruins.

"I'll do the talking," Stubble said as we approached. "We're here to make a deal and that's it. We get the boss and then we leave. I don't want this turning into an all-out brawl, so everyone just shut up."

Panicking, I uselessly struggled against my bindings and was rewarded with a smack in the back of the head. When the stars cleared, we had come to a halt and I looked up. We had stopped before the line of Pig Born, with Stubble at the head of our group. The rain cut a wall between us, but I could see the dripping, snarling faces of the creatures before us, hungry to tear us to shreds but cautious at our numbers.

Stubble raised his hands and his voice carried across the divide. "I have three Suicidals to offer you!"

The Pig Born shifted in the mud, naked feet and cloven hooves squish-
ıg wetly, unsure what to make of all this.

"I'll offer these three to you in exchange for one!" Stubble continued,
aving a hand at us. We were pushed forward to Stubble's side and I almost
ipped as I shuffled ahead. I felt malicious eyes fall upon me and I clenched
ıy teeth, shivering, terrified. I could feel their desire, their hatred, their need
hurt us. I worked my gag down past my mouth, allowing myself some
uch-needed air.

"I'm looking for one you took some time ago!" Stubble yelled. "A man!
e's about my age and build! A strong man! He has a scar along the side of
s neck!" Stubble surveyed the line of mutations before continuing. "Give
m to us and I'll give you these three to do with as you see fit! Blood for
ood! What do you say?"

One of the Pig Born stepped forward, a massive beast with human fea-
res and a warped snout that jutted out the side of his face. It spoke around
mouthful of broken teeth, its voice a gurgling growl.

"We kill you, we take, we win."

Stubble nodded as if expecting this. "Sure. Of course you could. But
ere are many of us and we've killed as many more. And we could take out
ite a few of you, if it came down to it. But why? Why bother? I'm offering
u more than you already have! Take them and give us the man we're look-
g for! It's a fair deal!"

The lumbering beast shook its head. "We kill. We take." The army bend him began to stir and grin, eager to start the bloodshed. I swallowed
rd, my knees knocking together as my weary legs shook.

Stubble's voice turned hard. "If you kill us here and now then we will
turn. But not alone. We will lure Berserker to your camp, to the Pits, and it
ll *annihilate* you. If you kill us, then the clouds will spit us out and we will
art again. But not you. The Pig is GONE! Who will give *you* life again?"

The line of Pig Born grunted and growled, suddenly unsure. I caught a
w fractured words muttered between them.

I could have sworn I heard the phrase "Mud Man."

The leader looked around and stamped its elongated hooves, snorting
grily. After a moment, it spoke, addressing its comrades at its back.

"Go. Get scarred man."

I saw Stubble's shoulders relax the slightest bit, exhaling a small brea of relief. We waited in silence, the rain thundering down around us. Wh I thought I would freeze to death beneath the weather, the line of Pig Bo parted and a man was shoved forward, a Suicidal. He was thin and battere his clothes torn, his face filthy. Stubble motioned for us to move. I was pro ded forward along with my two companions and I heard the man at n side begin to cry again. My mind raced with desperation, trying in vain conjure some plan to get out of this.

As we were shoved across the empty space to the other side, the P Born's captive was allowed to cross the distance to his rescuers. As we a proached one another, his face became clearer, his features more defined. M eyes suddenly widened and my mouth dropped open, our gazes locking a shuddering with recognition.

"Peter?" I gasped.

Disbelief swept across his face as we passed one another, his voice ragged whisper. "*You*?"

I couldn't believe it was him. Peter. A former member of the cult, t Hooves of the Pig, and the man who ushered me into their temple. The m who had placed his trust in me. The man I had killed trying to free Jess fro his religion's sick rituals. *He* was the leader of these Suicidals? How? And he was, then where the hell was Danny?

I realized I had stopped walking, shock rooting me in place feet aw from Peter who also had frozen, our eyes sparking the air between us.

"What the hell are you doing here?" Peter snarled, his voice a gra elly demand.

I stared at him, unable to believe my eyes. "Where's Danny?" I hiss urgently through the rain.

Peter sniffed at that, as if caught off guard. "Danny?"

A fist slammed into my back and I let out a cry, catching myself.

"Move," Stubble growled in my ear. "My time with you is over."

Before I could move, Peter stepped toward me, his voice a venomo whisper meant only for me.

"Don't think this is the last you'll see of me. I swore I'd never stop hur ing you and I haven't. I'll be back and I will bring all the pain of hell with m

And then he was gone, swallowed up by the Suicidals. My group reached the Pig Born and we were roughly pulled into their ranks, foul breath and angry grunts filling my world. I lost sight of my fellow captives as I was dragged forward, cries of victory rising and sweeping across the violent crowd as their prey was secured.

Chapter 5

I was pulled into the maw, a press of stinking flesh and filth. Hands and twisted fingers groped and prodded at me, a moving inspection as I was led deeper into the Pig Born camp. Spittle and drool and broken voices dripped from every side, a chaotic chattering that was only half-intelligible.

They're going to hurt you.

I kept my head low, my bound hands digging into my back. Terror took root as I heard one of the captors yell something about the Pits. This earned a joyous cry from the masses and I was led further into the sprawl. We passed a scattering of the crumpled constructs and I saw nothing but darkness beyond the open doorways.

Due to the cluster of Pig Born surrounding me, it was hard to make out anything past them, but I managed to steal a glimpse or two beyond the veil of diseased flesh. I swallowed hard as I realized we were passing massive holes in the ground, crudely dug circles about ten feet deep and twice as wide. From inside the pits, I saw men and women, Suicidals, two or three to each one.

And they were killing one another. The desperation in their eyes was enough to turn my stomach. They came together, howling in a violent clash as they tried to snuff the life out of their opponent.

That's where they're taking you. You're going into one of those pits.

I could feel myself shaking and knew it wasn't from the cold this time. I had to get away from this—escape and run...but how?

You're going to have to kill, Nick.

"No," I whispered into the horde, "no...no..."

Then you're going to get ripped apart.

"I can't do this again," I choked.

The sea of Pig Born parted before me and my eyes went wide. We had stopped at the edge of a pit. Down below, in the dirt, was a scattering of dead Suicidals. They were being cleared away, removed to make room for another brawl. Their bodies were covered in blood, sharp bone popping through the skin, angry gashes lining their features.

I felt hot breath by my ear, a single word uttered to me, a harsh command.

"Kill."

My bonds were cut and a heavy hand shoved me in the back. I fell down into the pit, bouncing and sprawling in the dirt, the wind knocked out of me as I reached the bottom. I coughed and blinked away stars, tasting blood. I spit it away and shakily got to my knees. I looked up at the circle of leering, grotesque faces that lined the hole and jeered down at me. I wiped mud from my eyes and stood. I felt sick and suddenly very exposed, my heart thundering in my chest, the taste of bile tickling the back of my throat.

Across the pit I saw two other Suicidals tumble down to join me. At first, I thought they might be the two I had traveled with but soon realized that wasn't the case.

The one closest to me was a young woman dressed in tattered clothes, her hair almost as wild as her eyes. She turned toward me, stealing my attention away from the big man on the other side who was now climbing to his feet.

I held my hands out, heart racing. "Hold on now," I said weakly, not entirely sure what to expect. "I'm on your side...I'm not going to hurt you..."

The woman took a step closer, a familiar, confident stride that did nothing to ease my fears. It was clear this wasn't the first time she had been cast down into one of these holes. I stepped back, trying to keep my distance. Above us, the Pig Born roared, an eager bellow that set my teeth on edge.

"I don't want to hurt you!" I yelled at the woman, trying to get my bearings, trying to make sense of all this. "I'm a Suicidal! We don't have to fight! I'm one of you!"

But the woman continued to advance, her fingers twitching at her side, er nails long and chalked with blood. Her bare feet sank into the mud, the round a swath of brown, earthy gore. A sharp stench invaded my head as circled away from the approaching woman, my hands still outstretched to er.

"Don't do this," I whispered vainly.

But my words fell on deaf ears as the woman suddenly let out a shriek nd charged me, teeth bared. I stumbled back, tripping over myself and amming into the wall of the pit at my back. I slumped down, half-fall-g, half-sliding, raising my hands to cover my face as the deranged woman mmed into me.

She was stronger than I had anticipated, and I felt myself seize in pain her shoulder connected with my chest. Stunned, I battered at her, trying y best to keep her flailing hands away from my eyes. She screamed like a ild animal and writhed like she had contracted some strain of rabies. Her outh foamed and I briefly wondered if there was anything human left side her.

A raking claw cut through my thoughts and I felt my cheek sting be-eath the blow. I reached out and grabbed at the woman's wrists, her assault relentless press against me. My vision was consumed by her madness, her roaty howls drowning out the drum of my own heartbeat.

"Stop it! Stop!" I cried, barely avoiding her lunging jaws. Her teeth apped loudly by my ear and I fought to stand. I planted one of my boots the mud and used the wall of the pit to push myself up, my hands still rapped around her wrists.

Finally feeling some semblance of control, I tightened my hold on her. owered a solid foot and a half over my attacker, but her ferocity made up r the difference in height. I went to twist her arm back, aiming to slow her tack, but before I could, the woman drove her knee into my groin.

I felt everything around me dim as pain exploded like dynamite be-een my legs. I lost my grip on the woman and sank down into the mud, pathetic wheeze escaping my lips. Vomit surged up my throat and I heard yself gag as pain overwhelmed me. I curled up in the fetal position and oked down any air I could find. My eyes watered and my vision swam, legs rning to jelly.

Sensing my defenselessness, the woman sprang on top of me and bega
to claw for my eyes. She panted and gurgled as she did so, her hands whi
ping wildly for my face. I balled into myself as tightly as I could, barely ab
to breathe, never mind fight back. I felt her nails dig into my neck and che
and then sweep over my ears and cheek.

She's going to find her mark if you don't get up and do something.

I tried rolling away with as much strength as I could muster, but sh
locked herself atop me and redoubled her assault.

Get up and hit her, Nick.

But the unending ache between my legs was like an anchor driven de
into the ground. I felt the woman grab a handful of my hair and jerk m
head up, trying to gain access to my eyes. This close, I could smell her filt
a combination of shit and dirt. I threw an odd elbow in her direction, but
only managed to graze her ribs.

Fight. Ignore the pain and fight.

Suddenly, without warning, I felt the woman's weight evaporate.
gasped down a breath of air and poked my head up, hoping she had decid
I wasn't worth the trouble.

Instead, I saw the woman being held from behind by the third perso
in the pit, the man from across the way. He looked calm as he bunched h
heavily muscled arms around the woman's chest, squeezing the fight out
her from behind.

The woman coughed and hacked and tried to wriggle free as her fa
turned blue, but the man didn't allow it. Right as I thought she was abo
to pass out, the muscled man heaved her up and then violently slammed h
down into the mud, planting her face-first in it. Without pause, he stoo
over her and stomped down onto her back as hard as he possibly could.

I heard her spine break from where I lay. The screams stopped and th
woman went completely still, except for her eyes, her back broken. Slow
the man got down on his knees, not appearing to be in any kind of rush, an
gently pushed the woman's paralyzed head deep into the layers of mud an
grime.

He held her there for as long as it took to die.

The Pig Born roared their approval as the man slowly stood and faced me, wiping his hands on his pants. His eyes held no emotion, his face unreadable. He began to walk toward me, his target marked.

I frantically scrambled to my feet, crotch throbbing, eyes pleading. "Don't..." I cried, backing away. "Please..."

You have to do something.

I backed into the wall of the pit again, my hands groping for purchase. I felt my fingers find a small rock and pried it from the dirt, trying to clear my head and ignore the insistent pain. The big man circled me as if trying to figure out the most convenient way to kill me.

I gripped the small rock in my hand, not quite sure what I planned on doing with it. Adrenaline coursed through my veins as I faced my attacker, dread and impossibility staring down at me.

Without warning, the man lunged, his movements so quick I let out a cry of fear and stumbled away and out of reach. I went down on one knee and rolled in the mud, feeling my attacker's hands miss me by inches. I came up in a crouch, fingers sinking into the wet earth. The man spun toward me, a spark of irritation in his eyes.

I closed my fists in the mud, the rock lost, a desperate plan forming. I waited for the big man to come at me again, stomach in my throat. Growling, he surged for me. Instead of rolling away this time, I flung a handful of mud at his face as hard as I could. Surprised, it caught my opponent across his right eye and the side of his face. He skidded to a halt, half-blinded, crying out in pain as the dirt did its work.

Taking advantage of my brief window, I dove for the man, catching him off guard. My shoulder took him in the midsection and he fell backward against the impact, his eye still clouded and running with mud.

I landed on top of him, his meaty hands already batting at me blindly, one of them catching me in the ribs. I felt the breath leave my lungs, but I stayed on top of him, my hands scooping for more mud. I shoved a massive glob down over his face, covering his eyes completely, taking the brunt of his wild blows across my arms.

Gritting my teeth, I gripped his head with my hands.

Do it.

I plunged my thumbs into his eyes and felt them erupt. Blood and yellow slime exploded from the man's popped sockets as I continued to sink my fingers into his head. His screams silenced my fear.

I pulled my hands away and bunched them into fists. Without thinking, I began to hammer them down into the man's throat. Once, twice, as many times as it took to turn his screams to gasps.

When he finally stopped clawing at me, his strength draining, I began to choke him to death. My heart thundered as the man's mud-smeared face began to wheeze, then gag, then drain of life.

I don't know when he died, but I sat there, hands around his throat, until the Pig Born pulled me away.

The world was a daze of blinking color, my mind lost in the sudden, unexpected violence. I felt my lungs burning as firm hands hauled me out of the pit. Color swam in and out of focus, my breath coming in long, desperate pulls. I suddenly wasn't sure what was happening or where I was, everything falling away in a collapse of logic.

My vision swam and I realized that I was shaking uncontrollably. Shock rose from the marshlands of my mind and slammed into me with a sudden detonation.

"Jesus Christ," I whispered as I was pulled along. "Oh Jesus god, what have I done..."

My legs didn't seem to be working and I sank, slowing. The Pig Born gripped me under my arms and dragged me onward, taking me to away to some new hell. I could hear them cheering, howling, roaring in satisfaction at my brutal victory. I felt like throwing up, the thoughtless murder rolling across my psyche like a tide.

You had to kill him.

My boots trailed in my wake, leaving divots in the mud as I was pulled.

Think about your family.

I focused my vision and looked ahead. The Pig Born were taking me to one of the houses, the doorless entry a dark mouth leading to the unknown. I looked to my left, panting, eyes bloodshot. In the distance, I could make out the shoreline, the beach a long stretch of sand before an endless ocean of shaded water.

Think about Theo. Think about Jess. Nothing comes before them. You've done this before.

I blocked out the voice in my head as we ascended the handful of rickety steps to the house, held tight by my captors, a flurry of disgruntled voices snarling around me. They took me into the house and my eyes adjusted to the gloom. It was an empty square of space divided down the middle by a wall of interlinked wood.

A cage.

I finally found my legs, the thought of imprisonment igniting a new fear. Memory of captivity roared through my head, thoughts of Muck and the torture I had endured during my first arrival at the Black Farm.

"NO!" I screamed suddenly, kicking and struggling. "No, let me go! Let me GO!" The Pig Born laughed at my feeble attempts at freedom and I was cuffed across the face, bringing stars to life.

Blinking heavily, I heard the cage open, the wooden door scraping across the floor. Terror coursing through me, I was shoved inside. I stumbled and fell, sprawling across the floor and banging my head against the far wall. Slivers of light filtered in through small slits of the hut and I spun around and saw my captors slam the door close at my back. Heavy chain was fixed around the cage, locking me inside. I stood, shaking, the blood draining from my face.

"Let me go!" I yelled pathetically, lunging for the sturdy wooden bars. "I WON! LET ME GO!"

The Pig Born ignored me as they turned away and left the house, headed back toward the Pits.

Heart hammering, I stared at nothing, fingers curving around the interlaced wooden bars. My chest rose and fell and I tried to get myself under control.

"Calm down, yelling won't do you any good."

Heart sputtering, I whipped around to where the voice had come from, unaware that my cage was already occupied. A man sat slumped in the corner, his face hidden in shadows.

"What is going on?" I asked, backing away from the bars. "What are they going to do with us?"

The man looked up at me, a finger of light stroking his face from a crack in the wall. "Buddy, you don't wanna—" he paused, his words snapping off at the lip. Slowly, he stood, his mood changing. "Wait a second…" he took a step toward me, his features coming into full view.

My eyes went wide and my jaw dropped open. "...Danny?"

The faded light illuminated a worn face, heavy with fatigue. His green eyes met mine and he slowly ran a hand over the stubble across his scalp.

"You've got to be fucking kidding me," he growled.

I stepped toward him, feeling the first glimmer of hope since arriving back at the Farm. "It really is you!" I gasped, taking him in. "Listen, there are things we need to t—"

My words were cut short as a fist plowed into my jaw. I fell backwards onto the floor, completely caught off guard, the taste of blood already growing familiar. Danny towered over me, fists shaking at his sides, the bags beneath his eyes falling like shadows over me.

"You son of a bitch," he snarled, quivering. "I never thought I'd see you again after what you did."

I raised a defensive hand. "Hold on! Wait! I'm not here to fight!"

Danny stomped down on my chest, driving the air from my lungs. He leaned heavily on it, keeping me in place, his voice like venom. "I have nothing to say to you other than go fuck yourself. Do you have any idea the hell you left me in when you pulled your little stunt and poisoned the Pig? Do you know what I've been through since it disappeared?! DO YOU!?"

I managed to wrestle him off my chest and took a gulp of air, quickly sitting up, coughing. "I-I know! I know all about it! I'm here to set things right!"

Danny looked like he was about to kick me again but paused. "Make things right?"

I nodded and took another shaking breath, rubbing the pain from my chest. "Yes...I have to find the Pig. Get it back...back to how things were before."

Danny just stared at me for a moment before spitting. "What the hell are you talking about?"

"I'm here to help, Danny. And I need you."

Danny snorted but backed off a step. "You need me...Jesus Christ, Nick I never thought I'd hear *you* say that."

I pulled myself to my feet and steadied my stance. "Look, man, I know I royally screwed things up here. I know the Pig is sick. I know the Keepers are unpredictable now. I know you lost your place and the Pig Born are taking it out on you for ordering them around for so long. I know you lost everything when the Pig disappeared. But I'm here to get things back. To put things as they were. I have to. And I'm going to need your knowledge of the Farm to do it."

Danny took another step back, his face swallowed by shadows. His voice came out as a whisper. "What the hell happened to you? Why do you care about any of this? You got out. You left. You escaped. Why the fuck would you come back?"

I said nothing, my chest rising and falling painfully.

"They found you," Danny said slowly. "They found you, didn't they?"

"It doesn't matter why I'm back," I said after a moment.

A sneer lit the corner of Danny's mouth. "What are they going to do o you if you don't get the Pig back in its place? What the hell has been romised to you?"

"It doesn't matter," I said again, voice hardening.

Danny shook his head. "It doesn't matter? Of course it does. You left me n the aftermath of your mess. And I can promise you that I have *suffered* for ." He advanced and jabbed a finger at me. "Whatever tortures they deliver you," he smiled, "I hope they're never-ending."

I let his words bleed out for a moment before responding, forcing my-lf to calm as much as I could. "Do you like this?" I asked, letting the words nk in. "Do you like being a plaything for these monsters?"

Danny grunted and leaned against the wall of our cell.

"I'm going to go ahead and guess you don't," I continued, keeping my ice low. "I'm guessing you'd do just about anything to get back to how ings were. This place is a nightmare, but at least you could avoid the worst the shit this place threw at you. I'm standing here right now, telling you at I'm trying to revive the Pig from whatever mess I left it in. I don't know here it is or what I'll have to do, but I know I'm going to need you. And I DO manage this impossible shit, then I'm guessing you'd get out of this llhole and back to the position you were in." I stepped toward him, teeth ming together. "In the short time I've been back, I have been beaten, bled, and imprisoned. So far, I've managed to keep it together. Barely. But I've managed." I felt an old darkness stir in my chest, a rising maw that crept up my throat. "But there's one thing I can't take and that's stupidity. I have too much to lose to tolerate idiocy. In case you can't tell, I'm a little fucking desperate. And if you don't take my offer and help me, then I swear to god Danny, I may just go mad." I stood nose to nose with him, letting the burning energy fill me. "Fucking *mad*."

Danny met my steely gaze, his breath hot across my face. "You're crazy if you think you can put things back the way they were."

"Are you saying you won't even try?"

Danny said nothing for a moment, then, "The thought of helping yo makes me actually want to vomit."

I suddenly grabbed him by the shirt, feeling an avalanche of frustratio and murderous desperation overwhelm me. "You'd be helping yourself, yo stupid FUCK! Don't you see!? If I actually pull this off, then you'll be fre from all this torture! Or do you like this? Have I completely misread th situation? Does this violence get you off or something?"

Danny shoved me away hard, his voice a snarl. "Get your goddam hands off me."

The maw, the shadow in my throat, growled at that, a long-suppresse stirring.

You can make him do what you want. You can hurt him.

I almost caved, the feeling, the need to strike out almost overwhelmin Danny must have seen it in my eyes, because he quickly raised his hands, h words coming quick.

"I didn't say I wouldn't do it, just that it'd make me sick."

"Yeah, well get over it," I said, barely keeping myself under control.

"Really got a way with words, don't you?"

I forced the tension from my shoulders, smoothing my tone as I did "I don't have time to stroke your ego or make you like me. Neither of us d

Danny waved a hand at our imprisonment. "You got some grand pl to get us out of here then?"

I looked at the bars. "I'm making it up as I go along. I'll thi of something."

Danny shook his head. "Jesus...what *was* your plan for all this?"

"Find you for starters," I said slowly, going to the wall and tracing my finger along the seams, "see if you knew where the hell the Pig went."

Danny said nothing.

Hand still on the wall, I looked at him. "What? What is it?"

"You really did a number on it last time."

"Be still my beating heart."

Danny turned and looked out of the cracks in the wood, out at the rain. "The Pig started to die, I think." His voice was soft now, his combatant nature ebbing away. "It got desperate. Everyone felt it. The Farm became unstable. Even more so than it is now. It's hard to explain. Things would just...happen."

I cocked an eyebrow. "Like what?"

Danny shrugged. "Just weird shit. Like, suddenly everything would go dark for a while. Pitch-black. Then the sky would turn red. Then back to the rain and gray. Random Pig Born would just explode, like something inside them detonated. Once, deep into it, the Pig went completely still. This was back when it was still at The Barn. It froze and didn't move for days. Didn't breathe, didn't communicate, didn't make a sound. When it returned back to its natural state...that's when things really went haywire."

"What do you mean?"

"I mean it started to vomit endlessly. Gallons and gallons of puke that spilled out and spread past the Barn and over the Farm. It just kept coming. Its form began to shrink and fall apart, like pieces of itself were rotting away."

I shook my head in disbelief. "That bad, huh?"

Danny stabbed a glare my way. "Yeah, that bad. Keep in mind, this is after shit already went sideways while you were still here. Remember the dead sun? Remember how the Pig blew it up?"

I nodded silently. How could I forget?

"Well, one of the Keepers got caught up in the explosion," Danny continued. "It took the full brunt of the blast. Call it bad luck that it happened to be in that part of the ocean."

"What happened to it?"

Danny grunted. "It was killed. I don't understand those things, what rules they abide by, but when that Keeper was destroyed, the rest abandoned the ocean. It wasn't immediate, but at some point they made landfall.

Sometimes they just walk aimlessly across the island. Other times they destroy us. You're never sure what they'll do." Danny lowered his voice. "There is one, though..."

"Berserker," I cut in. "I've heard of it."

Danny met my eyes. "Yeah. I don't know why, but that one...that one is a nightmare. If you see it coming, you better hide and hope you're lucky because it will annihilate anything in its path."

"Wonderful," I muttered, letting the conversation die.

I finished my inspection of the walls in silence, not finding any apparent weakness. I wrestled with horrible frustration and fear, the task before me seemingly impossible. Danny just watched me, his face masked in the darkness of our confinement.

I went over everything I had learned since my arrival on the Black Farm. So much had happened in such a shockingly short amount of time. And already I was imprisoned with barely a hope for escape. Every second I spent in here was another I wasn't solving the daunting problem before me. My thoughts drifted to my family, a small comfort in the misery I found myself in.

I knew Jess must have found my body by this point. And the note I had left her. It hurt to think about that, to think about the pain she was surely going through. The despair. The fear. The possibility that I might not return. I could almost picture her, clutching Theo to her chest, staring down at my lifeless corpse. Was she crying? Screaming? Or was she silent, pale-faced, and still?

You're doing this for them, I reminded myself, *whatever pain she's suffering, it doesn't compare to the pain she'd endure if you didn't.*

"We need to get out of here," I whispered distantly. Danny didn't respond, slumping quietly back down in his corner. Outside, I heard screaming.

"Danny."

"Mhm?"

"Can we do this? Is it possible to restore the Pig? To put things back the way they were?"

"I don't know, Nick. I don't know."

I went to him and crouched down, our eyes meeting in the gloom. "Danny."

"What?"

My eyes went as dark as the room. "Where is the Pig?"

It was a long time before he answered, his voice barely a whisper.

"On the other side of the ocean."

Chapter 6

' sat slumped against the wall, tapping my fingers against my leg, my mind .running wild. Thoughts clashed into one another, a vain attempt to form me kind of plan or way out of the cell. I knew they would come for me ain, take me back to the Pits to fight. That was my purpose here. To pro- de entertainment for the Pig Born. I had prodded Danny for more infor- ation on the Pig but he had fallen into silence, assuring me he didn't know uch more than where the Pig was.

Rain beat relentlessly against the roof of the shack. It dripped through e cracks in the ceiling and plopped loudly onto the floor. As I listened to around me, I couldn't shake Jess from my mind. She hurt to think about t remained present, a cloud of darkness intertwined with a pulse of light.

Time dragged on, a slog of misery and rain and distant screams. I could ar others being thrown into the Pits, Suicidals like myself who had the isfortune of getting caught. Danny just stared at the slits in the wall, our ly glimpse of the outside world and all the hell it had to offer.

At some point, I heard movement outside of our hut, a clatter of hooves d wet flesh slapping against the stairs. I stood quickly and saw Danny do e same. I pressed myself into the corner, like that would somehow hide my esence from whatever was coming.

The door banged open beyond the bars, casting a spill of gray gloom in- le. A trio of Pig Born pressed inside and came to the prison door, fumbling with the chains. My heart began to race, the fear of the Pits rising strong my throat. Danny just watched, his face set in stone.

The Pig Born opened the door and came for me, grabbing me rough by the arms. Terrified, I let myself be dragged from the cell, knowing it w useless to fight right now. Danny was taken as well, led by a single captor my back. My imagination went wild with fear as we exited the hut and I w temporarily blinded by rain as it fell into my eyes.

Where are they taking you?! My mind howled frantically.

As we clattered down the stairs of the hut, a Pig Born on either side me, I looked around trying to gauge what new torment was coming. Befo us was a large gathering, a circle of Pig Born all staring at whatever lie at t center. I was hustled through the ranks along with Danny and jerked to halt once we had passed to the inner circle. I saw other Suicidals around n as well—shivering, bruised messes. Our eyes met and then parted, leavi traces of hopelessness in our wake. We were all focused on what lie in t center of the ring. When I saw it, my heart sank and I felt my breath stutt

A man lay naked across the earth, his hands and feet hammered in the earth. He was crying, his body shivering violently in the cold rain. T Pig Born surrounding him snickered and shifted excitedly, making sure t other Suicidals were watching complacently.

Danny bumped into my shoulder and I heard him suck air between h teeth. "Shit."

"What is this?" I whispered quietly, unable to tear my eyes from t stripped man. Blood oozed lazily from his spread-eagle limbs.

Danny kept his head down as he answered. "This is what they do to y if you don't participate in the pits. If you just let yourself be killed withou fight. Once the clouds spit you back out, they'll find you. They make sure it." He shook his head. "Then they make an example out of you for everyo to see."

Before I could ask another question, the wall of Pig Born across fro me parted to allow a particularly huge one inside the ring. It was a massi mutation of bubbling flesh, snot, and limbs. Its mouth extended out fro its face and was pulled down into a snarl, a growth of jutting teeth cutti up from its lipless mouth. Its eyes varied in size and rolled without purpo in their sockets. Its thick legs took it across the wet ground on cloven hoofs, stopping before the naked Suicidal.

In its twisted hands, it held a colossal sledgehammer.

"Oh no," I gasped, squeezing my eyes shut. Something meaty thunked into the back of my head and I had to stop myself from falling on my face, pain spider-webbing across my skull. I blinked and felt wet breath in my ear.

"Watch."

The giant Pig Born circled the naked man, dragging the thick iron hammer across the ground so the Suicidal could see what was coming. I felt my heart thundering as the man's cries went from fear to terror, his eyes bulging. The other Suicidals' faces were pale and I spotted a few of them weeping silently. Around us, the Pig Born cheered, stomping their feet in anticipation.

"Whatever you do," Danny whispered urgently at my side, "keep your eyes open."

This is going to be bad.

I tried to steady my breath, but the man's howls of anticipated pain cut me to the core and drained me of all calm. I clenched my fists and prayed that it would be over quickly. The Pig Born began to chant in their broken dialect, a single, guttural word repeated over and over again.

"Break! Break! Break!"

Jesus Christ, my mind creaked, followed by something more cynical that made me sick to my stomach.

Better him than you.

The towering Pig Born stopped its circuit around the naked man and raised the hammer over its head, the helpless body before him convulsing with blind fear. The crowd roared with approval, their chants crescendoing above us.

WHAM!

I felt my legs almost give out as the hammer came down across the naked man's left knee. The smack of flesh was deafening, followed by the undeniable crunch of bone. The shrieks that followed turned my gut to rot and I clenched my teeth, bottom lip quivering as I watched.

WHAM!

The annihilation of the second leg brought the man's screams to new heights, blood and bone popping and squirting out from beneath the hammer's weight. The crowd jumped and jostled around me excitedly, whooping and calling out in energetic barks and snorts. The other Suicidals watched the mutilation with looks of absolute stunned shock, sympathetic tears escaping down their faces.

WHAM! WHAM!

The shins went next. It was like watching wood splinter and shriek and bleed.

WHAM! WHAM!

Feet next.

WHAM!

Right hand.

WHAM!

Left hand. Screaming so bad it hurt my ears.

WHAM! WHAM! WHAM!

More blood than rain now.

WHAM!

The Pig Born roared and cheered, spittle and sweat spraying across the back of my neck.

WHAM!

The naked man's face imploded beneath the hammer, finally silencing his suffering. The escalation of elation from the crowd almost blew out my eardrums. Now that the grisly spectacle was over, I sank my eyes to the ground, feeling my stomach turn. My fists remained clenched at my sides and I shuddered. Danny shifted next to me, silent. Before us, the Pig Born with the hammer began to prod at the shattered corpse, grunting with amusement as chunks of gore squished and squirted. The other Suicidals stood across from me, the trauma taking hold.

"Smashed!" the giant one cried, still poking the broken body. "Smashed! Smashed!" The others gurgled with glee and pumped their hooves and gnarled fingers into the air, their bloodlust sated.

Suddenly, without warning, the Pig Born began to quiet, a hush washing through them with jarring abruptness. Their faces went slack and their eyes rolled past me toward the ocean at my back. I saw something flicker in their gaze, some emotion I had never seen from them before. Fear.

I turned with the crowd, looking past my captors, across the rain-swept fields toward the distant shoreline and out into the dark waters. When I saw what everyone was staring at, I felt my blood turn to ice.

A Keeper stood motionless, watching us, its colossal form towering hundreds of feet out of the black sea. The glyphs lining its stone form pulsed the deepest crimson.

"Oh, fuck," Danny whispered next to me. All the blood had drained from his face and his eyes were wide.

The giant cross jutting from the shoulders of the great titan swayed slightly, scraping the ceiling of the sky. Even from this distance, I could see the chains that swung from the crossbeam, bodies dangling from the ends. Its arms dipped down into the waters, an unmoving monster, its presence absorbing the horizon.

"Berserker," I muttered when I found my breath.

The Pig Born surrounding us began to shift uncomfortably, their eyes locked on the giant golem in the sea. I could feel their fear seeping between them as they waited anxiously to see what the Keeper would do. I felt them step away from me, from the other Suicidals as well, our existence temporarily forgotten. I swallowed hard, the rain illuminated by the glowing red coming off of the mountain of stone in the sea.

An immense groan split the clouds, an echoing, grinding cascade of noise that made me wince, heart racing. I let out a silent breath between my lips, my captors growing more and more nervous.

"The trees," Danny whispered next to me. "If we get separated, run for the trees. I'll find you."

I kept my voice low. "What's about to happen here?"

Danny kept his eyes on the ocean. "A lot of us are about to die."

I winced as a jolting eruption blasted from the Keeper, a rumbling crunch roaring from its form, its body suddenly arching backwards, the enormous cross jammed between its shoulders shuddering.

It began to sprint toward us. Panicked chaos exploded around me as the Pig Born scattered, terrified squeals escaping from their mutated mouths. Great spouts of water rose around the Keeper's legs, its mammoth limbs churning through the ocean at a horrifying speed. The groan and grind of its movements were like the detonations of a clock ticking down the precious seconds between us and itself.

I felt a hand grab my arm, an urgent scream in my ear. "Nick, RUN!"

Danny pulled me along in a wave of dispersing Pig Born, the two of us becoming lost in the grunts and screams of the creatures. I felt myself jostled along, clumsily bumping and stumbling in the crowd as we fled, the thunderous monster growing closer at our backs. Danny steered us out of the pack, our boots splashing in the mud, directing us toward the treeline, seemingly forever away.

You'll never make it in time.

I mustered as much speed as I could and saw Danny do the same, the two of us sprinting as fast as we were able to. I chanced a glance over my shoulder and wished I hadn't, my heart leaping into my throat.

Berserker had reached the beach, its skyscraper legs pulling geysers of water out of the ocean with it. Its stone limbs pounded the sand, sending storms of the stuff exploding on contact. It was only a handful of miles away from us, from the Pits, from the terrified Pig Born who now split the four corners of the horizon in a desperate attempt to survive the coming onslaught.

"Don't look, just run!" Danny yelled as the rain whipped across his face. We were neck and neck, the rolling hills rising before us. It felt like they elongated as we ran, the space between us and the forest an impossibility.

BOOM! BOOM! BOOM! BOOM!

The earth shook beneath every colossal step Berserker took as it came for us, its towering form looming at our backs. The crunch and roll of stone as it moved sounded like a city crumbling, announcing our violent, impending death.

The mud squashed underfoot as I ran, sapping the energy from my legs. The air I frantically pulled into my lungs began to feel as if it were laced with glass, my lungs burning. Despite Danny's warning, I looked back just as Berserker reached the Pits and crude huts. It exploded through them like a bomb, annihilating the fragile structures like they were nothing. Wood erupted into splinters and whistled overhead and I saw a group of Pig Born get caught up in the collision, blood and flesh pulverized in an instant. The roar of the destruction pushed me forward, driving fear deep into my chest

I coughed, half-blind from the rain, and forced myself to keep moving. Danny's flayed gasps ripped from his lips and I knew we were both growing exhausted as the land sped past, each step pulling us closer to the trees.

Another eruption drove my eyes over my shoulder. Berserker backhanded a group of screaming Pig Born, taking out three huts in the process. Their flesh pulverized beneath the blow, spraying gore in an arch across the sky like dead crimson comets.

Keep...running, I thought, looking forward again. The forest was now only a couple hundred yards away, the promise of safety horribly close.

A shuddering groan rocked the heavens and I heard Danny curse at my side, rain streaking across his pale face. The land rumbled as Berserker moved once again, the tremors telegraphing its trajectory.

"It's coming this way!" Danny yelled, throwing a look behind us.

I dared to look and felt my eyes go wide. Berserker had turned its attention from the ruined Pig Born. It was now thundering toward us, its shape a massive structure of power and terror that rose up into the gloom-filled skies. Its colossal legs ate up the distance with ease, the cross-shaped head swaying as it approached. The grind of rock was so loud I felt like my skull would split beneath the noise.

I dumped the last of my energy reserves into my legs and practically ew, so close to the woods that I could make out the individual leaves.

BOOM BOOM BOOM!

"FUCK!" Danny screamed. "We're not going to make it!"

I felt a shadow fall across me, the screech of stone blasting like cannon re. I looked up and felt panic explode up my throat. Berserker loomed ove us like a collapsing tower, an arm the size of a cruise ship falling rapidly toward me.

"SHIT!" I screamed, diving to the left a split second before Berserker's m connected with the ground. The impact was massive, like something neath the earth had erupted, blasting me off my feet, sending me airborne. or a moment, as I flew through the empty air, stars slamming into my eyes, thought I had been killed and spit back out of the clouds. My vision filled ith gray and then rotated, allowing me a brief glimpse of the blackened sky the distance where the dead sun had once been.

As I began to come down, wind roaring in my ears, I caught a solita
snapshot of the maddened Keeper, its red glyphs pulsing like lava down i
titan-sized body. It was pulling its arm from the earth, its strike missing n
by mere feet. Great clods of dirt and mud came up with the limb, leaving
canyon in its wake.

I connected back with the ground and felt the air crushed from n
lungs. My shoulder hit first and I clumsily tried to roll with the impa
somersaulting painfully and skidding in the mud like I was carving a lan
ing strip.

My head rang and my system went into shock, paralyzing me where
lay, battered by the ever-present rain. I lay on my back, chest rising and fa
ing rapidly. In my periphery, I saw Berserker thundering away from me, ba
toward the Pits. The vermillion light of its stone-cast body blurred across r
stunned vision, leaving traces of red in its wake. I blinked, trying to clear r
head, convinced every bone in my body was broken. I felt the ground sha
as the Keeper stalked further across the island, searching for new creatu
to kill and destroy.

Get up, Nick. You have to move.

The thought was almost laughable. I coughed violently, blinking agai
the rain. Every part of me began to howl as the shock started to wear off. M
shoulder felt like it had been struck with a hammer, my legs like someo
had run them over with a truck.

Get to the trees. It's going to come back and finish you off.

In the haze of pain, the thought made terrifying sense and I brac
myself to try to sit up. Before I could even try, though, Danny suddenly a
peared over me, his face pale and grim. He dropped to his knees next to n
his hands running over my body.

"Jesus Christ, I thought you were fucked," he muttered. "Can you stan

"I can barely see," I gasped, wincing and forcing myself up.

Danny slid his hands under my arms and helped me to my feet, brin
ing a wave of pain jolting through my body. I placed a hand to my he
squeezing my eyes shut.

"Is it coming back?" I asked with my eyes closed, the sound of Berserk
thunderous footfalls all too present in the background of my pain.

"I'd rather not find out," Danny hissed. "Come on, tough guy, the treeline is right there, we need to get out of sight."

Forcing myself to move, I began to hobble forward, Danny trotting at my side. I was convinced I would collapse after only a couple steps but managed to keep myself vertical. At our backs, the continuous sound of death and destruction echoed as Berserker continued its rampage.

Finally, mercifully, we reached the treeline and crossed over into its protective cover. I almost tripped a dozen times as we went, each step sending rockets of pain shooting up my legs to detonate in my brain.

After a couple minutes, I slowed, darkness clouding my vision. I held up a hand for Danny to slow.

"I...I have to stop...catch my breath for a moment," I gasped, patches of ink swirling across my vision.

Danny turned to me, his face an impatient grimace. "We have to get further in, this is too close to the treeline still."

Dizzy, I felt myself sit down hard, back thumping against a tree. "Can't... just can't…" I could barely breathe, exhaustion flooding my system.

Danny shook his head. "For fuck's sake…"

I could feel myself blacking out, finally giving over to the pain. Before I did, though, I craned my neck up to Danny. "Why...why did you help me? Could have...gone…"

Danny turned away, his voice low. "Shit if I know…"

And then I was gone.

Chapter 7

I don't know how long I rested in the uneasy darkness before I came to again. My mouth was dry and my muscles bunched together, cramping and twisting uncomfortably. I pushed the groggy haze from my mind and forced my eyes open. It took a couple tries.

I was sitting against the tree still, bark digging into my back. Danny stood across from me, leaning against his own tree. When he saw I was awake, he grunted and crossed his arms.

"Thought you were going to die," he said without any emotion.

I rolled my shoulder and winced, the pain still present. "I'm sure that would have broken your heart."

"It would have been pretty inconvenient."

"Wouldn't want that," I groaned, testing the rest of my limbs.

"You good to walk?"

I looked up at him. "Just give me a second." I gingerly prodded my ribs, checking for breaks. "Have you seen anyone while I've been out?"

Danny crouched, shaking his head. "A couple Suicidals passed our way a while ago. They didn't see us. Not sure if they were innocents or part of that *group*."

I cocked an eyebrow. "What group?"

"There's a bunch of Suicidals that have banded together. Safety in numbers kind of thing," Danny sniffed. "They're almost as nasty as the Pig Born." He looked directly at me. "You remember the cult? The Hooves of the Pig?"

I nodded.

"Yeah, well, after you burned down their temple, they migrated to the woods. The actual temple is there still, but the Pig Born infest it now. It's one of the few places the Keepers leave alone. Not quite sure why."

I massaged life back into my stiff shoulder. "Is this the group that Peter leads?"

Danny grunted. "Yeah. Their numbers have grown recently. The Pig Born don't really mess with them anymore, which is the point, I think. Fucking assholes."

"So why didn't you ever join up with them? If they offer protection, I'd assume you'd be all over that."

He looked like I had just spit in his face, his voice a disgusted curl. "I would rather suffer in the Pits than ever join those pathetic fucks."

"What exactly is your problem with them?" I asked. "The Suicidals, I mean. You hate them so much, and yet you're one of us."

"So?"

"Seems a little strange."

Danny looked away. "It doesn't matter. But if we see them, we stay away, got it?"

"Whatever you say, Danny."

"So can we go now?"

Biting my lip, I slowly stood, carefully testing my legs. "You know where we're going? You have a plan?"

"You're the one hell-bent on putting this place back together. I'm just along for the ride."

I steadied myself, fairly sure I wouldn't collapse immediately. "At this point, you know more than I do. I was told to find you. I did. You gotta pull some of the weight now."

"Jesus Christ, Nick."

I shot him a hard look. "Look, I'm doing the best I can. I'm in uncharted waters here without a prayer in the world, all right? You think I *want* any of this responsibility?"

Danny stepped toward me, his voice dropping. "You know, you never did tell me why you came back—why you're so desperate to set things right."

I waved him away. "It doesn't concern you."

"Well, considering I'm now in this shit with you...I would say it does." He leaned toward me. "Which side got to you? Who threatened you?"

I was silent a long time before answering. "His name was Ramiel. He's an angel. Whatever that actually means."

"Ramiel," Danny repeated, chewing on the name. "Huh. I'm not surprised."

"You know him?"

"No, but I assumed it was heaven that got to you first. Cowardly bastards."

"Right."

Danny turned his attention back to me. "So, what? They threaten you with hell or something?"

I looked away. "Yeah, something like that."

Danny grinned suddenly. "They're playing dirty, aren't they?"

I exhaled wearily. "If there's one thing I've learned, it's that nothing about death is fucking fair."

"Boo-hoo," Danny snorted, "poor Nick."

"Fuck you."

"You done trying to impress me?" Danny continued. "Can we get on with it?"

I sighed, feeling frustrated and more than a little angry. "You keep saying that, like you're expecting me to pull out a magic reset button and press it."

"That'd be nice."

I ran my hands over my face. "Goddamn it...look...you said you know where the Pig went after it disappeared, right?"

"Maybe."

I bared my teeth, temper spiking. "You are seriously testing my patience right now."

Danny motioned away from us. "Yes, I know where it went. Jesus, calm down. I know you have a reputation to uphold, but relax, we're on the same side."

I clenched my fists, teeth grinding together. "Look...back at the Pits, you said you knew where the Pig went. You said it's across the ocean, right?"

Danny nodded. "Yeah...yeah, I might have said that."

I fought to keep my pulse under control. "Why would it go there? What's out there?"

Danny looked at me for a long time before answering, his voice even and quiet. "A mistake."

"What the hell does that mean?"

"It means that if we're going to make things right, we need to follow it."

I shook my head. "How? We can't cross the ocean. I tried that once." I paused, the memory slamming into me. "It didn't end well."

Danny kept his voice low, measuring his words carefully. "You're right we can't cross it. The Keepers would catch you."

"So how do we get to the Pig then?"

Danny met my eyes with darkness. "We go *under* the ocean."

I blinked, surprised. "Under?"

Danny just nodded.

"How on earth do we do that?"

Danny's eyes cautiously scanned the woods like he was afraid someon would hear. "There's a tunnel."

I leaned into him, keeping my voice down. "And where does this tun nel lead?"

Danny's face turned grim. "It leads down into the Abyss."

Confusion swept through me. "Is that where the Pig went? Down int this...Abyss?"

Danny shook his head. "No. There's something across the ocean that needs. Past the Abyss."

"Danny," I said as patiently as I could, "what's out there?"

"There's another island, Nick."

I said nothing, his words coursing through my head like freezing wat Another island? How? What purpose did it serve? Was it an extension of tl Black Farm? Were there more Suicidals out there? Pig Born?

A memory suddenly resurfaced, something Ramiel had told me.

I turned it on Danny. "This...this island. Does it have anything to c with the Mud Man?"

Danny's eyes fell on me with curious hesitation. "Where did you he that name?"

"The angel, Ramiel. He mentioned it. Said the Pig Born kept whispe ing about it."

Danny looked down at his hands. "Interesting."

"What is the Mud Man?" I pressed. "Who is he?"

Danny was quiet for a moment, then. "Let's...let's focus on one obstacle at a time."

I felt my frustration peak once again. "No, I want some answers here, Danny. If you know something that's going to help us, I need to know about it."

Danny shot me a look out of the corner of his eye. "I barely know more about it than you do."

"But you know about this...this Mud Man?"

"Not exactly."

"I swear to—"

"I don't know!" Danny growled suddenly.

I forced myself to calm as best I could. "There's still something you're not telling me."

"When I understand more about what we're dealing with, I'll be sure to write you an essay, OK?" Danny stepped away from me. "We have enough shit to get through without you drilling me about things I don't even fully understand, OK? Is that good enough for you?!"

I kept my voice even. "I guess it'll have to be. But I'm going to keep my eye on you."

"I'm shaking in my fucking boots," Danny snorted. "You know, you used to just charge into things head-first without a care in the world. When you royally fucked this place up last time, you didn't know shit about shit. But now you're afraid to barely take a step without discussing it for eternity. Where the hell is the old Nick? The one who punched first and asked questions later? Because I'll tell you what, buddy—you better find him and drag him back out or you're not going to make it this time around."

I met his stare. "Things are different now."

"You've gone soft," Danny challenged. "Back there in the cell when I hit you? The old Nick would have brushed himself off and knocked my teeth out. But what did you do? Huh? You tried to reason with me instead. I mean, Jesus."

Rip his throat out.

I swallowed hard. "I'm just not that person anymore, OK? I came back for a singular purpose, and mindless violence isn't it."

Danny waved a hand dismissively. "Sure Nick. Whatever you say. I just hope you have some fire left in you because we're going to need it before this is over. I can promise you that."

Gouge his eyes out.

I counted to ten and then tried again. "Listen...we have a long road ahead of us. I'm not going to fight you, OK? I can still hold my own if that's what you're worried about. But we have to be careful." I paused. "*I* have to be careful."

No you don't.

Danny's mouth twisted at the corners. "Sure. We done now?"

I nodded and tried to edge the anger out of my voice. "This tunnel you mentioned...where is it?"

"Past the mountain. The one that isn't there anymore."

"And this tunnel...it will take us beneath the ocean to the island? The one you think the Pig has fled to?"

Danny gave me a sharp look. "I don't think it, Nick. I know that's where it is."

I cocked an eyebrow his way. "Well, at least we know where we're going. That's a start." I continued to look at him, a question brimming. "How is it that you know that, though? What if we go all that way and you're wrong?"

"I'm not wrong."

"But what if you are? That's a long way for nothing."

"Jesus Christ, Nick, if you don't stop with the questions—"

"I don't want to linger here any longer than I have to," I cut in. "Forgive me for not completely trusting your word."

Danny squeezed the bridge of his nose, irritated. "It's out there. I can feel it. It's on the second island."

"You can...feel it?"

Danny's eyes snapped open. "When I began my service to the Pig, I was linked to it. It was the only way I could understand its wishes. It was the only way I could fulfill my role as a mediator between the Suicidals and the Pig." He looked directly at me. "I had to eat a piece of its flesh. To bind us, in a way, to one another."

My face drooped in disgust. "You...ate...a piece of the Pig?"

Danny nodded. "I had to."

"So can you like...talk to it?"

"No. Not in the way you're imagining. I can only...sense...what it wants. Not as words or even pictures. More like...flavors...it passes on to me. It's almost impossible to describe, and I don't see the point in doing so. But yes, I am connected to the Pig and I can sense where it is. Faintly."

I pushed my disgust aside. "Is that how you know about the island? Because of the Pig?"

"I think I know a lot I'm not supposed to. When I bonded with the Pig, we kind of...spilled into one another." Danny raised a hand to his head. "It almost overwhelmed me...the things I saw," he shook his head, "but through all that, I became aware of the existence of another island. I don't think I'm supposed to know about it, so I kept my mouth shut. But that's where it is and if we stand here talking about it for another second, I might just lose my shit."

I raised my hands defensively. "Fine. I'm convinced. If we have to travel to the mountain, we're going to have to cross a lot of open ground. I'll keep my questions to myself for now. But I believe you. Where exactly is this tunnel?"

Danny gritted his teeth. "Color me for a fool, but that sounded an awful lot like a question."

"All right. I trust you know where you're going. Lead the way."

Without another word, Danny pushed past me into the forest, a look of hardened irritation emblazoned across his face. I turned and followed, my feet crunching through the underbrush. My legs were stiff and my ribs thrummed, but it was more of a discomfort than actual pain. I pushed low-hanging branches out of the way as I followed Danny deep into the woods. He didn't linger and walked quickly, stepping confidently over fallen trees and over intrusive rocks. The rain overhead was slowed by the canopy of green and only faintly dribbled down to us.

As we walked, I inspected everything I had learned. The presence of another island was a shock. Why had the Pig gone to it? Was it really still there? What was on the island? I tossed these questions around and circled back to what Danny had said when I had asked that very thing.

A mistake. He said the island held a mistake. But what did that mean? I decided it was useless to guess and so I pushed it away. We had a long way to go before we even got there. First we had to get through this tunnel and pass through...what had Danny called it?

The Abyss. I dared not even guess why it was called that, but I knew I'd understand soon enough. The Black Farm was horrible enough on the surface...but down beneath it? For a second time, I pushed the subject aside, feeling uneasy. I knew the answers were ahead of me.

Time marched to the beat of our boots, distant noise trickling in from the dense woods. Occasionally I would hear the snap of a branch or a distant scream, immediately putting me on high alert. But the further we went, the more it seemed to fade. We were leaving the living and headed toward the part of the island that had been annihilated, the earth scorched beneath the detonation of the dead sun. The memory burned into my mind with haunting clarity. I had been at the end of my journey when the Pig had wiped out the streaking colors in the sky that had come to investigate. If it had the power to do that, then I couldn't imagine what it would do if it ever freed itself from the Black Farm.

Our trek remained uneventful as we crested the edge of the forest. The treeline thinned, giving way to an expanse of ash-soaked earth. Broken hills and shallow canyons expanded out before us, stretching toward the far-off mountain. It was a pathetic thing now, a rise of rubble that fanned out across the horizon. The rain came heavier now that we were out of the woods, the sky a spider web of black veins that grew from a tar-black smudge in the clouds.

Danny pushed forward, scanning the gray foothills for signs of Pig Born. Faint howls echoed with the rain as we walked, my eyes cautiously prodding every dip and rise. As we traveled across the open expanse, I realized how different the Farm felt now. It was as if it were holding its breath, its life force sheltered in the aftershock of the Pig's wrath. Things scurried now instead of sprinted. The shadows seemed filled with wary eyes. The gloom seemed quieter. Not because the dangers were gone, but because they were hidden now. The balance was off. Everything feared everything.

Except for the Keepers.

I wrapped my arms around myself and shivered in the cold wet. I followed Danny down a long slope and around a deep scar in the earth. I looked down into it as we passed the edge and saw only darkness down below.

Time slogged on like mud sliding into a river bed. The soundtrack of e Farm filled my head, the broken mountain growing closer and closer th every passing hour. Fatigue crept into my legs, but I knew we couldn't op. Not when we were wide out in the open. I blew rainwater from my lips th every breath, boots splashing and sliding across the soupy ash and rock.

Finally, after what seemed like forever, we reached the base of the ountain. Danny stopped and I took the opportunity to catch my breath. gazed up at the remains of summit and saw it was nothing more than a ister of fractured boulders and sliding rubble. I looked to the right and otted the Temple a couple miles away, its stone steeple peeking out over a umbling slope.

"The tunnel isn't over by that, is it?" I asked, nodding toward it.

Danny wiped water from his face. "No. Other side. We have to go ound a bit."

I eyed the far-off Temple. "You think we'll run into any Pig Born? I ow you said they're over here."

"I don't know, Nick."

I craned my neck and looked toward the summit once more. "You ow...despite everything...I'm glad this place was destroyed."

Danny said nothing.

I continued to stare, the rain beating down into my face, causing me squint. As I looked, something caught my eye. It was a flicker of light. othing more than a faint streak of blue that winked in and out of existence oss the heavens.

"You see that?" I asked quietly.

"See what?"

I didn't respond, fixated on where I had seen the light. It had looked e a falling star, as if a cobalt paintbrush had been flicked across the clouds.

Is that you, Ramiel? I thought. *Are you watching me?*

"We need to move," Danny said.

I nodded and we began to walk again, this time skirting the base of fallen mountain, away from the Temple. My legs ached, but I was get-g used to ignoring pain. The ground was filled with gravel and rock now, king the terrain harder to travel. I paid attention to where I stepped,

knowing a twisted ankle would make an already hard journey that mu
more treacherous.

It took some time, but we managed to reach the bend without in
dent or injury. The backside of the mountain looked similar to the front
shattered rise of natural debris. Danny led us inward, taking us up a slig
incline, the world a wash of gray clouds, rain, and rock.

It wasn't long when suddenly Danny held up a hand. I stopped, ha
sliding on some loose slate, and caught myself.

"What is it?" I asked, peering over his shoulder.

Danny pointed to something ahead of us. "Look there."

I did as I was told, eyes burrowing into the side of the mountain.
that...is that the tunnel?"

"No," Danny said quietly, "but it *is* a tunnel."

"Which means something is in there," I said quietly.

"Could be."

"Pig Born?"

"Most likely," Danny said. "We should avoid it. Go back down a lit
and give it a wide berth. We're getting close now, and I don't want to run in
an angry mountain horde."

I stared at the hole. It plunged into the side of the mountain, no bigg
than three or four feet across. As I studied it, a faint noise began to er
from the darkness. Danny noticed it, too, his eyes snapping back to the e
trance. It was only thirty or forty feet away from us, the echoing sound risi
in volume. I felt the hairs on my arms stand up.

"That's screaming," I said quietly, face paling.

"I hear it."

I waited for another howl from the mouth of the cave, and wher
came, I felt my stomach drop. "Oh Christ, Danny...that sounds like a kid

Danny looked at me, rain streaking down his worn face. "So what?
not our problem. We should go. Come on, follow me."

But I didn't move, the sound of the screaming child rooting me in pla
It sounded like something or someone was hurting them. Badly. My mi
tumbled over itself with thoughts of Theo, my little man. I couldn't stand
even imagine him in pain. I couldn't imagine leaving him to suffer.

That's not Theo in there. Leave this place.

Danny grabbed my arm. "Nick."

Another wave of agony echoed out from the mouth of the cave.

"I can't walk away from this," I said slowly, skin curling.

Danny gripped my arm tighter. "What the fuck are you talking about? This isn't our problem."

I shook my head. "I don't care. There's a kid in there that's getting hurt. I can't just leave."

Danny grabbed me by the shirt, mouth twisting into a snarl. "What the hell is this? What are you talking about? You some kind of saint now? What has happened to you!?"

I shook him off. "If that was my kid in there getting hurt, I sure as hell would want someone to step in and save them."

"Oh, for *fuck's* sake—"

"I'm going in there," I said, stepping toward the entrance, "and I need you to have my back."

Danny threw his hands into the air. "Are you kidding me? You have some kind of halo around your head I can't see or something?"

Another shuddering scream came from the mouth of the tunnel and I quickened my pace, making my way toward the gaping entrance. I heard Danny growl at my back, but then following me to catch up.

"You're a real pisser, Nick," Danny hissed in my ear.

"Shh!" I said, hushing him. I crouched by the tunnel entrance and peered inside. Another scream cascaded out, sending a shiver down my spine. Whoever was getting hurt in there sounded very young.

Taking a deep breath, I entered the tunnel. I crouched low, the ceiling pressing down overhead, almost forcing me to crawl. I heard Danny curse and then scramble in after me. I could make out a dim light ahead of us, a flickering flame that sent shadows dancing down the tunnel toward us. I slowed as we reached the end, the narrow passage opening up to reveal a small cave lit by a fire in the center. I stayed in the tunnel, pressing myself against the wall, Danny at my side.

My eyes widened as I stared inside. Two shirtless men stood with their backs to the fire, away from us. Tied to the cave wall was a small girl in a filthy white dress, no more than four or five years old. Her arms were stretched over her head, secured by a knot of rope. As I watched, my blood began to boil and I felt my teeth grind together.

One of the men, no older than myself, was holding an axe. He was laughing and pressing the blunt end of the head against the girl's crotch. The young girl cried out in pain and squirmed, tears rolling down her cheeks. The other man, the one without the axe, stepped forward and slapped her hard across the face.

"We told you to keep your mouth shut," He grinned, staring down at her. "When are you going to learn to listen to us?"

The man with the axe jammed it once again into the girl, harder this time. The girl screamed, her cries shrill and terrified. The man with the axe chuckled.

"Come on, now, we haven't even taken your clothes off yet. If you think that hurts, you better prepare yourself." He snickered and rubbed his crotch. "You're going to make a fine pet if you just learn to do what you're told."

The other man slapped the girl once again, the blow hard enough to daze her. Her head rocked to the side and she let out a choked gasp of pain, her little arms sagging in their restraints.

My jaw locked and I felt adrenaline explode across my body. I moved without thinking, a bolt of dark lightning coursing through my mind like a vicious current. I took four long strides across the cave and grabbed the man with the axe by the back of the neck.

He let out a surprised yelp as I pulled him backwards and down onto the fire. Sparks exploded beneath his weight, the flames springing up around him like burning ribbons.

"Jesus CHRIST!" he screamed, dropping the axe, thrashing to get off the fire.

Something thundered in my head, a throbbing pain that drove me, wiping out everything else. I raised my boot and brought it down into the man's face. He howled, his back on fire, blood and teeth exploding from his open mouth. I stomped down onto his face again. And again. And again. Each blow pulled my lips back into a snarl, each breath a hiss.

The man's face caved in on the eighth blow. The air crackled and stank of cooked flesh. I stepped away and looked at the remaining man. His eyes were wide and terrified, his back against the wall in the far corner. He raised a shaking hand to me, his voice a stutter.

"L-l-look man," he wheezed, unable to escape the sight of his dead accomplice. "I don't want any trouble...Jesus...you didn't have to...I mean Jesus..." he pressed himself against the wall again, shaking his head in disbelief, his ruined friend beginning to blacken over the fire.

Without speaking, I bent down and picked up the axe. My head pounded, the pain almost unbearable. I heard the man speaking to me, but it seemed muted and far away. The edges of my vision were tinted red. The cave suddenly seemed hot, way too hot.

I stepped toward the remaining man, hoisting the axe.

"Stop, STOP!" the man pleaded, raising his hands. "Look, you can have her! She's yours! Take her!"

I stopped, looming over the shaking man. I ran my tongue across my lips, everything dry and cracked and hot and miserable.

"I can...have her?" I croaked.

The man nodded vigorously. "Yes! She's all yours! Just, just...just take her and leave!"

I leaned down, the pain in my head beating against my skull. "She's a fucking *child*."

The man's eyes shot around with confusion. "Yeah...yeah, I know...we were just having a little fun, we weren't really going to hurt her! We uh...we were protecting her! From the Pig Born! You see—"

I swung the axe as hard as I could, the blade plunging into the man's gut, puncturing through his intestines with ease. The man let out a gasping grunt, his eyes bulging, blood spraying from his mouth. I yanked the blade away and he fell to his knees, hands going to the gash in his stomach. He looked up at me, blood running down his chin.

I flipped the head of the axe around and brought the blunt end down into his teeth like a hammer. They ejected from his mouth in a spray of red, the man's nose shattering in the process. Too stunned to scream, the man fell to the floor and onto his back, his body twitching, his hands shakily reaching for the holes in his gums.

Breathing heavily, my head splitting with pain, I stood over him and brought the axe up one last time. He raised a hand weakly, one last dazed attempt to stop his coming death. I brought the blade down into his face, cleaving his skull in two.

Panting, I stared down at the corpse. Everything swam with red and I closed my eyes, suddenly letting go of the axe. I clutched my head and gritted my teeth, stars exploding behind my eyelids.

A hand found my shoulder, Danny's voice in my ear. "You got 'em, Nick. They're dead."

I opened my eyes, throat incredibly dry, sweat running down my face. My voice was a gasp, a dehydrated croak. I looked down at the blood on my hands.

"*Fuck.*"

I turned around and came face to face with Danny. His jaw was set and his eyes were dark. He simply nodded.

I wiped my hands on my pants and dragged my shirtsleeve across my face. I looked at the little girl and saw she was staring at me, tears running down her face, a bruise standing out on her cheek.

I quickly went to her, my adrenaline draining. With shaking hands, I cut her free from the ropes. To my surprise, she stumbled back and away from me, retreating weakly into the corner of the cave. She huddled down into herself, crying quietly, and stared at me from between her fingers. Her small shoulders shook and I realized she was absolutely terrified.

I slowly outstretched my hands toward her, trying to keep my posture as relaxed as I could. "Hey...hey I'm not going to hurt you. You're safe now," I said gently. I took a tentative step toward her, keeping my voice low and friendly. "You can trust me. I'm going to get you out of here, OK? Do you want to go outside?"

What did you do?

The girl mopped her face with a grimy hand and then slowly nodded. It was a pathetic motion, her eyes stained with tears, bottom lip quivering.

"Come on, then," I motioned, holding my ground, not wanting to scare her. "I'll take you out of here."

Her big brown eyes traveled over me and I saw fear ripple through them. I looked down at myself, at the bloodstains and dirt and gore.

Jesus Nick. What did you do*?*

"Please," I asked softly, "come with me?"

Finally, cautiously, the little girl got up and walked toward me. I crouched down and opened up my arms to her, smiling as best as I could.

Suddenly, she fell into my arms with a whimper, an act of desperation with a need to make sense of all the violence and pain. I hugged her to me.

"It's OK, sweetie," I said quietly, stroking her hair, her face buried in my chest. "It's over. They're not going to hurt you anymore."

Her tiny arms reached up and wrapped around my neck. She began to sob into my bloody shirt and I felt my heart breaking.

"I got you," I whispered, still in a daze. "I got you, sweetie."

Slowly, carefully, I picked her up and hugged her to me. She was practi-ally weightless, her arms so tight around my neck I almost choked.

"You're going to be OK," I said, rocking her. "I'm not going to let any-hing happen to you. I got you."

Finally, she spoke, her voice a muffled sob against me. "T-t-they were urting me..."

"I know," I said softly. "I know they were. But they're gone now. They an't hurt you anymore."

I turned toward Danny, the little girl still clinging to me. "Let's get out f this place."

Danny looked hard at me. "What are you doing, Nick?"

I placed a hand on the girl's back. "I'm taking her out of here."

"Nick..."

"I'm not leaving her," I hissed. "Jesus Christ, Danny, look at her."

"She is not our problem," Danny said evenly, his voice hard. "You saved r. There's nothing more you can do for her. We have our own problems."

The little girl's voice was a trembling plea in my ear. "Don't make me be one again..."

I stroked her hair, eyes on Danny. "She's coming with us.'

Danny shook his head. "You have got to be kidding me."

I walked past him. "This isn't something I'm going to argue about. Now me on."

"You're just asking for trouble," Danny growled, following me.

Before I left the cave, I stopped. I looked down at my feet. Danny passed , grumbling. When he saw that I wasn't following, he turned.

"What now?" He called from the mouth of the tunnel.

With one hand, I bent down and picked up the axe.
"Might need this again," I said gravely.
The weight of it was all too familiar.

Chapter 8

We walked along the base of the broken mountain, three of us now. I held the little girl in my arms as we trekked across the uneven terrain. She remained tight against me, her head resting on my shoulder. Her dress soon became soaked from the rain, dripping trails of filth and dried blood from the hem. Danny was ahead of us and I knew he was pissed. Part of me couldn't blame him. The addition of a child to our small group wasn't going to make things any easier, but I couldn't just leave her. I couldn't. How the hell did a kid get to the Black Farm anyway? What had happened to her? I knew now wasn't the time to ask and so I kept my arms around the child and walked in silence.

Danny announced we were getting close to the tunnel entrance, the one that led down into the Abyss and beneath the ocean. The earth rose and fell with rock and shattered foothills, the canyons littering the landscape growing deep, vacant gashes that plummeted down into nothingness. The mountain remained to the right of us, our path skirting around its crumbling base. A time or two I thought I saw movement higher up, an odd rock tumbling down toward us. It set my nerves on edge. If we got ambushed out here, there would be nowhere to run. I quickened my step and caught up to Danny who just shot me a sideways look, irritated.

"How much further?" I asked, hefting the girl's weight in my arms. She squeezed me tighter.

"Just over the next rise," Danny said, his voice grating. Without slowing, he eyed the girl. "We can't take her down there, Nick."

"Let's just get there," I said, ignoring him.

The girl's mouth pressed against my ear, her voice sudden and soft. "Where are we going?"

Danny and I looked at each other.

"A bad place," I said finally. The girl let out the smallest of whimpers and I quickly changed the subject.

"What's your name?" I asked gently.

It took her a while to respond, her voice thin and frail. "Emily. My mom calls me Em, though."

"Well," I said as soothingly as I could, "my name is Nick. I'm your friend now. Is that OK?"

She nodded into my neck, her dirty blonde hair spilling over my shoulder. After a moment, she spoke again.

"Where's my mom?"

"She's not here," Danny cut in, his voice hard. "And we're not your friends. Cry all you want, but we can't take you with us."

The little girl, Emily, finally raised her head from my shoulder and looked directly at me, her big brown eyes shining with fear. "You're going to go away? You're going to leave me all by myself?"

I slowed a little, meeting her gaze. "Of course not." I shot Danny a hard look. "We wouldn't do that to you. I'm your friend, remember?"

"But he just said—"

"Never mind what he said," I interjected, "that's just Danny. He's a little grumpy right now, he doesn't mean it."

This seemed to calm her a little, her head slowly falling back to my shoulder, her cheek pressed to my shirt.

What are you doing, Nick?

We crested a small rise and Danny slowed, finally stopping. He put his hands on his hips as he looked down into the shallow rock pit below us.

"Shit."

"What's wrong?" I asked from his side.

He pointed down into the dip. "You see that pile of gravel?"

"Yeah?"

"That's where the tunnel was."

"Shit…"

"When the mountain collapsed it must have buried the entrance. I don't know why I didn't think of that." He shook his head. "Stupid…"

I looked down into the bowl of loose rock. "How are we supposed to get through?"

"I have no idea."

"We've come a long way; there has to be something we can do."

"Like what?" Danny spat.

"We have to reach the Pig…"

"You think I don't know that?!" Danny yelled.

"I'm just saying there has to be another way. Another entrance maybe?" I asked defensively.

Danny clamped his teeth together. "Why don't you and your new friend go down there and start digging? Because that's the only entrance I know of."

"He's mean," Emily whispered in my ear.

I hugged her. "He's just frustrated. It's OK."

"Don't do that," Danny scoffed. "Don't try to protect her. You're not her father and there's nothing you can do for her. She's here in this goddamn place, same as us. She's NEVER getting out, so don't waste your breath by feeding her bullshit."

"Knock it off," I growled, stepping away from him.

Danny stepped toward me, ignoring my warning. "Are you listening, little girl? You're dead and you're never getting out of this place. What those men did to you in the cave? That's going to happen to you over and over and over again and there's nothing Nick here can do about that. So why don't you climb down out of his arms and fuck off?"

"That's ENOUGH!" I screamed. My voice echoed and bounced off the mountain, ringing through the air around us.

Danny's eyes narrowed, the air silencing once more. "You might want to keep your voice down, idiot. Screaming like that—you might as well shoot up a signal flare."

"Then leave her alone," I hissed. "You don't have to scare her."

Danny cocked his head at Emily, who was peeking at him through her bangs. "Am I scaring you?"

She nodded.

"I'm one of the friendliest faces you'll see around here, kid," Danny said, finally mellowing out. "Enjoy your new friendship while it lasts. He's the only protection you'll get in a place like this."

"Can we focus on the issue at hand, asshole?" I snapped. "Because it seems to me we have a serious problem."

"No shit."

"What the hell are we—"

Before I could finish, a small avalanche of rock slid down the slope to the right of us, stealing our attention. Danny and I simultaneously snapped our heads in the direction of the noise, my heart exploding up my throat, the axe gripped in one hand. Coming down the mountain was a lone figure, their stride casual and unhurried.

"Who the hell is that?" I asked, heart racing. "Pig Born?"

Danny, on high alert, whispered back, "No...no that's a Suicidal. A man. The hell is he doing all the way out here?"

"Should we run?" I asked, tensing.

Danny shook his head. "No...no he clearly sees us. Let's see what he wants."

We waited, the air tense, each passing second bringing the man closer At twenty yards away, I could see that he was smiling and holding a large makeshift spear in his hands. It bounced lightly on his shoulder, his body clothed in a filthy pair of overalls. Strapped to his back was a large pack loudly clanking with whatever sat inside. As he slowed to a stop before us recognition erupted across my face and I had to force myself to stay calm.

"You fellas are a long way away from anything safe," the man chuckled hoisting his crude wooden spear. His face was covered by a thick beard, th brown hair curling with gray.

Pudge. Jesus Christ, it's Pudge.

I met his eyes and held my breath, the memory of our last encounte exploding through my mind with terrifying clarity.

The mountain. He climbed the mountain with you.

Pudge looked hard at me, his head tilted at an angle.

You stole his gun and blew his brains out.

"Not a talkative bunch, are ya?" He said, the smile never leaving his face. His eyes never left mine.

"Who are you?" Danny finally asked carefully.

"Who, me?" Pudge asked, jamming a meaty finger into his chest. "I'm the king of this rock pile, that's who! Name's Pudge!" He looked at Danny and then dragged his eyes back to mine, something flickering behind them. 'So who are you all?"

"We're looking for something," Danny continued, "something that was upposed to be here."

Pudge chewed on his lip. "Well, that's fine and fuckin' dandy, but y'all never answered my question." He gripped the spear in both hands now. Who the hell are ya?"

I cleared my throat, praying. "My name's Jack. This little girl here is Emily and that's Danny."

Pudge squinted hard at me. "Do I...know you from somewhere, miser Jack?"

"Can't imagine that's possible," I lied, mentally crossing my fingers. "I ot to this place not too long ago."

Pudge continued to chew on his lip. "Hmmmm. I suppose. I guess you ot one of them uh," he snapped his fingers, thinking, "uh, one of those failiar faces. No offense, you're just kind of genetic-looking."

Danny cocked an eyebrow. "You mean generic?"

"That's what I said, wasn't it?"

Danny took a measured breath, summoning his patience. "Look... idge was it?"

"Yes sir, that's me."

"Right. Pudge. There used to be a tunnel here, before the mountain me down. You know anything about that?"

Pudge kicked at the rocks beneath his feet. "What's it to ya?"

"We just need—"

"And what're y'all doing with that little lady, huh?" Pudge cut in, pointg with his spear at Emily who still clung to me.

"We got her away from some bad men," I said. "We're keeping an eye her."

Pudge's eyes pressed into Emily. "You wouldn't be doing anything fun
with her, would ya?"

"Of course not," I said sharply.

Pudge leaned on his spear, his voice rising. "They being good to y
kiddo?"

Emily peered at Pudge from my shoulder, her big brown eyes cautio

"They nice men?" Pudge asked again.

Slowly, Emily nodded. "Uh-huh. Nick saved me."

Pudge looked up at me. "Nick? Thought you said your name was Jac

I swallowed hard, clearing my throat. "She's just confused. There wa
man with us named Nick. He was killed when we freed her."

"Uh-huh…"

I chanced a glance at Danny and found him staring intently at m
begged his silence and he thankfully kept his mouth shut.

Pudge looked back to Danny. "So y'all are looking for the tunnel, hu

Danny nodded. "It was supposed to be here."

"Well, things changed when the mountain came down. It ain't here
more," Pudge said matter-of-factly.

Danny gritted his teeth. "Clearly, genius."

Pudge narrowed his eyes. "You're not very polite, mister."

"It's been a long day," Danny shot back. "I'm freezing my ass off in t
rain and very recently we became babysitters. So I'm sorry if I'm not exa
tipping my cap to you every time I open my mouth."

Pudge suddenly chuckled, shaking his head. "Well shit, that's fair, m
ter Danny. And here I am running my mouth asking y'all questions inst
of helping some fellow Suicidals out."

"We'd really appreciate any help you could give," I said soothin
hoisting Emily in my arms. "It seems like you might know your way arou
this part of the island...being the king and all?"

Pudge suddenly blushed and waved a hand at me. "Aw, I'm not reall
king. I was just fibbin'."

"But you know this part of the island, right?" Danny interjected.

"Shore do. Been hunting Pig Born in these parts for ages now," Pu
said proudly, raising his spear. "This ol' thing has seen its share of bloodsh
let me tell ya."

"You're...hunting Pig Born?" Danny asked, raising an eyebrow. "Why?"

"Why not? You got something better to do?"

Danny snorted and shook his head. "You're a strange one."

"So I been told."

"But why out here?" Danny asked, spreading his arms to the barren landscape. "Doesn't seem like there's many Pig Born around. Wouldn't you have better luck over in the forest?"

"You would think so, wouldn't ya?" Pudge laughed.

"Unless you're hunting the wandering Keepers? Berserker?"

Pudge shook his head violently, eyes wide. "No, sir! Are ya crazy? No one can kill that thing!"

Danny twirled a finger in the air, confused. "Soooo?"

Pudge sighed. "Well, it comes back to what you were asking about. The tunnel." He suddenly stepped toward us, his eyes lighting up. "You see... that's where all the really weird shit crawls out of. Regular ol' Pig Born? Killing them gets old after a while. You wanna hunt something a little more sinister? You gotta go to the tunnel." His voice lowered, like he was sharing a secret. "You gotta wait for something to crawl outta the Abyss and poke its head out."

Danny suddenly came to life, his voice urgent and pressing. "The Abyss. You know about it?"

"I certainly do," Pudge said almost proudly. "Ain't anything else like it on the island."

"And...you've been down there?"

Pudge's face suddenly got very serious. "I have. Though if this is going where I think it's going, I'm going to have to stop you right there."

"Why? What's wrong?" I asked.

Pudge looked at Emily in my arms. "It's no place to be taking a little girl. I'll tell you that right now."

Danny barked a laugh. "Well, on that we can agree."

I hugged Emily tightly against me. "She has no one else. You have no idea what we rescued her from. I can protect her. Where we go, she goes."

Pudge nodded to the axe in my hand. "You going to protect her with that little thing?"

"If I have to, yes."

Pudge shook his head. "Hoo boy, you fellas really have no idea wha you're getting into, do you?"

Danny stepped forward, rain streaking down his face. "One way o another, we have to get to that tunnel. A little girl isn't going to stop us Nothing is. Now please, Pudge, where is it?"

"Well, at least you said please this time," Pudge said, mulling our reques over, "but you boys clearly have no clue about what goes on down there." Hi voice dipped low, his eyes suddenly sharpening. "Down in that deep dark— when you haven't seen the sky for hours or days even. When things start t mess with you. Talk to you. When you can't tell if you're alive or dead."

"You're not going to talk us out of this," Danny said sharply, "so sav the pitch."

"Whachoo boys wanna go down there so badly for, anyway?" Pudg asked, snapping back to his default state.

"We have to get to the other side," I said, hoping Danny would just shu up for a second. "We're trying to get this little girl someplace safe."

Pudge's eyes widened. "You wanna go…all the way across?"

I nodded.

Pudge shook his head. "There ain't no way you'll make it. It's impossible.

"Why?" Danny asked.

Pudge's eyes roamed back to Danny. "Mister Danny…if you've seen hal the shit I seen down there, you wouldn't be asking me that."

"Look," Danny said, forcing patience between his snarls, "we're not ask ing you to go down there with us. We just want to know where the tunne is. That's it. Then you can go back to killing Pig Born or whatever else it i you do out here."

Pudge stewed that over for a moment before answering. "Hmmm…it true the tunnel used to be here. You weren't wrong about that. But when th mountain came down, it caved in the entrance."

Danny threw his hands into the air. "We know that already!"

"Now calm down. Geez Louise," Pudge grumbled, "you're a miserabl one, aren't you? I didn't say there wasn't a tunnel, I just said it wasn't her anymore. When this entrance closed, another one opened up."

"What?"

"If you'd breathe instead o' losing your marbles, you'd have lower blood pressure," Pudge instructed, "and if you'd let me finish, I'll tell you fellas where it is."

"Thank you!" I exclaimed, hoping Danny would calm down.

"There's just one condition," Pudge said.

"Here we go," Danny grumbled.

"I'm coming with you."

Danny looked at me before looking back at Pudge. "What? Why?"

Pudge pointed at Emily. "I wanna make sure the little one is looked after. No offense fellas, but you both look like a pair of prepubescent pussies. There's no way you can handle half the shit down there."

"As much as I appreciate your concern," Danny said, his voice edged, "that's not at all necessary. We'll be just fine without your protection."

"Good," Pudge said unfazed, "'cause I ain't coming to protect you. Just the girl."

"Danny," I said slowly, "it might not be a bad idea. He's been down there before. He knows what we're up against. Any kind of help is a good thing."

Danny rolled his eyes. "This just gets better and better…"

"We should get a move on, then," Pudge said, pointing past us, "before company arrives."

I turned and felt my throat tighten. A lone Keeper lumbered in the far distance, its stride taking it left to right across the horizon. It was miles away still, but I felt a sudden need to make myself invisible.

"I don't like those things," Emily whispered in my ear.

"That makes two of us," I muttered.

Pudge motioned for us to follow him. "Come on now, let's git to it then, shall we?"

"How far away is this new entrance?" Danny asked as we all fell in line.

Pudge used his spear to point toward a large mound of rubble a couple dozen yards away. "Just over that ridge."

I could practically hear Danny blow a blood vessel. Thankfully, he kept his mouth shut, content to just grind his teeth.

Pudge took the lead and walked a couple paces in front of us. Danny strode to my side, opening his mouth to speak, his voice quiet and intended for my ears only.

"Do you know this abomination of man?"

I kept my arms around Emily, the axe still in hand as I answered. "Let's just say we had a run-in during my first trip here."

"What happened?"

"I stole his gun and shot him point-blank."

Danny almost snickered. "Of course you did." He looked ahead of us at our oblivious leader. "So what the hell? He doesn't remember you?"

I shrugged. "It's been a long time. Do you remember everyone you've come across here?"

"Fair enough."

"Let's just see what happens," I said. "We really could use his help."

In front of us, Pudge cocked his head over his shoulder. "Hey, don't take this the wrong way, but you three weren't ever with that band of Suicidals in the woods, were you?"

"What's he talking about?" I asked quietly.

Pudge answered the question for me. "You know the group I mean, right? Those crazy bastards? The mean ones? They're led by that rude asshat, Peter?"

"We're not with them," Danny answered. "Wouldn't be caught dead with that bunch."

"Well, I'm glad to hear that," Pudge called loudly, our boots crunching over the rough terrain, beginning to crest the rise. "I don't know much about them, but I've seen the way they treat their own. I think they're a bad bunch. Like their brains have been scrambled or somethin'. They're all just so dang mad all the time. Guess that can happen to folks who have been here a while, ya know?"

"Sure," Danny said, not paying attention.

We reached the top of the rise and came to a stop. The four of us stared down into the gravel pit before us, Pudge smacking his stomach proudly.

"Yup! See! I told you it was there!"

Burrowed into the stone was a lone circle of darkness. It was about ten feet high and half as much across. Rain washed across my face as I gazed down at it. For some reason, I expected something more.

"That's it?" I asked.

"That's it!" Pudge said, shooting a glance behind us at the distant Keeper. It was still quite a ways off, its lumbering stride absorbing our attention for a brief moment.

Grunting, I pulled Emily away from me, my arms sore. "Sweetie, I'm going to put you down, OK?"

"OK," she said timidly, letting go of my neck. I placed her on her feet and she quickly reached for my free hand, the one not carrying the axe. I accepted it, surprised at how small it felt.

Pudge unslung the pack from his back and rummaged around in it, inally pulling out a pair of large sticks, the ends wrapped in cloth.

"Bet you suckers didn't think of these, did you?" he asked, handing one of the sticks to Danny.

"A torch?" Danny said, turning the piece of wood over in his hands.

"You boys planning on stumbling around down there in the dark?"

Danny and I exchanged a look. He was right; we hadn't thought of that.

Pudge squatted down and addressed Emily, a smile lining his chapped ps. "I'd give you a little flashlight if I had one, little lady. Unfortunately, I'm esh out. But you just stay close to Uncle Pudge and you'll be OK."

Emily peeked out at him from behind my leg. "I'm not even afraid of e dark."

Pudge blinked and then threw his head back and laughed. "Well, all ght, then! Maybe we should have you lead the way then!"

"Can we please get out of this goddamn rain?" Danny said moodily.

Pudge hoisted himself back up and shouldered his pack once more. "All ght, ya sourpuss, we're going, we're going."

Together, our odd party descended over the lip of the ridge and down ward the gaping hole in the earth. As we approached it, I couldn't help but el my nerves begin to bunch. I kept Emily's hand tight in mine, the patter rain and crunch of rock filling the silence. I looked down at her, a wave of sponsibility suddenly overwhelming me.

Am I doing the right thing?

The entrance loomed before us, a pitch-black oval, like a mouth ready accept us down its throat. One by one, with Pudge in the lead, we entered. e ground changed almost immediately from rock to hard packed dirt. The n and gray skies disappeared and all sound save for our footsteps vanished.

It was as if we had entered a vacuum, the panting of my lungs suddenly ve
loud in my ears.

Pudge stopped and reached into his pocket. He flicked something
his hands, and a spark danced onto the cloth wrapped around the end of l
stick. A sickly sweet smell filled the air and light bloomed out around
Pudge motioned for Danny's torch and they brought them together, birt
ing even more light. Shadows rose and danced across the narrow passa
expanding down and into the open maw. I looked ahead of us, seeing o
dark walls and high ceilings.

"Now listen," Pudge said softly, suddenly very serious. "There's a cou
things you all need to know about this place before we go on." He turn
and looked down the tunnel before continuing. "There's going to be a lot
things you see and hear in here that you aren't going to understand. Wh
these things happen, you need to just keep moving. Don't speak or listen
anything. We're going down, deep, deep down into the belly of the Fa
We're going to be walkin' along its seams, so to speak. Things get a lit
kooky. Unnatural. But no matter what, just keep moving and keep your e
ahead of you. You got that?"

"We got it," I said, his words bringing new worry. Just what the hell v
this place?

Pudge looked down at Emily. "If you start to get scared, you just
on your friend's hand, OK? I don't want you to start crying or anythi
We're not going to let anything happen to you, sugar. Just be as brave as y
can be."

"I'm pretty brave," Emily piped up. Her hand never left mine.

"Course you are," Pudge said, smiling slightly. "Now let's get a move c

Together, we stared down the expanding hole of darkness and then t
the first heavy steps into the Abyss.

Chapter 9

I don't know how long we had been walking, but at some point Pudge applied more cloth from his backpack to the end of the torches. The tunnel continued down, the decline sloping at a consistent angle, shoveling us deeper into the guts of the Abyss. Pudge led the way with Emily and myself in the middle while Danny brought up the rear, his torch held high overhead. The silence was eerie and I felt it crawl across my skin like an inky bug. The shadows and darkness seemed endless, our path seemingly eternal. I kept waiting for something to change, to happen. But the void offered nothing but a lonely hallway, tilted down and funneling us toward the unknown.

I readjusted the grip on my axe for the hundredth time, choking up on it just to give my hands something to do. Emily looked at the blade and then away. She still clutched my hand in hers. She hadn't talked much, content to let the silence fill the air.

"You doing OK?" I whispered down to her.

She looked up at me, her brown eyes dancing with reflected flame. "Uh-huh. This is far. How much longer?"

"I don't know, sweetie," I said, "but you let me know if you get tired and I'll carry you again."

Emily shrugged. "I can walk. Mom says walking makes you strong."

I raised my eyebrows. "Oh, yeah? Sounds like your mom was a smart person."

Emily's shoulders suddenly drooped. "Yeah...but Mom is sad a lot. I can hear her cry sometimes when I go to bed." She looked back up at me, her face unexpectedly distraught. "Do you know why she gets sad?"

I shook my head vainly. "No, I don't. Sometimes people just get sad, though."

"Mom always ate vitamins when she got sad," Emily said quietly, "but I don't think they made her happy."

I looked back at Danny and was met with a stony gaze. I licked my dry lips and gently whispered, "Emily...did you ever take your mom's vitamins?"

Emily said nothing for a long time, her hand fidgeting in mine. After some time, I heard her speak again, very gently. "I'm sorry. I know I'm not supposed to."

I squeezed her hand. "It's OK, Emily. You're a good kid."

Pudge shot a look over his shoulder at us. "Cut the chatter. You're getting too loud."

We fell back into silence. The walls around us seemed to be expanding slightly, the passage widening. After a couple minutes, I deduced that my assumption was correct, but the ceiling remained a solid ten feet above our heads, the bare-faced rock and dirt offering nothing but our singular route.

Ahead of us, Pudge began to slow, bringing his torch up. I stopped at his side, squinting down the gullet of black ahead of us.

"What is it?" I whispered.

Pudge pointed a finger down the tunnel. "You see that?"

I squinted and after a moment, I noticed something new. It was a dim red light that faintly illuminated the area ahead.

"Did we make it?" Danny asked from behind us.

Pudge snorted. "Don't you wish? We've barely gotten started."

"Then what is that light?" I asked.

"We're almost to the first drop. Come on," Pudge said, trudging forward again without further explanation.

Danny and I looked at one another and then followed, Emily quietly shuffling along at my side. As we approached the light, I began to see what the cause was.

Gashed along the side of the tunnel was a long cut of red. Light pulsated from inside the gap, the source hidden. What caught my eye, though, wasn't the strange fissure, but what appeared over it.

"Jesus, it looks like the wall has stitches," Danny said, "doesn't it? Pudge, what is this?"

Pudge looked at the oddly patched crevice. "I told y'all we were going to be walking along the seams of the Farm. This here is what I was talking about. Things tend to get funny when you see a seam, so best stay close. The drop is just ahead, OK?"

"What drop?"

But Pudge was already moving. We hurried to follow his light, but I stopped, realizing Emily had let go of my hand. I had a brief moment of panic and then saw she was standing behind Danny.

"Emily, we need to go!" I said, pushing around Danny who clenched his teeth with irritation at the delay.

I got to Emily's side and crouched down next to her. "Hey, what's going on?" I asked quietly.

Emily was staring down the tunnel at the way we had just come. Her eyes were wide and her skin was pale. I gripped her arm and she looked at me, fear overwhelming her features.

"What's wrong?" I asked.

Her voice was thin and faint. "Somethin' saw us."

Goosebumps crept up my arms. "What do you mean? Where? Did you see something?"

Emily nodded and then pointed down the tunnel. "It was there."

Danny was suddenly standing over us, his voice urgent. "Nick, we have to catch up to Pudge."

But before I could say anything else, Emily leaned into my ear and whispered something that sent my skin crawling.

"It looked like you."

"*Nick.*"

I took one quick look into the darkness and then grabbed Emily's hand. Together, we double-timed it down the tunnel toward Pudge, his torch blinking ahead of us. Danny jogged at our back.

"What the fuck was she talking about?" he whispered hoarsely.

"I don't know," I breathed, still trotting, "and I don't want to. You heard what Pudge said about the seams."

We caught up to Pudge and slowed. He looked back at our faces and saw the unease.

"You need to stay close," he scolded. "What'd I tell you about looking around?"

"Sorry," I said, breathing heavy, "Emily thought she saw something back there."

"No doubt she did, but I can assure you it ain't anything good. Now watch your step up ahead, we've reached the first drop."

We shuffled forward further into the tunnel and came to a halt as the ground suddenly vanished ahead. Pudge scooted toward the gaping black and shoved his torch into the tar-thick darkness.

"A hole?" Danny asked.

I peered around Pudge and felt my stomach sink. Danny was right. W had reached a hole, a thin circle of gloom that dropped down, plunging dee into the bowels of the Farm. The sight of it made me extremely uncomfortable, the diameter of the lip barely wide enough to fit a single person. looked ahead of us, down the tunnel and past the hole, and saw a blank wa that impeded any further progress.

"Only way is down," Pudge said.

"I am not going down that thing," Danny said, suddenly on edge. H shifted from foot to foot, casting nervous glances at the tight gap in th floor. His whole demeanor changed in an instant upon sight of the hole. H face went white and his eyes shifted around erratically, his tongue flickerin between his lips.

"You gotta," Pudge said. "Hope you're not claustrophobic."

"There has to be another way," Danny said, his words coming out in rush.

Pudge shook his head. "Nope. I reckon you could go back, but I would advise it."

"Why?"

Pudge looked down at Emily. "You saw something back there, did ya, sugar?"

Emily's brow furrowed with concern and she nodded. "Uh-huh…"

"A scary thing?"

"I didn't mean to see it…"

"It's all right," Pudge said, squatting down next to her, "but that means we got to keep moving forward. You think you're brave enough to go down that hole with me?"

Emily looked up at me. "Are you going to come?"

"Of course I am," I said, taking a knee. "I told you I wasn't going to eave you."

Danny was shaking his head, though, growing more and more upset. No, no, no, there's no way I'm going down that thing. I won't do it. I won't."

Before any of us could say anything, Emily suddenly stepped toward)anny and took one of his hands. "Don't be scared. We'll all be together."

Her touch practically paralyzed Danny, his eyes wide as they stared own at her, his torch frozen in his opposite hand.

"It's scary back there," Emily continued, gazing up at him with all the nnocence in the world, "and it's dark. Stay with us. Please?"

Danny finally shook himself free and pulled his hand back, scratching is neck. "For Chrissakes…"

"I'll go last," I offered, trying to calm Danny's sudden nerves. "Keep the rch with you, though, that way you won't feel so trapped. Deal?"

Danny shot a venomous look at the hole in the floor, a mixture of loath-g and terror. "Ah, *shit*...."

Pudge positioned himself over the hole and then dropped his torch wn the throat of darkness. Together, we watched it plummet down, down, wn, the black almost swallowing it completely from sight before hitting e bottom.

"Oh my god," Danny stressed, running a hand over his head.

Ignoring him, Pudge slowly began to lower himself into the hole. His oulders brushed the narrow opening and he looked up at us.

"It's a little tight, but you'll make it." He looked at Danny. "There's tches in the rock for your hands and feet, just like a ladder. Keep a tight p on it and you'll be just dandy. Let me get down a bit and then let the le lady come next. If she falls, at least she'll hit me first."

"I won't fall," Emily said confidently. "At my school there's a jungle gym l I'm really good at it."

Pudge smiled. "Well, OK then. See you at the bottom."

I waited for him to get a couple feet down before motioning for Emily to go next. She padded into position and then lowered herself down, expressing no outward fear. I reached out to help her, but she had slipped into the gap before I could.

"Go slow," I cautioned, watching her with some concern.

"I know," she responded, still descending.

I turned to Danny. "OK, you're up."

Danny took a deep breath. "Goddamn it…"

"You wanna ditch the torch? It's pretty tight. Plus it'd free up an extra hand."

Biting his lip, Danny nodded and let it fall, pushing shadows back. patted him on the shoulder.

"You got this. It'll be over before you know it."

"I doubt that."

Hands shaking, Danny got down on his hands and knees and gent lowered himself into the narrow pit. His face was almost completely white i the torchlight, sweat standing out on his brow. Hesitantly, he began to clim down, a string of curses following him.

I waited a couple seconds and then took my turn. I crouched an reached with my foot into the hole, feeling for the first notch. When I four it, I swung myself in and began to follow the group down. The walls presse in tight against my shoulders, just barely wide enough for me to move. Ro bumped and scraped against my back, each rung bringing with it a sen of growing claustrophobia. It wasn't easy trying to maneuver with the a in hand, but I wasn't going to leave it behind. Not in a place like this. Fo rungs down and I felt my heart begin to race, a trickle of sweat runni down my spine. Beneath me, I could hear a more vocal hysteria growing.

"Just keep moving, Danny!" I called, my voice sounding way too co fined in the tight space.

You're going to get stuck.

"Stop it," I muttered nervously.

What if the walls cave in?

"Can we go a little faster?" I begged.

"Doing the best I FUCKING can!" Danny half-screamed, his voice cracking.

Emily suddenly cut through the panic, loud and unafraid. "Be brave like me!"

I gritted my teeth and stopped for a moment, forcing myself to calm. Everything was fine. I wasn't going to get stuck. I was doing it. The bottom wasn't that far down. I could do this.

I took a deep breath and closed my eyes. When I was ready, I opened them again and looked up to see how far I had come…

…and saw something staring down at me. As soon as my brain registered the shape, the thing vanished, disappearing back over the lip.

What the hell was that?!

Swallowing hard, I continued to descend, going as fast as I dared. Whatever that thing had been, it had seen me. It knew where I was, where I was going. If it wanted, it could drop a boulder down on me and end my life instantly.

You cannot die, Nick.

The thought held unexpected gravity. If I died, I would have to do this all again. The entire journey. The woods, the broken mountain, the tunnel, this damned hole…

I willed myself to block out the rising panic. I concentrated on the rungs, the placement of my boots, the grip against the wall. I began to count in my head, ignoring the scraping of rock at my back. When I reached thirty, I realized it was working, that my bubbling hysteria was beginning to gray.

When I reached one hundred and thirty-one, I felt my feet settle over solid ground. In disbelief, I looked around, letting go of the rungs with overwhelming relief. I turned and saw Pudge, Emily, and Danny staring at me, a new, wide tunnel at their back.

"See, that wasn't scary," Emily announced up at Danny. Danny just looked at her, the corners of his mouth drooping.

Pudge had retrieved his torch and was delicately wrapping more cloth around the burning end. I looked down the new passage and saw more red scars lining the wall, along with the strange stitched patchwork. The gashes gave the tunnel an eerie red hue, the silence around us incredibly still. I noticed this time, though, that there were multiple passageways branching off from the main tunnel.

"We all still have our sanity?" Pudge asked as he finished with the torch.

"More or less," Danny mumbled.

"How far down are we?" I asked.

Pudge shrugged. "I dunno. Pretty damn deep, though."

"You've been here before?"

"Mhmm," Pudge said, sliding his spear out from where he had stuck it to his pack. "Lot of nasty things down this way. Stay close. Let's move."

Our footsteps echoed down the passage as we followed our guide once more. Emily found my hand and took it. I was surprised by how much comfort it gave me. I looked down at her and she smiled, her hair bouncing across her shoulders.

She has no idea what's going on, I thought sadly.

We began to pass the red scars in the rock, the light coming out almost like a mist, bleeding its dim light into the tunnel. I found that when I looked directly at it, I began to feel dizzy. I turned away from the light and stared at Danny's back, the light from Pudge's torch mixing with the strange red. We passed multiple tunnels that snaked away from us, disappearing into whatever lie beyond the silent black openings.

Just focus on Pudge, I reminded myself, *eyes ahead, don't look around, keep walking.*

Time became an unreadable metric, the constant march forward blurring my sense of direction and perspective. I knew we had a long way to go, but I found myself very much wishing for an incline, something, anything, that promised a way back up and out of this place.

After some time, with the eerie red light washing over our faces, Danny began to jerk his head from left to right, stealing glances down the branching tunnels that burrowed away from us.

"Keep your eyes forward," I whispered cautiously.

But Danny didn't listen, his head twisting frantically from left to right.

"Do you see them?" he whispered back.

His words sent a shiver down my spine. Against my better judgement, I glanced down one of the tunnels. My blood turned to ice and I almost stopped dead in my tracks.

There was something in the tunnel and it was looking directly at us. It didn't move, its human form clothed in shadow, its face a featureless wash of dull gray. It stood a couple feet back from the mouth of the tunnel like a statue, its arms hanging motionless at its sides.

Heart racing, I looked to the right and saw that the other tunnels hosted the same chilling vision, each passage occupied by a single, featureless, human-shaped entity. They just watched as we passed, never moving, never uttering a sound.

"What do they want?" Danny hissed.

"It doesn't matter," I said with more confidence than I felt. "Just keep your eyes on Pudge."

As we passed more of the branching tunnels, I felt a growing sense of danger, like we were trespassing and shouldn't be here. I kept Emily's hand tight in mine as we skirted by more of the red-stitched gashes in the wall. The floor continued to dip, taking us down the eternal slope, further and further into the Abyss.

Without warning, Pudge suddenly altered our course, taking the four of us down one of the side tunnels. I felt a worm of worry squirm through my guts as we left the wide tunnel and entered a twisting burrow of rock, the walls collapsing, the ceiling dropping to a mere foot above our heads. As we entered the passage, I noticed this was one of the few that didn't hoist one of the strange, faceless creatures. We were forced to walk single file, Emily ahead of me while I brought up the rear.

"You sure this is the right way?" I called up, the sound of my voice causing me to jump.

"Yup" was all that echoed back. I looked behind me as we rounded a bend and caught the last fleeting glimpse of the tunnel we were leaving.

This doesn't feel right.

With no choice but to trust Pudge, I continued to follow him, the four of us winding deeper and deeper into the rapidly closing passage. After a couple minutes, the walls became so narrow that we had to shuffle sideways a number of times. As we passed through one of these constricted gaps, I realized that the ceiling was beginning to dip, forcing us to crouch now. I could hear Danny worriedly muttering beneath his breath. Emily was the only one who didn't have to duck down and she looked back at me, offering a little smile.

"Keep going, Emily," I coaxed, trying to fight my rising sense of claustrophobia. My shoulder brushed against the tight rock and I tried not to think about how much trouble I was having just breathing.

"Pudge, are you SURE this is the right way?" Danny cried hoarsely as we were forced to duck lower, the ceiling pressing us almost to our hands and knees.

"Yup," Pudge responded, his voice hollow.

I felt like a piece of meat passing through an intestinal tract, our bodies twisting and bending through the hardened guts of the Abyss. After the four of us slid through another crack, something caught my attention.

It was a noise. Something skittering at my back. I didn't catch it at first dismissing it as paranoia, but after the fourth time, I knew I wasn't imagining it. I glanced nervously into the tight void, my axe held tight at my side.

Skitskitskitskitskit.

I paused for a moment, holding my breath, waiting for another. I ran my tongue across my lips, every muscle in my body bursting with tension.

Skitskitskitskitskit.

Closer now.

Something's coming.

I turned back down the tunnel, pressing forward with new urgency voice raised. "Hey, I think there's something following us!"

I heard Danny curse profusely and we picked up the pace, Pudge's torch cutting through the tight darkness. Without warning, the ceiling dipped impossibly low, driving us to our hands and knees, and then to our stomachs Ahead of me, Pudge squirmed through the smallest of holes, huffing and puffing, pushing his torch ahead of him across the ground.

Skitskitskitskit.

"You need to go faster," I urged Emily, pushing her ahead of me.

"Danny's in the way!" she called back, one foot almost connecting with my face as we all wriggled desperately in the dark.

Skitskitskitskit.

"Danny, move your fucking ass!" I yelled, panic starting to settle in.

"I'm trying, goddamn it!" he bellowed back. "I think I'm stuck up here! JCK!"

"If Pudge's fat ass can fit, so can you!" I practically screamed, the deep ıck licking my ankles.

I could hear Danny grunting ahead of me, his voice almost a whining :a as he struggled to move. Inch by inch, we scooted ahead, my head bang- ; against the miserably low ceiling. I didn't want to think about what was ming up behind me or how close it was or if it could see me.

"We're through!" Pudge called back to us. "Come on! It opens up! Just ıttle further!"

I heard him scramble to his hands and knees and then stand, stooping pick up his torch, bringing night into the tunnel I was trapped in.

"Thank god," I heard Danny exhale, squirming free from the ht confines.

Skitskitskitskitskit.

"Go Emily, go go go!" I pressed, shoving her forward and out of the :row mouth of the passage.

Something brushed against my foot and I let out a shriek, kicking wild- adrenaline surging through my veins. I banged my head and scraped my ees and elbows, frantically clawing my way out of the coffin-tight gap and o a small cavern. Gasping, I got to my feet, backing away from the gap.

"I felt something touch me!" I yelled, grasping my axe with both hands w. Pudge raised his torch up above our heads, casting a warm glow around small rock crusted cavern. We peered at the hole we had just squeezed : of, tense and waiting.

After a couple pregnant seconds, Danny glanced at me. "I don't think re's anything there."

"I know what I felt," I shot back, eyes glued to the tiny passage.

"What do you think—" Pudge started, but stopped mid-sentence. His s widened.

A pair of pale hands slithered out of the hole, thin, bony things that ended outward toward us exposing ghost white arms and bending joints.

"What the hell?" Danny hissed, jumping backwards.

The hands and arms continued to grow from the mouth of darkness, t
fingers prying and probing the floor at our feet. We could hear moveme
following the hands, like a body being dragged across the floor.

"Stand back!" Pudge ordered, tossing his torch to the floor and bra
dishing his spear.

We scooted away from the entrance as a massive body oozed out of t
gap and into the open cavern, the hands rising up into the air as it did
In the dim light, my eyes absorbed the monstrosity before me and I felt
stomach twist in disgust and fear.

It looked like a four-foot ant, its flesh a phantom white. It scuttled t
rest of the way out of the hole using tiny appendages that lined the und
side of its body. The pair of arms connected to the creature rose from t
floor and blindly twitched in the air like antennas, the joints bending a
contorting back into the massive crawling sack of flesh.

Emily screamed at my side and I quickly stepped in front of her, shie
ing her from the monster. As I did so, the giant flesh ant curled its to
backwards, exposing its underbelly at us. Shock rattled through me a
gazed upon it.

Its belly looked like a massive oozing vagina, pink flaps of flesh peeli
outward from a cut of darkness down the center. Before I could react,
folds of flesh parted slightly to reveal a small human body slotted sidew
into the vagina, one human eye bulging from a face dripping with a v
cous slime.

"Pudge!" Danny screamed, stumbling away from the abominati
"Do something!"

I stood my ground, heart thundering, feet planted. Pudge appeared
my side, face grim, spear in hand. We stared down the monster as it hiss
at us, spraying goo out of its exposed vaginal cavity. It moved from side
side, its tiny legs scraping against the bare rock floor. Its long antenna har
swayed dangerously in the air, as if waiting to strike.

Without any kind of warning, Pudge suddenly roared and charged
thing, spear held high. The flesh-ant scuttled to the side and swiped at h
with one of its arms, catching the big man across the chin. I heard him gr
and stumble, falling to the floor, his spear clattering out of reach.

Help him!

I launched myself at the monster, axe raised, adrenaline pounding in my ears. Its attention was momentarily on Pudge, giving me a split-second advantage. I used it to swing the axe down into its body with all of my might. Thick pink goo exploded from the fleshy gore as the blade made contact, biting deep into the massive ant. Its reaction was immediate, screeching and spraying slime as it spun around to face me, severely injured, but not dead. I yanked the blade free, ready to confront the thing, pink slime running down the handle of the axe.

Before I could strike another blow, though, one of its fists came pummeling into me from the shadows, catching me across the temple. Stars erupted across my vision and I slumped to the floor, the axe falling away. I tasted blood and realized I must have bit my tongue, everything shrouded in a haze.

Trying to recover as quickly as possible, I fumbled blindly for my weapon, blood and drool dripping from my chin. My fingers brushed across the axe handle, but before I could grip it, something thudded into me, flipping me onto my back.

My vision cleared and I felt a scream crawl up my throat as the giant vaginal ant crawled on top of me, rearing back to expose the person slotted into the flesh. The folds parted further and a massive stinger protruded from the pulsing viscera.

Axe—get your axe!

I reached for it, fingers bumping and sliding over the handle, the stinger bobbing dangerously over my face, preparing to strike.

You can't DIE, NICK.

A solitary second before the stinger came plunging down into my throat, the creature let out a sudden scream as something thick slammed into the exposed face of the ant. Pink goo poured down over me as the monster screamed and stumbled off of me, Pudge's spear protruding from its vaginal slit.

Rough hands grabbed me and pulled me to my feet and I turned, expecting Pudge, but found Danny, his face flushed.

"I got it good, now finish the fucker off!"

I quickly stooped down and picked up my axe, the ant's gurgling cries echoing across the tight cavern. In its death throes, I waited for its body to flop away from me before stepping toward it, swinging the axe like a bat. It connected with a sickening crunch, the blade buried in the things back. Without waiting, I ripped it downwards, parting the flesh like raw steak. The ant's pink insides bubbled and splashed out of the deep gash, the creature's jerking movements spitting organs out and across the walls.

Thirty seconds later it died, crashing to the floor, leaving me coated in gore, panting, teeth on edge. Silence swept through the small, dark space save for the tug of air into my lungs.

You did it. You got that fucker.

I wiped goo from my eyes and spat to the side. I stared at the thing I had killed, its opened cavity still dribbling slime.

I hated how alive I felt.

Across the room, Danny was helping Pudge to his feet, a large welt already growing from the side of his face.

"What the hell were you thinking, charging at that thing like a maniac?" Danny yelled, brushing goo from Pudge's shoulder. "Fuckin' idiot. Think next time would ya?"

"Don't know what came over me," Pudge said, actually having the audacity to smile sheepishly.

I suddenly snapped back to reality and spun, searching for Emily. She was huddled in the corner of the room, crouched into herself, hands over her eyes. I dropped the axe and forced the horribly energetic feeling from my mind.

Don't hide from it.

I hurried over to Emily and knelt in front of her, hands gripping her shoulders. "Are you OK? Are you hurt?"

Tears trickled down her face, her lip quivering with terror. "W-w-what was that?" she cried.

I hugged her to me and stroked her hair. "A bad thing. But it's dead now You don't have to be scared. It's gone. It's not going to hurt you."

She pulled out of my embrace, wiping a swath of pink goo from her cheek, her voice shaking. "Y-y-you have blood on you."

I looked down at myself and grimaced. My entire chest was coated in streaking pink. I looked apologetically at Emily.

"Sorry about that."

"Nick?" she whispered.

"Yeah, sweetie?"

"Where is this?" she asked quietly, eyes brimming.

Instead of answering, I stood and took her hand in mine. Danny and Pudge walked over to us, still recovering from the encounter. Danny handed me my axe.

"You still swing like a champ," he said darkly.

I took the axe and appraised Pudge, whose cheek was starting to bruise. "Promise me you won't be that stupid again."

Pudge shrugged. "You don't gotta be so dramatic."

"I thought you hunted these things for sport? How are you not better at this?" Danny snapped.

Pudge shrugged again. "I ain't ever seen one of those things before. Guess I got a little excited. We're all still here, right?"

"That's not the point," I interjected. "You're our guide. If you die down here, we're kinda screwed."

Pudge suddenly looked directly at me, his eyes locking with mine. "Yeah...I wouldn't wanna screw you bunch over now, would I?"

I felt a chill run through me and I quickly lowered my eyes.

"Anyhow," he continued, now enthusiastic, "we killed that nasty creation and we're no worse for wear."

"Whatever you say," Danny muttered, shaking his head.

"You all wanna keep on trucking or do you wanna continue with this intervention?" Pudge asked.

Danny and I looked at one another, my voice careful and quiet. "Lead the way."

"That's more like it," Pudge smiled. He went to the ant corpse and yanked his spear out of its gullet. Grumbling and wiping it off on his pant leg, he bent and retrieved the flickering torch.

"OK, team, let's boogie," he said almost proudly.

Chapter 10

The darkness was starting to get to me. Even with the torch, I could feel the pressing claustrophobia squeezing in around me. I was at the back f the pack again, with Emily, Danny, and Pudge leading the way. We had ntered another tunnel, this one sending us spiraling downward, the Abyss vallowing our small group. In front of me, Emily kept her head down, her ood tempered by the violent confrontation we had just survived. I didn't ame her. Our dreary disposition seemed to grow with every step. I kept my e in hand, praying I wouldn't need to use it again.

Liar.

The longer we walked, the harder I tried to keep track of where we ere going, what passages we were taking, but it became impossible. This ace seemed to be an endless nest of snaking throats, pulling us deeper and eper without end.

I went into an almost dream state, my mind curling with doubt and eping hopelessness. I was growing tired the further we descended, my dy sore and worn from the bloody fight. As we rounded another bend d entered another tunnel, I pondered the possibility of our mission. At the rt, I had known this would be a hellish task, one filled with overwhelming ds and death. But I had clung to hope—as small a sliver as it had been. I stulated that if I kept my family at the forefront of my mind, a constant ninder of why I was here, then I could overcome just about anything.

But that optimism could only take me so far.

Trapped in my head, I almost ran into Emily, unaware that the pa
had stopped. I looked up and saw Pudge looking down at something,
rock walls hovering around us like a curse.

"What is it?" I asked, shuffling forward.

"Stairs," Pudge said, turning back to us. "It's been a long time since I
been this deep, but I recall these."

I pushed between Pudge and Danny, already dreading what I was ab
to see. Stone steps spiraled down into the earth, burrowed into the rock fl
Red scars illuminated the open hole, crimson stitching casting an eerie gl
over the slate walls. I looked down the looping staircase and kicked a sm
rock over the edge. It plummeted into the open space between the stairs a
fell for entirely too long before echoing back up.

"Just how far down do we have to go?" Danny mumbled, shaking
head and eyeballing the empty space before us.

"I want you to hold my hand, Emily," I instructed. "I don't want y
tumbling over the edge." Silently she obeyed and locked her hand arou
mine. Pudge hoisted his torch and began to stride down the long, curl
staircase. Danny went next, nervously hugging the wall, staying as far av
from the empty plummet as he could. Emily and I went last. I kept
slightly ahead of me and against the rock. My fingers grasped her small ha
in a vise-like grip, praying she wouldn't trip.

The four of us curled and twisted down, down, down, and after a wh
I began to hear Pudge panting ahead of us. We passed multiple red gashe
the wall, each one emitting that dizzy haze. I made sure not to look into
crevices, keeping my eyes at my feet.

After a couple minutes, I began to hear something. It snuck up on
a slow build of noise that caused me to slow. It was a deep rumble, lik
pained exhale, and it came from down below. It rose and fell in a pattern,
something massive was breathing—inhale, exhale—the low groan steal
our attention.

Pudge stopped dead in his tracks, the rest of us following suit. Pu
leaned over the edge and peered down into the emptiness.

"Shit."

"What is that?" Danny whispered.

Huuuhhhhhhh...hoooooooom....

Pudge looked at us, passing the torch between his hands. "We have to stop."

Danny raised an eyebrow. "What? What are you talking about? What's making that noise?"

"Should have known better," Pudge muttered, almost to himself.

"Why? What's going on?" I asked quietly, the rumbling climbing up the darkness.

"Something's down there," Pudge answered, a whisper. "Something you don't wanna meet."

Danny peeked over the edge nervously. "Can it get us up here?"

Pudge shook his head. "If it's what I think it is, then no. It's too big. Can't fit on the stairs. Musta found its way down here by some other means I'm not aware of. But we can't go any further until that thing goes away. You understand?"

"It sounds like it's pretty far down still," Danny observed.

"We don't wanna be anywhere near it," Pudge stated, "so for now, we wait. If we're lucky, it'll move on without knowing we're up here. Just don't go shoutin', and pray it moves along."

Huuuuuhhhhh....hoooooom....

"What is it," I asked quietly, "another one of those ant things?"

Pudge plopped himself down on the stairs and leaned against the rock wall, shaking his head. "Nah. Something way worse. They call it The Maw. Some nasty thing the Pig birthed when it first got sick. I haven't seen or heard tale of it in quite some time. Now I get why. The bastards been hiding out down here." He motioned for us to sit. "Might as well park it here and get some rest. We could be here a while."

"Of all the places to get trapped," Danny muttered nervously.

"You're free to go up or down," Pudge offered, resting his head back against the rock, closing his eyes. "Though I wouldn't advise either. Take a load off and rest your eyes. Ain't nothing we can do right now until that noise stops."

I looked down at Emily. "You wanna rest a little? Are you tired?" She nodded and so I took a seat on the stairs, planting my back against the wall. Danny slumped down next to me, exhaling loudly. I leaned the axe against the wall and Emily curled up beside me, resting her head on my lap. It was unexpected, but not unwelcome, and so I stroked her hair and watched as her eyes closed.

"That's good," I said gently, "you get some sleep while you can, OK? I'll be right here."

She nodded in my lap and after a couple minutes, her breathing evened out as sleep took her. I glanced over at Pudge and to my surprise saw he was dozing as well, his mouth hanging open, his chest rising and falling peacefully.

"Don't know how the hell that hillbilly can sleep in a place like this," Danny grumbled, "especially with that thing breathing just a couple hundred feet below us."

I looked down at Emily. "Well, this little thing didn't have any problem, either, it seems. She's out cold."

Danny glanced at her. "What's your endgame with her, anyway?"

I let a couple seconds tick by before answering. "I don't know. Maybe I can take her back with me. Shit, I don't know. I just want to keep her safe for as long as I can."

"Take her back with you," Danny mused, shaking his head. "This place isn't some amusement park where you can come and go as you please."

"Yeah, well I have a ticket out of here," I said quietly.

"That angel you talked about? What was his name? Ramiel?"

I nodded.

Danny snorted. "You actually trust his word? You really think if you find the Pig and get this place back to how it was that some angel is going to swoop down and save you? Jesus, Nick. I knew you were a fool, but you're pushing it."

"What the hell else can I do but trust him?" I snapped back, suddenly irritated. "It's not like I have much of a choice."

We were silent for a moment before Danny spoke again, his voice softer. "Trust...right. Your one ticket out of here. Again."

"I'll find a way."

Danny leaned his head back against the rock wall. "Can I ask you something?"

"Fire away," I muttered.

"What year is it?"

I cocked an eyebrow at him. "Why?"

"Humor me."

I told him.

Danny stared at me and then exhaled slowly. "Jesus Christ…"

"What's wrong?"

Danny ran his hands slowly down his face. "I thought it had been longer than that. Much, much longer."

"Longer?"

Danny looked at his feet dangling over the lip of the stairs. "If you're telling the truth...then I've only been here for eight fucking years."

I said nothing. Danny's mood was turning.

"What a mess," he breathed, "what a stupid fucking mess…"

I cleared my throat. "What uh...how *did* you get here?"

Danny shot me a look that could have frozen hell. "Excuse me?"

I shrugged. "We got time to kill. I was just asking. Obviously, you weren't very happy with your life. Something drove you to suicide. What happened?"

Danny looked away, his face sour. "Don't ask me questions like that, Nick."

I looked down at Emily's sleeping face. "Sorry. I know that's not exactly something you probably wanna relive. God knows I can't stand thinking about what drove me here. The first time, at least, when I made the choice."

"Your kid died, didn't they?"

Shock forced my eyes open and I slowly turned to stare at Danny. "How the hell did you know that?"

Danny pointed to Emily. "You're good with her. You want to keep her safe, no matter how stupid of an idea that might be. You got a soft spot for kids. That usually comes from a place of abuse or loss. I'm guessing it was loss."

I ran my hand gently through Emily's hair. "You guessed right."

"Which also explains why you're so hell-bent on seeing this insane thing through. You mentioned you had a family. Another kid, right? A second chance?"

I felt a weight settle over my chest. "His name's Theo." I smiled sadly. "He just turned one, actually."

Danny sniffed. "Yeah? And you left him to come back here? Seriously?"

"If I didn't, him and his mother would die. Horribly. The bastards running this crazy existence aren't exactly fair or kind when it comes to getting what they want."

"For once, I agree with you."

I looked over at him. "So which one were you?"

"What?"

"You have a reputation for hating the Suicidals, despite being one. You probably weren't born with that baked into your DNA. So. Which one are you? Abuse or loss?"

Danny stared at his hands for a long time before answering. "Both, I guess."

"What happened?"

"Didn't I tell you I didn't want to talk about it?"

I retreated slightly. "All right, I get it. Just thought it might help or something."

"Help what?" Danny snapped, growing angry once more. "There's nothing you can do to help my situation except get the Pig back running things. If I'm lucky I'll get to take my old place at its side. My best-case scenario is an eternity of feeding horribly broken human beings to an entity that was put in charge by a god that didn't want to be bothered. In the grand cosmic scheme of things, we're nothing more than a fucking *headache*. "

"So how would you change things?" I said after a while.

A darkness entered Danny's eyes. "I'd wipe the Black Farm from existence. This is an evil place filled with people who deserve some goddamn peace. One of the most complicated and horrible events in someone's life shouldn't be punished with such wickedness. I've never met God, but to send Suicidals to a place like this? He's either lazy or just as evil as the Pig."

I let his words sink in before responding carefully. "If you pity the Suicidals so much, then why do you hate them with such ferocity?"

Danny sighed miserably, like he was examining something long dead. "Because they're not any better than me. They made the same mistake I did. They killed themselves. And while I understand the need, that fucking miserable promise, we're all stuck in the same place."

"Sounds a little hypocritical, doesn't it?" I asked.

"I need people to be *better than me*," Danny suddenly exhaled, almost urgently, a finger pointed to his own chest. "I need people to be able to make the hard choices I couldn't make. And every single new Suicidal I see here is a reminder of my own weakness. And I can't-fucking-stand-that." He enunciated each word with venom, his lips curing into a snarl.

"How can you hold people to a higher standard than yourself, though?" I pressed. "You want to talk about things being fair? That's not fair at all."

Danny scooted closer, his voice a hiss. "Imagine that every person in our life reminded you of the worst thing you've ever done. Wouldn't you ate them? Wouldn't you grow to loathe their existence?"

I stared hard into Danny's eyes, searching. "What...what did you do, anny?"

Danny's voice came back clothed in burning hatred, so thick it brought ed to his face. "What did I do? You really want to know what it was that rought me here? OK, Nick. I'll tell you." He leaned in even closer. "I didn't ill my father."

I blinked, taken back. "What?"

"That fucking monster plagued my life. He was a daily disease, each assing year bringing more and more misery. He terrorized my mother and e in ways I can't even fucking *think* about anymore. But I got out. I esped. Ran away when I was fifteen. I left my mother with him, the sole ceptor of his wrath. With me out of the picture, she was his only target hen his temper turned. You're probably asking yourself, why didn't she just ave? Get out like I did?" Danny shook his head. "My mom was a saint. She ore an oath before God to stay with him, in sickness and in health. And she stayed, despite the hell he put her through." Danny looked away now, e heat in his voice cooling. "For ten years I tried to summon the courage go back there and get her out, no matter what it took." His voice began shake. "But I couldn't do it. The thought of going back...of setting foot in at fucking house again, even for a minute...I would throw up just thinking out it. *Fuck*."

"What happened to her?" I asked somberly.

Danny looked back into my eyes. "He killed her. I was too late."

"Jesus, Danny..."

Danny leaned back against the wall, his voice now growing holl
"Wasn't long after that I killed myself."

"I'm sorry," I whispered.

"Keep your pity," Danny muttered heavily, "just...keep it..." He fell i
silence for a while before continuing. "I think that's why the Pig chose m

"Chose you? What do you mean?"

"I tried to feed the Pig. But as soon as I climbed into its mouth,
bastard spat me back out. Something about how I tasted, I think. I thi
the Pig could taste my anger. My hatred. So instead of sending me to hel
decided to use me. That's how...that's how all this shit started..."

I looked down miserably at Emily, my chest heavy.

"Ironic, isn't it?" Danny muttered. "The god my mom believed in c
demned her to that house until it killed her. How can you believe in som
thing like that?"

"I don't know, Danny," I said softly. "I don't know..."

"Fuck," Danny breathed, "it doesn't matter. None of that matters a
more. Those are problems long dead. We have our own shit to deal wit
He looked over at Emily and then past me at Pudge. "Might as well
some rest while you can. If you want. I'll keep my eyes open in case son
thing comes."

"You don't have to."

"It's fine. Get some sleep while you can. I have a feeling we're going
need your axe arm again before this is over."

I decided to give in and shut my eyes, despite my nagging paranoia.
red light dimmed behind my eyelids and I realized just how exhausted I w
Emily was warm against me and I focused on her soft snores to lull me i
an uneasy slumber.

When I felt something nudge me, I could have sworn I had only b
asleep for a couple of seconds. I forced my eyes open, blinking myself i
alertness. Everything rushed back in a moment and I nearly jumped to
feet in a panic.

Pudge stood over me, poking my side with the blunt end of his sp
"Rise and shine. We gotta move." I looked around and saw Emily
crawled up from my lap and was now standing next to Danny.

"How long was I out?" I asked thickly, climbing to my feet.

"'Bout an hour," Danny said.

Pudge tapped his ear. "And do you hear that? The Maw has moved on which means it's time for us to as well. You wipe them cobwebs from your eyes and we'll be on our way."

"You sure it's gone?" I asked. Even as I said it, I realized I couldn't hear the low grumble from the depths below us.

"If it's not, then we're going to have a nasty surprise waiting for us at the bottom of these stairs," Pudge said, shouldering his pack, "but I don't hear nothing, do you?" I shook my head.

"Lead the way, Pudge," Danny said, "I'm getting real sick of this place."

I reached out to Emily and she took my hand. "You sleep OK, Em?"

"I had weird dreams," she said quietly.

Yeah, I remember those.

Pudge started down the stairs once again and we followed in stride. The steps continued to wind deeper and deeper into the darkness, the empty air illuminated by the strange crimson cuts in the stone. As we descended, Pudge got quiet and I sensed a heavy tension rolling off of him. It set me on edge and I fought the urge to ask him what was wrong. From behind, I noted the way he gripped his spear, his knuckles white against it. He also moved quickly, his pace hurried and deliberate. Emily had to practically jog at my side, and I heard Danny grumble something about breaking Pudge's neck.

To my relief, it wasn't far until we reached the bottom, the end of the stairs suddenly appearing before us. As we reached the end, I observed a pair of massive tunnels leading in opposite directions, one left and the other to the right. But between them, in the center of the large room we found ourselves in, was a massive hole. Its circumference was almost as wide as I was tall, an empty drop into pitch-black. I peered into the abyss, searching for a ladder or more stairs, but only saw rough rock walls.

"Please tell me we're not going down there," Danny said, peeking over the edge. Emily let go of my hand and went to his side, grabbing a handful of his pant leg and looking down as well.

Pudge didn't answer, his face flushed, his head quickly turning from side to side. He hefted his spear and walked behind us like he was waiting for something to come charging out of the tunnels.

Danny turned to face him. "Pudge, where the hell are—"

Before he could answer, Pudge lunged forward, spear held across both hands. He used it to shove Danny and Emily backwards hard, and my heart leaped into my throat.

"What the fu—SHIT!" Danny screamed, stumbling backwards, one foot dropping into the open hole. Emily cried out in fear and her hands flailed wildly as she was forced backwards.

Losing his balance, Danny wrapped his arms around her, his face whit with terror, and then they were gone, their screams following them dow the massive hole.

I stood frozen in place, my hands wrapped around my axe. My eyes wer wide and I felt like there was something, a scream, trapped in my throat. M ears rang with Emily's cries of terror, the space she had just occupied hor ribly empty.

"Did you really think I'd forget what you *did* to me?"

The blood drained from my face and I snapped out of my trance in a instant. I spun and saw Pudge leering at me, circling me, jabbing his spear a he positioned me dangerously close to the lip of the hole.

"What the hell have you done!?" I yelled, vein pulsing in my temple.

Pudge continued to circle me, holding me in place, the open abyss inch es from my heels. "You must think I'm pretty goddamn dumb, don't you he snarled.

"What the fuck are you talking about?" I lied, smacking a jab away wi the head of my axe. My heart crawled up my throat and I heard my heartbe pounding in my ears.

"Don't act like you don't remember me, ya goddamn dog," Pudge sp closing the distance. "You're name's not Jack. You're Nick. The same Ni that stole my gun and shot me in the face. I did nothin' to ya, but you mu dered me in cold blood just the same."

The axe handle turned slick beneath my sweating palms, the h horribly close. "I don't know what you think I did to you, but you got t wrong guy."

Pudge jabbed at me again, forcing me to jump back toward the ed "When I saw you, it took a second, but I remembered, same as I remem the sky is blue. You're a bad person. A mean, nasty bastard."

I pointed behind me, down the hole. "And what about Emily!? What about HER?! Was she bad!? What the FUCK DID YOU DO!?"

Pudge shrugged, his face ugly and furious. "I don't give a good goddamn about her or the other guy. That's on you. I have a bone to pick with YOU, and THEY were just in the damn way. You did that to them, not me."

I felt my foot slip into the hole and I quickly caught myself, deflecting another strike from the spear. Sweat stood out on my brow now, my voice hot. "What the hell was all this, then? Why not kill us? Why take us all the way down here? WHY!?"

Pudge suddenly grinned, but the expression held no humor. "Cause I ain't ever been further than this. That drop won't kill ya, but it's going to hurt. And when you come to, I think you're going to find there ain't any way out." He jabbed at me again. "I wonder what will kill you first? The madness or the monsters? What do you think, *Nick*?"

"You son of a bitch," I growled, pulse quickening. "You chicken shit mother*fucker*..."

"I wanted to make sure you paid for what you did to me," Pudge said, advancing, his spear poking the air wildly, "and whatever's down there? I think it'll make sure of that."

Pudge surged toward me, spear aimed for my stomach. I cried out and swung my axe, deflecting it by inches. But Pudge charged forward behind the blow, shoulder lowered, attacking my exposed side. He thundered into me and I felt myself falling backwards into open emptiness. A scream rattled through me as I became weightless, plummeting down into the mouth of darkness. The last thing I saw before striking my head and blacking out was the snarling face of Pudge watching me from above.

Then the darkness became complete.

Chapter 11

Pain shuddered through the inky clouds filling my head. It was a sharp, insistent stabbing at the back of my skull. I felt as if my bones had been ıattered and carelessly put back together. Something warm encased my kin as I slowly came back to life. As my eyes fluttered open, stars dancing, realized that I was alive and still in the Abyss. It was a blessing I wasn't ıre I wanted, the drop damaging my body in ways I wasn't sure I wanted explore.

Dim red light swarmed the haze before my eyes and I shifted in whater I was lying in, something thick and wet sloshing around my elbows.

Pull yourself together, Nick. Get up, you have to get up.

I groaned and tried to sit up, a lance of agony shooting through my ain and piercing the back of my eyes. I gave myself a moment, letting evything focus and settle. I stared up at a faint red ceiling, a thin vermillion sh lining the rock up above.

Where are you? Where is this?

I groaned again, begging my body to cooperate and sit up.

What's down here with you?

Gritting my teeth, I made myself sit up, biting through the pain. I sped as I managed to get upright, leaning back against the wall. Panting, swimming across my vision, I looked up at the hole I had fallen down d saw a small circle of light up above.

How are you not dead?

I let my eyes drop to my legs and saw that I had fallen into some kind of oozing black liquid. I raised a hand to my face and watched the goo run between my fingers. It smelled like sulfur and sent a faint buzzing sensation across my skin.

What is this shit?

With my senses returning, I began to test my throbbing muscles fo breaks. Mercifully, I didn't find any, just a mass of bruised skin and sore muscles. Wincing, I got to my feet, the action taking far longer than it shoulc have. When I finally stood, sweat stung my eyes and I had to lean against th wall for a moment to catch my breath. As I pulled in hungry lungfuls of ai I looked around and saw a lone tunnel leading away from the dead-end hol I had fallen from. More of the black ooze slithered across the floor, a coupl inches deep, the decline draining toward the unknown.

Hazy red light lit the way, a foggy blur of color. I squinted, my eye catching something standing in the tunnel. It was dark like a shadow an looked human in shape.

"Danny?" I gasped.

The figure didn't move.

I cleared my throat. "DANNY?! Is that you!?"

Slowly, the shadowy shape walked down the tunnel away from me ar disappeared out of sight.

What the hell was that?

I squeezed my eyes shut, pain spiking through my battered hea "DANNY!? WHERE ARE YOU!? EMILY!?"

My voice echoed off the walls and bounced down into emptiness. chilled me to the bone, and I felt rising panic begin to rear its ugly head.

You're alone down here, Nick.

"No," I gasped desperately, "no, they fell! They should be down here!"

There's no one.

"Please," I begged, spittle spraying from my lips, "oh god, *please*."

The black goo swirled around my feet and lazily flowed down the pa sage like some kind of rotting river. I stared at it, trying my best to cont my panic. I knew I had to follow it, down that dark slope to wherever it l Taking a deep breath, I steadied my nerves as best I could and began to wa my boots sloshing in the muck. As I went, I began to see more of the strar shadow forms ahead of me. They made my blood curdle, each one appearing just seconds before walking out of sight. I couldn't be sure, but it appeared as if they were rising from the shallow stream of inky slime, like they were brought to life by its churning flow.

The tunnel twisted and snaked further downward, branching paths splintering off to the left and right. But for some unknown reason, the black goo remained in the central tunnel, as if it were alive with a destination in mind. I decided to continue following the current, convinced it had to lead to something other than endless wandering.

Where the hell are Danny and Emily?

I thought about calling out to them once more but voted against the idea. I didn't want to draw any more attention to myself. The red gashes continued to line the wall, sending red shadows down into the stream.

After a while, I slowed, my ears picking up a distant sound. It was a low whine, like a foghorn from a hidden boat. The noise rose and fell in a constant pattern, each note sending dread deeper and deeper into my bones.

You're going to die down here.

"Shut up," I hissed, throat dry.

The tunnel banked left ahead and as I reached the bend, I heard movement behind me. I spun, heart surging in my throat, and saw a trio of dark shapes rise from the small river and begin to walk toward me. They made no sound, their movement robotic, like their joints were frozen. Something held me in place, their presence cementing me in the slime. My mind screamed to run the closer they got, but for some reason I remained transfixed.

The dark shapes approached me, their stride never slowing or quickening. I pressed myself against the wall, eyes wide, as they passed. They were featureless, a mold of darkness in human form. If they saw me, they made no sign of it. The three passed without contact or acknowledgement, walking silently and disappearing around the corner.

What the hell was that all about?

I gave myself a couple seconds before moving once again, my senses heightened.

There's something terrible going on down here.

The thought came with such conviction that I didn't even try to combat it. This whole island was evil, but this place, the Abyss…this place held a darkness that I could feel with every breath.

The deeper I walked into the Abyss, the louder the sound grew, that low blaring pattern of noise. I continued to follow the stream, catching snippets of more figures ahead of me, always going the same direction as the goo.

Finally, after what seemed like ages, I emerged into an absolutely titanic cavern, the walls lined with red scars that lit the place like a cursed cathedral. The ceiling opened up and expanded up toward an incredibly high roof of rock. The walls pushed back hundreds of yards in every direction, the ground littered with towering structures of stone that bloomed at the top to exhale plumes of glowing blue light.

"What the hell is this place?" I muttered, taking a couple tentative steps forward, my attention enraptured by the dozen-odd pillars of rock. They varied in size, the open mouths coughing up mouthfuls of that eerie blue fog glow.

I looked down and saw the river of ooze led to the center of the cavern where it pooled around an odd structure of jumbled rock that ran almost the length of the expanse. I squinted, the colored light mixing, and saw the congregation of shadow forms all walking toward the rock. As they reached it, they didn't stop, but instead passed through inside like they were entering through some invisible door.

The source of the noise, that odd horn, came from the pillars of smoke. Each time another cloud wafted from the opening, the noise rumbled across the cavern, so loud I felt gravel shift beneath my feet.

I looked to my right and saw the ground rise slightly to form a natural peak. I quickly went to it and climbed the slope, hoping to get a better vantage point. When I reached the top, I was sweating, the exertion causing me to pause and catch my breath for a moment.

"Nick?"

I almost cried out in surprise as I whipped around to see who had called my name. Relief flooded through me as I spotted Danny and Emily sitting against a boulder, watching me with unbelieving eyes.

I scrambled over to them. "Jesus Christ, I thought you two were gone! What happened? Are you OK?"

Danny winced and rolled his shoulder. "I've been better. Landed hard on my side, but nothing's broken."

I looked down at Emily, who was curled up next to Danny, one hand clutching his arm. "You OK, sweetie? Do you hurt anywhere?"

"I'm OK," she said softly without looking at me. "Danny saved me from the fall."

I looked at Danny, who shrugged. "Didn't want to crush her. Don't make a big deal out of it."

"You told me not to be scared," Emily mumbled, still clutching him, "and that you'd help me find Nick again."

Danny looked away. "Ah, I was just talking…"

I offered Danny a grim nod. "Thank you."

"Oh, relax."

"Can you walk?" I asked, appraising him for obvious breaks.

"I'm fine. Just came down hard on my side. Lost my breath for a minute when Emily dropped onto my chest. I tried to catch her." He winced. "It worked."

"Are you OK with Danny?" I asked Emily, noticing how she hadn't moved.

"I don't like it down here," she whispered. "There are people covered in sticky stuff and I don't like them."

"I saw them." I nodded. "They're following the river straight into the center of this canyon."

Another blast of noise echoed across the open space, and I saw Emily wince and grip Danny's arm tighter.

"The noise can't hurt us," Danny mumbled awkwardly.

I scanned the expanse of the cavern, eyes searching. "Did you happen to see a way out of this pit?"

Danny pointed to his right. "I think there's a tunnel over there. A big one."

"Does it lead to the surface?"

"The hell would I know that?" Danny asked, then softened. "I don't know, Nick. But something tells me we've reached the basement."

I looked to where he was pointing and saw a large open circle of darkness leading into the rock.

"That looks prom—" my words were cut short as another blast of sound shook the cavern, the loudest yet. I slammed my hands over my ears, wincing, the ground shaking.

And this time it didn't stop.

"What the hell is happening?!" Danny yelled over the din, small rocks trembling beneath us. He climbed to his feet and took Emily by the hand leading her over to my side to stare down into the center of the cavern.

"Something's happening!" I yelled, deafened. "Look! That massive rock formation! It's moving!"

Danny's eyes went wide as something swept through him. "Oh *no*..."

Struggling to remain standing beneath the quake, I looked at him, pulse racing. "What!? What is it!?"

"LOOK!"

I followed his finger toward the wall of the cavern where the rock formation ended. It was beginning to light up, a strange pattern of blue light sparking the edges. When I realized what was happening, what I was looking at, I felt my blood turn to ice.

"Jesus fucking Christ," I gasped, trembling. "It's a goddamn Keeper."

BROOOOOAAAAAHHHHHMMMMM.

The ear-splitting blast rocked us, and Danny had to hold Emily to keep her from falling over. My eyes were locked to the massive construct lying along the ground, hundreds of feet across. More glyphs activated and I realized it was coming to life, the constant stream of dark shapes disappearing inside acting like pulls of oxygen.

"They built a new fucking Keeper!" Danny screamed over the gale of noise. "Jesus FUCK, they built a new Keeper!"

A bellowing groan of rock joined the hurricane of sound as the colossal creature shifted, raising its massive cross-shaped head, roaring its first breath of life. The earth rattled beneath its movement as the titan slowly sat up, its body alighting as its glyphs activated.

"Nick!" Danny screamed, stumbling. "We have to get the FUCK out of here!"

BROOOOOAAAAAHHHHHHMMMMMM!

The Keeper climbed to its feet, bringing with it a crunch of stone, part of the ceiling exploding as its head struck the roof of the cavern. Grea ınks of slate slid and plummeted, erupting across the floor like bombs. : Keeper, bent over double, let out another deafening wail and slammed back of its cross-shaped head into the ceiling, splintering a massive crack t snaked left to right.

"We have to run!" Danny screamed, ushering me toward the new tunnel h Emily in tow. "It's trying to get out! It's going to bring this whole fuck-place down on us! NICK!"

I snapped out of my trance, ears ringing, legs shaking beneath the blows. n right behind you, GO!"

We took off toward the far side of the cavern, stumbling and tripping as earth shook beneath our feet. The ground trembled and our ears shud-ed as the Keeper brought its head up again, further widening the crack it making in the roof. I shot a glance at the damage and felt my stomach p.

"Danny, we have to go faster, LOOK!"

Wide-eyed, Danny threw a look over his shoulder and I saw fear fill his :. Streams of black ocean water had begun to trickle in, each blow causing re to filter through.

"Grab Emily, we don't have much time!" Danny yelled, half-skidding vn a slope and adjusting his course back toward the new tunnel. Mid-run, ooped Emily up in my arms and threw her over my shoulder.

"Hang on!" I screamed.

BOOOOOOOOM!

I could hear the water now, cascading down to the cavern floor in a en different waterfalls. I focused on Danny, snaking our way through the lder-filled cavern toward the tunnel. We had almost reached it, our path ıbing toward the open mouth.

As we reached it, I felt my ankles engulfed in water. I almost fell but ıaged to right myself without dropping Emily in the process. Danny ted ahead, sprinting head-first into the wide mouth of the passage.

BOOOOOOOM!

"All the water is coming!" Emily cried in my ear. I didn't need her to tell my steps slowing as the water rose up to my calves. I sloshed through it, ing my muscles begin to buzz as they numbed, submerged in the danger-liquid.

"Danny, get us to higher ground or we're going to get swept away! bellowed, pulling myself through the rising tide.

"This way!" he yelled, his words swept up in the rush of crashing wa "There's a rise just ahead! The tunnel is leading up! We're getting the fu out of this place, just keep running!"

BRRRROOOOOAAAAAMMMMM!

The roar of the Keeper was accompanied by a colossal crunch of ro the passage shaking as bits of stone fell away above us. I coughed and sp tered as it splashed into the growing river at our feet, temporarily blindi me. Blinking furiously, water clinging to my face, I felt Emily's small ha reach for my eyes and wipe my vision clear. I didn't have time to thank as I struggled for air, my legs burning.

Just as I was about to give up hope, I felt the ground slope up, angle growing steeper, my boots taking me up and out of the rising wat Danny's hand found my arm and hauled me ahead, out of the sloshing fr

"Let me take her!" he yelled as the tunnel shook around us. I felt Em slide out of my arms and into Danny's, his voice rising over the chaos.

"It's a straight shot!" Danny cried, wrapping and arm around Emily a pointing up the tunnel, "we just have to stay ahead of the water!"

I sucked down a breath and looked ahead of us, horribly aware of rising threat below us, just feet away. The tunnel almost looked man made its design, a burrowing hole lined with red gashes that climbed straight to what I hoped was the other side of the ocean.

BOOOOOOOM!

"We're right at the end of this!" I yelled, "now RUN!"

We took off, the constant detonations at our backs fueling every ou of energy we had, pushing us up toward the surface. The water at our b snarled mere feet behind us as it gave chase, a gasping, relentless threa knew that if we stopped, even for a second, we would risk being overwhelm

I gritted my teeth and doubled down, keeping Danny and Emily ah of me in case one of them went down, Emily bouncing over his shoul like a sack of flour. The Keeper's cries echoed up to us from the depths it struggled to break free from its womb, an unearthly wall of sound t pushed at our backs and drove us to the surface.

Sweat stood out on my brow and my legs began to burn furiously, the constant rise digging into my muscles. I noticed Danny panting heavily, his face pale and haggard. I gave it a couple more minutes and then I snatched Emily from him. He shot me a thankful look and wiped sweat from his nose without slowing.

Time seemed to stretch out before us like melting taffy, a long, seemingly endless sprint that threatened to take me to the floor. Each breath rattled from my battered lungs and I fought off a growing sense of dizziness and complete exhaustion. The water growled from behind and I locked away thoughts of slowing, knowing it would be a death sentence.

"I can feel a breeze!" Danny yelled from ahead. "Just a little further! We can make it!"

My vision blurred and my legs turned to fire as I injected my muscles with everything I had. Spittle flew from my lips and I felt a relentless nausea creep up my throat. I risked a look ahead and felt something cool wash across my face.

Just a little more, Nick. Don't give up.

Wheezing, we climbed the final distance, the length of time unknown as we exploded out of the tunnel. Immediately, my skin was swallowed in chilly night air and the ground beneath my boots turned from rock to sinking dirt. The change was so sudden, the night so dark, that I wasn't aware we had made it out immediately. I stumbled as the terrain softened and then I went sprawling face-first into the mud, losing Emily in the process. I heard her squeal and then strike ground next to me, Danny only a second behind. Mud sprayed my face and I coughed as it entered my mouth. I rolled onto my back, feeling like a corpse, chest heaving as I wretched and then vomited, my lungs and stomach absolutely spent.

After a moment, I felt liquid running across my body, tingling on contact. I looked up, tears running down my face, and saw the open mouth of the tunnel gurgling the remains of the ocean waters as they escaped the dark passage.

Wiping my eyes, I searched for Emily and saw her struggling to her feet, her face confused and scared.

"Stay away from the water!" I cried, trying to get to my feet. "Get away from it! Don't let it touch you!" My own legs were beginning to numb as they were swallowed up, the gushing, inky liquid cascading over me. I splashed around, beginning to panic, begging my body to cooperate.

Suddenly, a pair of hands hauled me to my feet and dragged me away from the growing river, pulling me toward a rise of grass next to Emily.

"Can't have you dying after that all-star sprint," Danny grunted, face coated in dirt and sweat, his grip powerful. We reached the grassy hill and collapsed next to Emily, who stared at us with wide, frightened eyes. I lay there, convinced my chest would collapse, as I struggled to recover. I felt like I had been beaten within an inch of my life, every part of me aching and throbbing and gasping. Danny lay down next to me, wheezing, the two of us unable to believe we had made it out. Emily sat down between us, crossing her legs.

"Are you OK?" she asked, her voice shaking. "Can you breathe OK?"

I offered her a weak thumbs-up and then let my hand fall back to the grass. I closed my eyes and forced the stars out, feeling the burn in my chest finally start to fade. I looked around, rolling my head in the dirt and saw the ground continue to slope up at our backs, rising up only to be devoured by dark woods. I looked to the sky and realized that it was almost pitch black, the open air devoid of stars or sun. Instead, tiny slivers of golden ligh peeked through the blanket of oppressive tar, offering just enough illumina tion to light our surroundings.

Finally, I sat up and stared down the slope, down where we had com from. I spotted the mouth of the tunnel, now dribbling the last of the wate out of the opening, a singular hole reaching deep into the earth. I swept m eyes around and saw the quiet ocean only a hundred yards away, the beac speckled with golden light from the clouds. I scanned left to right, min stretching with disbelief.

"Danny," I panted, "where are we?"

Danny sat up next to me, wiping filth from his eyes, his voice raw ar weathered. "I'd say we made it across." He snorted in disbelief. "We made to the second island."

I continued to stare out at the strange new landscape, absorbing it all best as I could in the strange light. I paused as I looked toward the beach to our left. I squinted and felt something turn in my stomach.

"Danny," I said without taking me eyes away, "are those campfires?"

Danny turned toward the pocket of small fires. "I'll be damned…"

"It doesn't look like there's anyone by them, though."

"Empty campfires," Danny mused. "Well, it tells us one thing at least."

"What's that?"

"That we're not alone here."

"Wonderful," I hissed. turning to Emily. "You doing OK, sweetie? I know it got a little crazy there."

"That was really scary," she said softly. "I don't like those big monsters. Why was it down there?"

"I think that's where they're born," I said, "or at least that one was."

She looked up at me, her big brown eyes shimmering. "Nick? What... what is this place? Where's my home?"

I knelt down next to her, one arm wrapping around her shoulders. "It doesn't matter where this is. I'll keep you safe, OK?"

"But where is my house? Where's my mom? Why is it so scary here?"

I squeezed the bridge of my nose and closed my eyes, searching for the right words. "Listen, Emily, I know you probably don't understand a lot of this, but something bad happened to you. And because of that, you were sent here. But that's OK, 'cause I'm here, too, right?"

Emily shrugged, unconvinced. "I guess...but when can I go home? I miss my mom…"

"Well—"

My words were cut short as something roared from the sloping forest behind us, a squealing howl that set my teeth on edge. The cry echoed around us and slowly faded back into the darkness of the trees. Wide-eyed, I turned to Danny, trying to understand what we had just heard.

"I think we found the Pig," Danny whispered, face pale.

Chapter 12

After some discussion, we decided to head toward the campfires. We knew the Pig was in the woods, up the massive hill and past the grass-d. Charging head-first toward it would accomplish nothing but getting selves potentially killed, so we headed for the beach. We needed to un-stand this place better before we could set a plan in motion.

Our feet took us over the rolling foothills beneath the night sky, the ee of us stretched out in a line, shoulder to shoulder, with Emily in the ldle.

As we approached the fires, Danny glanced at me. "What happened to r axe?"

I looked down and realized I wasn't holding it. "I...I don't know. I must e lost it in the chaos."

"If there ever was a time we could use it," Danny muttered.

"I was a little busy trying to save a certain small someone," I said, tilting head down.

"We'll make do," Danny said calmly. "It just would have made me better."

"You've never been to this island, have you?"

"I'm a tourist, same as you. Seems to be relatively similar to the first nd, though."

"I don't know," I said. "It seems...quieter here. Almost like we're be-watched."

Danny nodded toward the forest on the slope to our left. "Could be t
Pig. That noise we heard...that was definitely it. I'm sure of it."

I shook my head. "No, it's not that. It's something else."

"Could you be any more vague?" Danny muttered, mildly irritat
"What did your good buddy say about this place? Anything?"

"Good buddy?"

"That angel fucker guy."

Emily giggled behind her hand.

"Ramiel," I said, keeping the campfires in focus ahead of us. "He di
say anything about this place."

"Didn't he give you like a clue or something to look for? I seem to re
you mentioning...something."

"The only thing he mentioned was someone called the Mud Ma
have absolutely no idea who that could be or where we'd find him, but
stressed that he could be important."

Danny's brow furrowed. "So we really have nothing to go off of, w
walking toward what could very well be a trap, the Pig you poisoned mi
be watching us, and you lost your axe." He snorted. "Wonderful."

I felt a tug at my sleeve and looked down to see Emily pointing tow
the sky. "Look! A shooting star!"

I craned my head back and saw a streak of blue travel across the i
canvas above. It only lasted a couple seconds before winking out of existe

"Speak of the fucking devil," I muttered.

"Friend of yours?" Danny said, noticing the light.

Why don't you come down and say hello, you bastard?

"It's not important right now," I said, dismissing it, trying to change
subject. "Look, Danny, this whole shit with the Pig…"

"What about it?"

"What would happen if we just...let the Pig die?"

"What?"

"It's sick, right? What would happen if we just did nothing and
it die."

Danny said nothing for a while before answering. "Do you actu
think the Pig can die?"

"Everything dies."

"No, not everything. Some things just get meaner."

"Is there a pig here?" Emily asked suddenly.

Danny looked down at her. "Yeah, do you want to go pet it?"

Emily nodded enthusiastically.

"Knock it off, Danny," I warned.

He shrugged. "Hey, she may get the chance."

"I wanna pet the pig!" Emily announced.

"It might bite your arm off," Danny continued.

Emily's face drooped. "I don't wanna pet a *mean* pig..."

"Hey, what're those over there?" I said, noticing something past the campfires. "You see those?"

"I don't see shit," Danny said, squinting. "What are you talking about?"

"Look further down the beach, more inland. That cluster of rises coming out of the ground? They kind of look like—"

"They look like anthills!" Emily announced loudly.

"Oh, I see them now," Danny said. "Those tall mounds?"

"Yeah, there's a whole bunch of them. Should we look?"

"I suppose we should. Doesn't look like we're going to find much at the fires anyway."

The campfires weren't far now, a trio of empty pits that silently flickered in the sand. Nothing about them stood out or gave clue to their purpose. Had someone lit them and been forced to flee? Where were they now?

Danny saw me watching, his voice suddenly sharp. "Nick, I don't want to get any closer."

We stopped and I shot a glance at Danny. "You see something?"

Danny pointed out toward the ocean. I followed his finger and felt my heart skip a beat. A Keeper stood offshore, waist-deep in the ocean, almost invisible in the thick night. It faced the campfires, staring down at them like it was waiting for something. Was this the same one from the Abyss? Was it following us?

I felt Emily curl against my leg. "It's the monster again," she whispered, her voice fearful.

I looked at Danny, voice grave. "I don't know what the hell is going on here, but we need to be careful. Let's go check out those mounds. But keep your eyes open." With one more look toward the immobile Keeper, we changed course and headed inland, aiming for the strange, tall mounds of earth. As we drew closer, I realized that Emily was right. They did resemble anthills, but on a much greater scale.

The darkness of the second island pressed close as we traveled across the silent grasslands. The thin flickers of golden light from above didn't even seem to emit light outside the path of their beams. The quiet was terribly obvious and I began to feel extremely exposed, like we were trespassing in a place we were never supposed to find.

I looked toward the rising forest nestled on what looked like an endless mountainous slope. "What do you think is in there?" I asked Danny quietly.

"Nothing we want to find," he answered, eyeing the distant trees, their trunks pressed tight against one another. "This whole place makes my skin crawl."

"You think anyone has ever made it through the Abyss like we did?"

"Fuck if I know. Don't know why the hell anyone would be foolish enough to try," he finished, sliding me a look out of the corner of his eye.

"You say a lot of bad words," Emily stated from between us.

"Yeah, well there's a lot a good reasons to use them," Danny said, unaffected.

I continued to stare at the forest, feeling frustration unexpectedly bubble up in my chest.

"I wish we knew what we're supposed to do here."

"We'll figure it out," Danny said calmly. "I honestly never expected to make it this far, so we got that going for us. And we heard the Pig earlier, we know it's here, somewhere in those woods. No clue what kind of condition it's in, but we're on the right track. We're doing OK, Nick; don't get mopey on me now."

Danny's unexpected optimism caught me off-guard and the corners of my mouth twisted into a grim smile. "If we ever get through this, remind me to buy you a beer."

"That's not even funny."

"It's the thought that counts."

"Keep those thoughts to yourself from now on," Danny said. "Some of us aren't going to get to leave when this is all said and done."

Still walking, I raised my eyebrows. "So now you actually think I'll make it out? That's a change of tune."

Danny waved my comment away. "Don't get corny on me, asshole. We have a long way to go."

"You said another bad word," Emily said softly.

"For Chrissakes…"

Before another one of us could speak, our attention was drawn back to the forest, a rumbling crunch filling the night air. The three of us stopped and I felt unease tickle my spine as the sound continued, like something massive was walking through the mountainside forest.

"You think that's the Pig?" I asked quietly as the crack of wood continued.

Danny's eyes bore into the far-off trees. "At this point, I almost hope it is."

I looked back toward the ocean and saw the Keeper was gone. For some reason, this unnerved me more than if it had still been there. I swiveled back to the treeline and kept my mouth shut until the crunch of trees subsided and silence took the night once more.

"That sounded like a really big pig," Emily whispered.

Danny looked down at her and then at me. "Let's maybe move a little faster toward those mounds."

"Couldn't agree more."

We began to trot across the rolling landscape, icicles of gold dripping down the ladder of the sky toward us. Emily didn't complain as we went, her little face screwed up with determination to not fall behind. It didn't take long to reach the first of the dozen odd rises.

They looked like small towers made of dirt stemming from an igloo-shaped base. Each one stretched about ten or fifteen feet into the air. Dug into the face of each base was a hole that burrowed into the mounds, exposing nothing but darkness inside. As we passed through them, staring up at the odd unnatural constructs, I realized that they formed a rough circle with an open clearing in the center. We entered the space, our feet traveling over packed dirt, and turned around slowly to take in the entirely of the strange phenomenon. The beach was only a couple hundred yards away from the first structure, the mountain forest a similar distance from the last.

"What are we looking at?" I muttered, turning in place.

"I told you they're anthills," Emily said matter-of-factly.

"I hope not," Danny muttered. "I had my fill of ants back in the Abyss."

"Something or someone made these," I said quietly, eyeballing the shape and form of the igloo bases, "and I'm guessing whatever it is or *was* also made those fires down at the beach. Maybe they fled once the Keeper appeared. I know I would, especially now that they're coming out of the ocean."

"I don't like this," Danny said, voice low, "not one fucking bit."

Emily wandered away from us and approached one of the igloo openings, her neck craned back to take in the dirt spout that extended from the rounded roof. "They're chimneys!" she said loudly. "So the smoke goes out!"

"'Cept there's no smoke, kid, but good try," Danny said quietly. "Nick, we should leave. I don't know what lives here and I'd rather not hang around to find out. I'd bet you every axe on the Black Farm that this place is bad news."

"Goddamn it," I hissed, "what the fuck are we supposed to do then?"

Danny looked at me, annoyed. "Sorry, I left my travel guide back on the other island."

I curled my hands into fists.

Before I could respond, a sudden voice gurgled from the darkness of the igloo Emily was standing next to.

"We mean you...no harm…"

I jolted in surprise, reaching forward and snatching Emily away from the opening. "What the hell!? Danny, there's something in there!"

"Thanks, I heard," Danny growled, going on full alert.

The voice continued from the mouth of black, a wet, dribbling sound. "Please...we don't want any trouble."

I looked at Danny, heart hammering. "We?"

"Show yourself!" Danny demanded, pushing Emily behind us. "Come out so we can see you!"

"Just don't harm us...please," the voice begged.

"NOW!" Danny yelled.

Slowly, a figure began to emerge from the dirt igloo. As it came out into the open, my eyes tried to make sense of what I was seeing. I felt Emily's arms wrap around my legs as the thing made itself fully visible.

"What the fuck?" Danny hissed.

The creature looked like a blob of mud with stubby arms drooping from its gooey body. A pair of massive eyes sunk into the rotund figure along with a wide mouth that seemed to ooze brown slime. As it slid across the ground toward us, it raised its pathetic arms in a defensive posture.

"Don't hurt us," it gurgled, its large eyes rolling wildly.

I stepped back, unnerved by its grotesque appearance. "What...what the hell are you?"

The blob shuddered and smacked its lips wetly. "We are a mistake... nothing more."

Danny's eyes roamed across the multitude of igloos. "Are the rest of your kind hiding inside these...these dirt piles?"

The thing nodded, a roll of dripping ooze up and down. "Yes. They are afraid. It has been a long, long time since we've seen your kind."

"Our kind?" I asked cautiously.

The thing smiled, or at least I thought that's what it was trying to do. "You are the ones God chose, are you not? The clay he created to walk the Earth?"

"I have no idea what you're talking about," Danny said carefully, "but I'm going to need all of you to come out. I don't enjoy feeling like I'm about to get ambushed."

"Oh, of course!" the thing assured quickly. "I can promise we wouldn't dare harm you." It raised its soggy voice. "It's all right, everyone! You may come out!"

After a moment, more of the gross blobs began to slither from their holes, eyes wide, watching us intently. They varied in size, the smaller ones clinging to the bigger ones like deformed children. I turned slowly in place, assessing their posture and expressions, gauging just how screwed we might be. All in all, there were roughly thirty of them. And they all looked terrified of us.

"You see?" The first one declared. "We don't want any trouble. We haven't seen your kind in quite some time so you'll have to forgive our bewilderment." It turned and addressed the crowd. "We mean them no harm, right?"

A chorus of wet voices echoed hurried assurances, dozens of massive eyes appraising us with worry and caution.

"Hold on a second," I said, memory dawning and reforming. "Danny..."

"What?"

I stared at the oozing blobs, eyes wide. "What Ramiel said to me...I don't think we were looking for the Mud Man...we were looking for the Mud *Men*."

Danny let the words sink in before answering, his voice only for me now. "These...things? Are you sure?"

"Look at them. What else could they be?"

The first blob became worried, its voice rising. "I uh...I hope we haven't done anything to upset you?"

I turned to it. "No, no, everything is fine. More than fine. I think we've been looking for you, actually, without even knowing it."

It swept its eyes around at the small crowd. "Us? But why? We are nothing."

Before I could answer, the far-off woods ignited with noise, a rising screech that blasted up into the night sky and then quieted into the sti calm. The Mud Men's reaction was instantaneous, the small group retreatin into themselves, eyes wide and terrified, anxious looks cast behind us.

I pointed to the hilly forest. "That's why we've come. The Pig."

The creature's large eyes brimmed with fear. "Its presence here plague us. Threatens our very existence. We just want it gone."

"So do we," I assured. "That's why we've traveled here. We need to g it back to how it was. In power, back on the other island like it should be."

"We would like nothing more."

Danny stepped forward. "Sure, but...why is it here? There must a reason."

The Mud Men shuffled in place, globs of filth running down their dri ping bodies.

"I suppose if you're here to help solve our problem then we should t you exactly what we are," the creatures said slowly.

"I'm listening."

The thing cleared its throat, a sickening gurgle. "I guess I should start the beginning. My name is Yurt. I've been here, on this island, for as long a can remember. All of us have been, each one you see here." The crowd star at us with large, wet eyes as Yurt spoke.

"We have been called many things. Mud Men is the most common, but it was not the one assigned." Yurt sighed and looked directly at me. "We are the First Race."

Danny cocked an eyebrow. "First Race? What does that mean?"

Yurt looked at the ground. "It means...that humanity was not the first form of life to be created by God. We were."

Danny balked a laugh. "You? Are you serious?"

Yurt's eyes filled with hurt. "There's no need to remind us of our grotesque fragility. We are all well aware of it—of our failed state. We were an experiment, a test. God's first attempt at life. And each and every one of us is a failure. We are nothing more than blueprints that were built upon."

"Wait a second," I cut in, mind reeling. "Are you telling me you've been alive since the birth of humanity?"

Yurt wiggled his mass, a nod. "Yes. It didn't take God long to realize he could do better and so he cast us aside, opting to create something more..." he looked up at us, "beautiful. Life that reflected not only his intellect, but his image. We became an embarrassment, useless lumps of life that were dropped here on this plot of land to be forgotten."

"You have got to be fucking kidding me," Danny muttered, shaking his head.

"We are not a proud race," Yurt continued, the group sadly nodding at his words, "but we try to keep one another's spirits up. We know of the Black Farm, the island from which you came, but our contact with it is minimal. On occasion we'll spot a Keeper wandering the ocean in the distance. We light fires when they get too close. For some reason it holds their interest—covers our escape. But now," Yurt paused and lowered his voice, "now the *Pig* has come."

"But why?" I pressed. "What is it looking for?"

A shudder ran through the crowd before Yurt continued. "It is hunting us."

"Hunting you?" Danny said slowly. "Why on earth would it do that?"

A look of shame filled Yurt's dark eyes. "Because of our flaw. Because of how we were created."

"I don't understand."

"The Pig is sick, is it not?"

"It is. Very."

Yurt's voice grew soft. "When God made us, he overlooked one very important thing. He forgot to make us mortal. Do you understand what that means? We cannot die. Our flesh, the fiber we were created with, it carries that immortality. That life."

Yurt locked eyes with me. "The Pig needs that to heal itself from this sickness. The Pig needs to feed on us."

Danny and I slowly looked at one another. I felt a slow, dawning sense of dread fill my stomach.

"It is desperate," Yurt continued, "and yet so far we have been able to hide from it. We slide about, from here to there, going anywhere it is not. These *pyrels* you see here, these mounds—they fill this island. We have made them, pockets of home that we travel between. I don't know how much longer we can last, but we have managed so far."

Emily suddenly poked her head out from around me, her voice curious and careful. "Are you...sad?"

Yurt looked at her, surprised at the unexpected question, and then he smiled, a weary thing. "Sad? No, child...we know our place in this existence. We have come to terms with it. We only wish to continue, left alone to keep one another company until the end of days."

Danny leaned in toward me, his voice a careful whisper. "Nick…"

I looked at him sharply, my thoughts slowly turning grim.

Yurt looked at us intently. "We were planning on moving again. Very soon, actually. We fear the Pig knows where we are once more. We must stay ahead of it. The three of you are welcome to join us. It would be an honor."

Danny continued to look at me, his eyes boring into my own. "I need to talk to you. Right now."

I closed my eyes, beginning to feel sick. "Danny…"

He grabbed my arm, turning to the Mud Men. "Give us a second, I have to talk to my friend here." He dragged me away from the cluster of dirty blobs, leaving Emily standing in the middle of them. I saw her approach Yurt and begin to ask him questions, but it was Danny's voice that filled my ear instead of hers.

"Do you understand what is happening here?" h hissed when we were a safe distance away. "Do you get what has to happen?"

"You are jumping to *massive* fucking conclusions," I growled back.

"We have a goddamn solution to our problem right here," He spat, casting a look over my shoulder at Emily. "I mean, look at them. We can do this."

"I am not serving them up to the Pig on a silver platter," I snarled. They don't deserve that. I mean, Christ, they've done nothing wrong!"

Danny's face filled with fury. "What the *fuck* is wrong with you? Don't you want to go back to your family?"

"Of course I do!"

"So what's the issue?"

I turned and looked at Emily. "I just...I have to be better. I have to be able to live with myself when this is all over."

Danny grabbed me by the shirt. "You don't get to fucking walk away from this without some blood on your hands. That is not how this place works. You of all people should know that. This might not be the pretty little magic button you've been looking for, but it's a means to an end. An END, Nick. You hear me? So dig deep, grow a spine, and help me do what needs to be done. This is the answer we've been looking for. This is how we get the Pig back in power, fully healed and where it belongs."

I looked at Yurt, who was now smiling and conversing with Emily. "Look at them. Just *look* at them. They're a pathetic, self-loathing mess, but they care for one another. They've made the most of things, despite their lot in life. How the hell can I take that away from them? There has to be another way, Danny."

Danny leaned in close, his breath hot. "Sometimes you have to be the *goddamn* bad guy."

I ran a frustrated hand over my face, my stomach pooling with rot. "Fuck...*FUCK*."

"What else are we supposed to do here, Nick?" Danny continued. "What other option do we have? Because I'll listen if you can think of another. But from where I stand, there's only one solution to this mess."

I stared at the group of muddy creatures, dread blooming. "They don't deserve this."

"And you don't deserve to be here a second time," Danny said sharply. Isn't that right? Sometimes shit isn't fair and you have to do things you wouldn't otherwise."

What else are you going to do, Nick?

I continued to watch Emily and Yurt, hands curled into fists.

"I can't do this alone," Danny continued, studying me intently. "You're going to need to keep them put while I draw the Pig here. Are you listening to me?"

"I'm listening," I said softly, bile staining the back of my throat.

Don't fight this. Don't even think about it. You've done worse. This is nothing.

"The Pig is in those woods," Danny said, pointing. "It shouldn't take long to find it. I can feel it. It's close. But you have to make sure these things, the Mud Men, don't leave. Can I count on you?"

Remember how easy this used to be?

"Nick."

"What the hell am I supposed to tell her?" I whispered, staring at Emily who was happily chatting with Yurt still. "She's not going to understand what's happening."

Danny shook his head. "You chose to bring her with us. I'll let you choose how to explain this."

"Goddamn it."

Danny grabbed my shoulder. "Nick, the clock's ticking. If we're going to do this, I need to leave right now. Are you with me?"

These creatures are not your responsibility. You didn't put them here.

I exhaled, fighting with myself.

This might be your only chance to fix this mess. How badly do you want to see Jess and Theo again? How much longer can you last here before you're stuck? If you don't do this, what other horrible shit are you going to have to do to get out?

"Fucking talk to me, man," Danny said, snapping his fingers in front of my face.

"Go," was all I said, my voice thin and full of self-hatred. Danny looked into my eyes hard and then nodded, taking off toward the forest at full speed.

I ran my hands down my face. "Goddamn it."

God was the one who put them here.

I clenched my teeth.

This isn't your fault. It's his. Hate him, not yourself.

I raised my eyes to the sky. "You watching this?"

Slowly, I walked back to the small group of Mud Men. As I entered the :le, Emily turned and smiled at me, her face alight.

"Mr. Yurt is really nice!" she announced cheerfully.

Yurt smiled, a grotesque pull of his muddy cheeks. "This young lady is te the delight. It sounds like the three of you have had some adventures."

"Adventures...right," I muttered, distracted.

"They said we can go with them!" Emily said, coming to my side and ging on my arm. "Can we go? Please?"

"What?" I asked, tearing my eyes from the woods.

"Can we go with Mr. Yurt and his friends?"

I blinked and looked around at the group of thirty-odd creatures, each staring at me with wet, brown eyes. I found no hostility or ill inten- —nothing but hope and warmth.

Don't do this to yourself. Don't pity them.

Yurt approached me, his movements sluggish. "Like I said before, you're re than welcome to come with us." He looked around, brow furrowing. y, where is the other one? Your friend? Did we do something to of- d him?"

"He's, uh, checking on the fires you mentioned. He's worried about the :pers," I stuttered. "We saw one of them before we stumbled on this camp."

Yurt chewed on his lip with blackened teeth. "There shouldn't be any d. Is he returning soon?"

"Shouldn't be long."

No. It shouldn't.

Yurt looked around at the other Mud Men. "I don't mean to be rude, but can't wait long. It is becoming increasingly dangerous to stay at this site. understand, don't you?"

"Just give him a little bit," I said. "He'll be back. Promise."

"I suppose we could spare a few minutes," Yurt said worriedly, "but I will nit it makes me uncomfortable."

"We'll be fine."

Sure we will.

"Where did Danny go?" Emily called from the group, her small frame ounded by the curious Mud Men.

"He'll be right back."

"OK!"

Five minutes turned to ten, then twenty. Mercifully, Emily kept t
small crowd amused with her antics and constant chatter. All except Yu
who continued to look around with nervous eyes. Finally, he approached r
looking almost sheepish.

"Sir, I'm so sorry, but we really need to move."

"Just a little longer," I said, fingers tapping my leg. "I don't know w
he's taking so long. Please."

"I understand, but the longer we're here—"

"I know," I cut in. "We're in danger. I get it." I closed my eyes, gu
spreading.

Yurt bobbed his mass. "I'm so sorry. I don't mean to keep repeating m
self. It's a nervous habit. But I have to watch out for my own, just like y
wouldn't you agree?"

Come on, Danny.

"I think we're OK here," I said slowly. "We haven't heard the Pig aga
have we? Maybe it moved away, deeper up the mountain."

"I really must insist, please," Yurt said, "this just doesn't...feel right."

"What does that mean?"

Yurt avoided my eyes. "It's just...the fires...he would have return
by now."

He knows.

"Do you have something to say to me?" I asked, forcing iron into
voice, hating myself.

"Of course not," Yurt babbled, "but for the safety of my people, we rea
must go. I'm sorry."

I placed myself in front of him. "I...I can't let you do that."

Remember this is not your fault.

Yurt finally met my eyes. "W-what?"

"We're not leaving without my friend."

Yurt tried to slither around me. "I can appreciate your loyalty, but I
ally must insist—"

I sidestepped, blocking his path. "No one is going anywhere."

The crowd had gone quiet, every pair of eyes on me. Emily step
toward me, her face scrunched up with worry.

"Nick?"

I loathed how she looked at me. "Stay close, Emily. You understand?"

"What is going on here?" Yurt asked, concerned.

"I told you," I stated, "no one is going anywhere. We wait for Danny."

Emily touched my hand. "W-why are you being angry at Yurt?"

"Just stay with me, OK, sweetie?"

"They're nice!" Emily said. "So be nice to them!"

Hurry the fuck up, Danny.

Yurt appraised me with fearful eyes. "You know...I never did learn why ou came here to this island. Why you *really* came."

Uh-oh.

"Relax." I snapped, "Just fucking relax. We're just waiting for my friend."

Yurt narrowed his bulbous eyes. "Are we? Then tell me—where did he eally go? Because something tells me it wasn't to the beach."

"Stop talking to each other like that!" Emily suddenly cried, grabbing ny arm. "Don't be mean, please!"

I looked at Yurt, feeling every ounce of hatred I possessed turn inward nd drain into my own stomach. "How about you cut it out with the ques- ons and behave like I asked. OK? Got that?" I turned to the crowd, feeling ke a monster. "And that goes for everyone here! No one moves until Danny eturns! Don't test me on this!"

Emily tugged at my hand and I finally looked down to find her tearing p. "Stop it! Please be nice!"

You can't afford to be nice. She doesn't understand that. This isn't your fault. God hurt them by casting them aside. You're just finishing his dirty work.

It was a thought all too familiar, and it set my teeth on edge.

"We're leaving!" Yurt announced loudly, waving his stubby arms at the rowd. "Everyone, we head east! Form up!"

Do something.

I stepped in front of Yurt once again, voice raised. "I said no one moves!"

Yurt weakly tried to push past me, mud staining my sleeve. "Please get ut of my way!"

DO SOMETHING.

Stomach rolling, mind fraying, I steeled myself, pushed past my self- isgust, and slammed my fist directly into Yurt's eye. The gelatinous orb exploded on impact, covering my arm with black sludge, my knuckles sin ing deep.

Yurt screamed, his short arms wailing against me, mouth agape in te rible pain. The Mud Men gasped, horrified, cries of concern and fear echoi around me. Somewhere in the mix, I could hear Emily screaming.

She doesn't matter, Nick. You're not here for her.

I pulled my fist away, the ejection bringing a wave of thick slime wi it. Yurt clawed at his ruined socket, his good eye rolling back in agony. H howls crowded my head, reminding me of the trust I had betrayed.

"ANYONE MOVES AND I RIP OUT THE OTHER ONE!" I be lowed, facing the crowd.

Atta boy.

"Shut up," I hissed, vision blurring. I searched for Emily, her cries dra ing my eyes to her. She huddled with the Mud Men, now a cluster that clu to one another like a large mass of quivering Jell-O. The way she looked me drove a spike of murderous self-hatred through my skull.

"I told you all to STAY PUT!" I yelled, voice cracking the nig "I WARNED YOU! This is what happens when you don't do what FUCKING SAY!"

Comes easy once you remember what it's like, doesn't it?

I marched around Yurt, who was still weeping sludge. "I know you're immortal, but I can make eternity a blind hell for EVERY ONE of you! I you understand!?"

The crowd just stared at Yurt with looks of horrified fear, the violen rooting them in place.

I grabbed one of Yurt's arms and bent it back, hard. "If I don't get so affirmation here, then I'm going to rip this goddamn thing off! Now— you all understand?! NO ONE MOVES!"

It was Emily's voice that spoke for the crowd, a thin wail that sliced in my chest and burned into my heart. "Don't hurt him anymore! We wo move! Promise!"

I bit back against my rising bile. "Emily! Come over here with me! C away from them!" Emily didn't move, her eyes large and wide and wet.

"Why...are you doing this?" Yurt coughed, slime spraying from muddy lips.

"It's nothing personal," I growled, keeping a grip on his arm. "I'm just trying to get back home."

"Let him go!"

Emily's demand burrowed into my ears and plunged deep into conscience. I turned my attention to the small crowd, feeling a mental timer continue to tick down.

"I didn't condemn you to this island!" I cried, feeling my anger slowly turn to growing desperation. "I didn't want ANY of this! I'm doing this because I have to! So everyone just calm down and sit tight, OK!?"

"They are our friends!" Emily cried again, firing the statement like a bullet. "You hurt our friends!"

"What...a sad...creature you are," Yurt breathed wetly, each pull of air a labored affair.

"Shut up," I snarled. "I'm no worse than you. If you want to get angry, then get angry at the bastard who made us both. I didn't stick you here on this empty island. I didn't throw you aside like some ruined school project. In fact, the only reason I'm here is because the big bastard upstairs threatened me into submission. So if you want to bite someone's head off, then I offer you his. Just let me watch, 'cause I have no love for the fucker."

Yurt winced beneath my grip, gasping thick, heavy breaths. "Do not speak evil of our creator. He is not the one inflicting punishment on us. You are."

"Stop. Talking."

"You are his chosen race. How can you spit in the face of your creator with such contempt? He did not birth you to revel in sin such as this."

"I'm going to break your goddamn arm off if you keep this up."

"He has given you life and access to heaven. How can you just throw that away? Do you know how desperately I wish to be in your position?"

"You have no *fucking* clue what kind of god you're talking about. But I can assure you—the bastard that put you here is not the saint you think he is."

"There is such hatred in your heart," Yurt wheezed, his form still leaking black sludge. "Such overwhelming hatred."

Before I could respond, a deafening roar split the night sky, an exaltation of rage and sound that blasted from the mountain forest at our backs.

It turned my skin cold and I loosened my grip on Yurt, a great thundering following in the footsteps of the roar. It sounded like the trees were being ripped apart, a great cracking, splintering eruption.

The Pig.

"Have mercy on us," Yurt whispered miserably.

Suddenly Danny burst from the wall of night at full speed, skidding to a halt in the midst of us, eyes wide. He gasped for air, face covered in sweat.

"Jesus, Danny!" I cried, stepping away from Yurt. "What the hell happened to you? What took so long!?"

Danny looked up at me, his face sickly pale, his words a fearful hush. "It's coming. And it is not as you remember it." He licked his dry lips, still panting. "Nick, the Pig has *evolved*."

Before I could ask what that meant, another squealing howl blasted from the woods and the ground began to shake.

"Run," Danny gasped. "RUN!"

Chapter 13

grabbed Emily and began to run, throwing her over my shoulder as I fled. The Pig continued to bellow from the woods, its thunderous approach nounced beneath a crash of trees and shuddering earth. Danny sprinted at y side, the three of us bolting for the shoreline, away from the Mud Men.

I could hear their cries of fear at our back and knew they would not be le to escape the coming violence. I looked back, clutching Emily, and saw e small group fleeing as quickly as they could, left to right. But they were t fast creatures and their sluggish bodies oozed thickly across the ground e a pack of slugs.

Another roar came from the forest, and through the slivers of light I w an absolutely titanic form emerge from the woods. It slithered out of debris, ducking below the falling trees, catching pockets of gold that il- ninated it from the dark heavens.

What the...?

The shadowy form crawled across the ground with terrifying speed, aded straight for the group of panicked Mud Men.

"We have to help them!" Emily yelled in distress, pounding at my back.

We had almost made it to the shore, Danny in the lead, hell at our ks. A squealing howl cut into the night and I could hear the Mud Men's tant cries of terror as the abomination approached.

I looked again, knowing the Pig was almost upon them, and when I saw at towered before them, I felt my heart sputter.

The Pig was not the same creature I had left a year ago. Time and sic ness had changed it, mutated it, warped its appearance into something out a nightmare. As I turned back to look, the Pig rose from the ground to sta on its hind legs, a wash of golden light spilling across its form to expose new existence.

The first thing I noticed was how big it was, its snapping jaws swa ing over a hundred feet above the earth. My eyes fell down across its bo and then widened at what they found. The Pig's torso was bone-thin, elongated mutation that looked like flesh wrapped around an arcing spi Jutting from the smooth stretch of bone were dozens of wriggling hoov giving the Pig the appearance of a centipede in distress. It thundered towa the Mud Men on its hind legs, its balance perfect, its lower appendages thi with muscle that ended in hooves the size of cars. Taking it all in, it look like something had pulled the Pig in two to reveal a squirming bug betwe the two halves, the tiny hooves lining the thin spine appearing to act of th own accord.

"It's going to get them!" Emily cried in my ear, her tiny fists assaulti my back.

We reached the shore and Danny pulled me behind a low dune, t three of us dropping to our stomachs, panting, only to peek over the crest watch whatever came next.

Daggers of gold lit the scene before us, the howls of the Mud M rising as the Pig reached them, its massive snout falling toward them lik steel trap waiting to spring shut.

"What the hell has happened to it?" I gasped, eyes wide, sweating ru ning down my face. "It doesn't look anything like it used to!"

"I told you, you really fucked it up," Danny answered without looki at me. "But even so, it wasn't this bad the last time I saw it. I mean, Chr it's *huge*."

Emily was between us, shoulder to shoulder, her bottom lip quiveri as she peeked over the dune."You tricked them. You tricked them and n they're going to die!"

I said nothing. I watched as the Pig opened its dripping maw and c lected the first of the Mud Men into its mouth. Their screams were all t familiar and I closed my eyes as the Pig slammed its jaws shut, crushing the life out of the frail creatures.

"Don't look, kid," Danny muttered, "just...don't look."

Emily buried her face in Danny's shoulder and I heard her crying softly. I forced my eyes open and turned back to the carnage. Even from this distance, the presence of the Pig was enough to send shivers running down my spine. It swallowed the first mouthful of Mud Men and then fell upon the rest with a vigor. It was like watching a colossal tree fall upon innocents, only to rise and chew, howling and squealing into the night.

After the third mouthful, I noticed something begin to change. It was subtle, but enough to inform me that something was happening. Its eyes began to emanate a soft orange light, as if some long-dead ember was being restored to life.

"Christ, it's almost gotten them all," Danny whispered from the sand, "just like that..."

"I wish it didn't have to be like this," I said quietly, watching as the Pig stomped over to the last of the fleeing shapes, leaning down to collect them into its waiting jaws. I wondered if Yurt was in that group. Or perhaps he had been spared the fear of the inevitable and had been devoured in the first mouthful.

"You see its eyes?"

"Yeah."

Danny shot me a look. "You think?"

"I don't know what to think," I muttered, watching the giant creature gobble down the last of the Mud Men, bringing their screams to an eternal end.

Emily continued to sob into Danny's shoulder.

"I feel sick," I said, lowering my face into my hands.

"It was the only way," Danny stated. "We didn't have a choice."

"There's always a choice," I said, eyes closed, listening to the distant roar of the Pig as it finished its meal.

"Well, it's over now. It's done. There's no use lamenting."

I looked over at him, eyes bloodshot. "Will you just shut up?"

Danny sniffed but said nothing.

The roar of the Pig rattled my teeth, its meal devoured, its life force returning. It craned its head up into the darkness, jaws wide, eyes alight. Its titanic hooves crunched into the dirt as it digested its prey, their imperfect bodies seeming to work an almost perfect magic on the beast. It shook its limbs, growling and writhing, coughing and heaving, the glow of its eyes burning brighter with every second that passed.

And then it turned and looked directly at us.

I felt my stomach tighten, fingers digging into the sand. The Pig stopped howling, stopped moving, and just stared. The night seemed to die, a sudden stillness sweeping over the island, rushing over the dunes to take my breath away.

You got what you wanted.

"It can sense I'm here," Danny whispered, voice dry.

The Pig remained motionless, bits of gore dripping from its cavernous jaws. Tendrils of ember orange wafted from its eyes like smoke. I felt its gaze drill into my sockets and bore through my skull. Did it know who I was? Did it remember me?

"What is it doing?" I asked, voice hardly present.

Danny continued to stare. "I have no idea. But it sees us."

Leave us alone, you bastard. Go back to the Black Farm where you belong.

I clenched sand in my fists.

Let me go home.

After a moment, the Pig let out an ear-splitting roar, its limbs spread as if to challenge us, its stance aggressive. A second later, it doubled over and vomited. It was like watching a damn burst, a massive eruption that flowed out of its mouth like wet tar. It splashed to the ground and swam over the earth like a wave thinning along some poisonous shore. It coughed and spat, then lurched again, its enormous body bending double to release more of the cancer and venom that had plagued it for so long. After it recovered, it snorted twice, a sound like cannon blasts, and then it slowly stood tall, its form rising high into the black heavens.

"My god," I heard Danny whisper.

The Pig took two long steps away from us, and then without warning, it slammed its face into the ground and began to burrow deep into the earth. Its limbs flailed wildly, its hooves sinking into the dirt, pulling its long, squirming body beneath the ground like a worm slithering back home. Huge clods of soil rained down around it, its movement frantic, almost hungry. I watched it with bewildered dread, observing its form as it slipped further and further beneath the surface.

Until it was gone, leaving a gaping hole in its wake.

Danny and I didn't speak for a couple seconds, the spectacle locking our lips. I stared at the hole, expecting the Pig to pop back out and come roaring for us. But it didn't. Minutes died beneath the silence until finally Danny stood, brushing sand from his clothes. He said nothing as he pulled Emily to her feet and swished grains of sand from her hair.

She looked up at him with wet, bleary eyes, her voice thin and fragile. "Is...is it gone?"

Danny stared down at her, his voice even. "It's gone, kid."

"Where did it go? Where are my friends? Did it?"

"They're gone, too," Danny said quietly, staring off at the distant hole. "Everything is gone."

I climbed to my feet, feeling shaken and stiff and exhausted. "What the hell did we just see? What was that?"

Danny didn't look at me. "I think it's going back to the Farm."

I stared at the circle of darkness in the ground and then swept my eyes across the ocean. "You mean...do you think?"

"I don't know, Nick. Maybe. Maybe not."

I looked at the black tar that the Pig had thrown up, still sinking into the dirt like a shadow. "That vomit...was the Pig rejecting the Mud Men? Or was its body purging the poison I infected it with?"

Danny turned and stared at the ocean with me, a breeze curling around us. "I can still sense it. It feels...different." He looked at me. "It feels stronger."

Something rose up from my stomach and wrapped around my chest, a feeling so foreign that I almost couldn't comprehend it. Hope.

"Did we...set things right, then?" I asked very slowly, measuring out my words carefully.

Danny sniffed. "Right? No, Nick. There's nothing right about what we just saw. But things are...different now. We did something here. What effect will it have on the rest of the Black Farm? I couldn't tell you. There's only one way to know for sure."

I let my eyes travel across the waters. "We go back."

"We go back."

I ran a hand over my weary face. "When is this going to end?"

Danny looked down at Emily, then back up at me. "You know, there's an easy way to return. We don't have to walk. We don't have to go through any more tunnels or caverns."

"What are you?"

Danny drew his thumb across his throat.

I blinked. "But..." I looked down at Emily.

"We let the clouds do the work," Danny said softly. "End it here and get spat back out over there."

I shook my head. "But we have no idea where we'll end up. And we most certainly will be separated."

Danny shrugged. "We did what we needed to do here."

I narrowed my eyes at him. "What, so that's it?"

"Gotta break up the band sometime."

"And what about her?" I whispered. "Now that it's over, am I just supposed to leave her to fend for herself?"

"She was your choice in this, not mine. You're here for your family, right? Isn't that enough?"

"She's just a kid," I shot back. "There's got to be something we can do. She didn't even mean to kill herself, so how is it right that she's here?"

Danny chuckled and it threw me off-guard. "Jesus Christ, man. Do you really expect the cosmic rules to bend to your sense of what's right and wrong? Is your ego so big you think you actually have a say in what rules God puts in place? This is how things are. These are the parameters we have to work in. Do I agree with them? Of course not. But I've learned how to bite my tongue and take my beating. Maybe it's time you did, too."

"I cannot accept that," I said. "I don't believe existence is that cruel."

Danny stepped toward me, his voice lowering. "Are you serious? After everything you've been through? Think about why you're here. Right now. Who put you here? Who forced you to come back? Who always gets what they want? Because I can tell you right now, it ain't you buddy. It's the big guy upstairs, our eternal puppet master and rule-maker."

"You really think he's that much of a bastard?"

Why are you trying to pretend you think otherwise?

Danny smiled at me, a knife's edge. "Of course I do. He's an egomaniac ith little patience for failure. I mean, look around us. What did we just see ere? The Mud Men? His failed experiments left to wander for eternity on is lonely island? And what about you? What about us? What about what ou've been through, what I've been through, what brought us here the first me? Nick...how can you *not* think he's a bastard?"

I met Danny's gaze. "I'm not saying I don't. I'm saying maybe someone ould tell him that sometime."

Danny snorted. "Oh, I do. All the time."

"Please don't get mad at each other," Emily suddenly begged. I looked own and saw her eyes streaming with tears, her face in anguish. "I don't ant anyone else to be mad."

I sighed and felt my fatigue ignite all over again. "I'm not mad, Emily." reached down to stroke her hair, but she shied away from my touch and rled herself into Danny.

"You got mad at my friends," she said, her eyes glistening, "and now ey're gone. Are you going to make me go away, too?"

I opened my mouth but then closed it again.

"You're bad," Emily whispered up to me. "You're a bad man."

"Emily..."

"I don't want to be friends with a bad man," she said again, bunching her nds around Danny's pants. "Mom says I shouldn't talk to people like you."

You haven't seen anything.

I locked my thoughts away and squatted down, trying to edge the ten- n out of my voice. "Listen, Emily. I don't expect you to understand, but at happened to your friends had to happen. They had to go away."

Emily pressed her face into Danny's leg and refused to look at me. I ard Danny sniff, but he didn't move.

"Never mind," I muttered, feeling sore, beaten, and mentally exhausted. ached out and touched Emily's arm, earning me a peek.

"Do you want to go back with me? Will you come back to the other nd with me? Please? You don't have to be my friend if you don't want to, I can't just leave you here."

Emily curled her head back to look up at Danny. "I want to st
with him."

Danny finally broke free from her grip. "I don't think you do, kid. I
taking the fast pass back to the Farm. I think you're going to want to
with Nick here. Or don't. You could always stay here by yourself. Might g
lonely, though."

Emily stared up at him with hurtful eyes. "Where are you going?"

Danny returned the look, his face stone. "I'm going to kill myself."

"Christ, Danny," I muttered, standing up, "go easy."

He shrugged. "Listen, you two do whatever you want, but I have to g
going. If the Pig has returned to reclaim the Farm, then I have a very sm
window of time before my former position gets filled. And I'd rather n
have that happen."

"You really want to return to the Pig's side as its conduit to the Suicidal
I asked quietly.

"What the hell else am I going to do here? Besides, once the Pig is ba
in power, the Pig Born will listen to me. And let me tell you, I got a bone
pick with a couple of those cultist fucks."

I exhaled heavily and looked at him, then down at Emily, then back
him. "I guess this really is goodbye, then."

"Seems to be the case."

"Do me a favor?"

Danny cocked an eyebrow.

"Go somewhere else before you...you know. I don't want her to have
see that."

Danny looked down at Emily. "Sure...whatever you say."

"Hey, listen," I said slowly, easing the edges.

"What is it now?"

"Thanks for all your help," I said quietly. "Couldn't have done this wit
out you. I know we don't exactly see eye to eye, but I mean it. Thanks."

"Yeah, I'm going to go before I start tearing up," Danny said sarcas
cally. But before he went, he paused and looked at the ground, his voice so
"I, uh, I hope you get back to your family, Nick. I hope you get out of t
goddamn place."

And without another word, he left.

"Where is he going?" Emily asked after a little while, her voice panicked, the two of us watching his retreat toward the woods. I said nothing, the darkness swallowing Danny. A breeze kicked in from the ocean, filling the silence between us. I suddenly began to feel very alone. It was an unexpected sensation, one I didn't welcome. I looked around us, at the empty island, my eyes falling on the giant hole the Pig had left behind.

"We got some more walking to do, kiddo," I said gently, prodding Emily. She sighed heavily, almost angrily, her face creased with dismay.

"Look, I'm sorry about before. I don't expect you to understand what's happening or why I did what I did. But all of this...it's almost over. And I intend to continue watching out for you. I'm not going to leave you, all right? Now, you don't have to talk to me or even like me, but you're stuck with me. You think you can handle that?"

Emily crossed her arms and stared off into the middle distance, her tiny lips locked.

I cocked an eyebrow. "Emily? You hear me?"

"I'm tired of walking," she finally sighed, her cheeks drooping.

The breeze caressed my face. "So am I. But I think this is going to be the last hike we take. I can carry you if you want. If you're tired."

Emily shook her head. "No, I don't need you to. Where are we going?"

"Back to the Farm."

"Why? It's quiet here."

"You wouldn't understand," I said wearily.

"I'm not dumb, you know," Emily sulked, crossing her arms.

I smiled a little. "I know you're not. We have to follow the Pig. We have to make sure it gets back to where it's supposed to go."

"Then what?"

I let out a long breath.

Yes, then what, Nick? What happens after that?

"You want to hold my hand?" I asked after a moment, offering her mine.

She looked at it once, then shook her head. "No."

I pulled my hand back, then asked after a moment, "Are we still friends?"

Her brow furrowed. "I don't know."

I rubbed my eyes. "Come on, we have to go down that hole."

We walked across the rolling field, our steps illuminated by frozen bolts of gold reaching from the sky. When we reached the lip of the hole, I stopped and stared down into the long dark. Flecks of red lit the descent, the island scars giving off a calm glow.

"It looks scary down there," Emily said, mostly to herself.

"I still got two open hands, if you want one," I offered, gazing down into the abyss. The decline was steep before it leveled off. The expanse of the hole was wide—huge, even—the burrowed walls smooth and clean, like a tunnel along some major highway.

Emily glanced at my extended hand and after a moment, she took it reluctantly. I smiled internally and together, we entered the hole and began the long walk back.

Chapter 14

The tunnel was eternal. The smell of dirt blended with the odor of the Pig's passing, mixing together to form something that made my head swim. It swirled up my nostrils and settled over my mind, pushing my troubled thoughts to the front of my skull.

What the hell are you doing here?

It was a thought that seemed to be on loop. No matter how many times I combated it with the obvious answer, it never seemed to stick. Jess and Theo were the reason I was here. I was protecting them, saving them from a promised hell.

And yet, that seemed...hollow. The longer I remained here, the more something nagged at me. Something beneath the reason. I mean, what had I really done here? Why was it so crucial that I come back? What power did I possess that others didn't? I reflected on my actions since my arrival, the path I had taken, the steps I had chosen. What had my presence here *really* changed? Sure, I had distracted the Mud Men to lure the Pig to its recovery, but so what? Wouldn't the Pig have reached the same outcome at some point anyway? Hadn't that been inevitable?

Maybe. Maybe not. Why are you wasting your time on this?

It was because I was exhausted. The tunnel was wearing me down, and Emily was still wary of me. I had betrayed her fragile trust, leaving us in limbo.

I continued in silence, my boots kicking up clods of loose dirt. I kept thinking about Yurt's face, the way he looked at me when he realized what I planned on doing. His eyes had filled with such accusation, such sorrow. I knew I should feel guilty, but now that the moment had passed, I realized I felt almost nothing for them.

Of course you don't. You've never felt bad about harming others. Just so long as you got what you wanted. Isn't that right? No? You don't agree? You keep playing this game—why? What part of you are you trying to save? You can't erase all the terrible things you did the first time you were here.

I looked down at Emily, her shoulders drooping.

She's not your redemption, Nick. Stop trying to use her to make up for what you've done. Stop using her to prove something to yourself.

I tried to block out the intrusive thoughts. They were starting to wear on me.

If you make it out of here, are you going to be able to hold it together enough to be a functioning parent?

Stop. Enough.

Do you think you'll just snap one day? Do something that'll scar Theo for life? I think that's probably how it'll happen. I mean you have killed a lot *of people for almost nothing…*

Everything was different here. It wasn't the same.

Of course not. No, you're absolutely right. Just keep thinking that. And while you're at it, you better figure out how to stop those nightmares you've been struggling with. That'll get Theo asking some questions, won't it? What are you going to say when he asks what you're dreaming about? About why you keep waking up screaming? What are you going to tell him? You going to tell him about the time you burned an entire temple? Gored their obese leader with an axe and left him to cook? That'd be a good one to start with. Sorry, is this bothering you?

I forced my eyes closed and counted to ten, blanking my mind. I exfoliated the poisonous thoughts and continued walking.

I was numb by the time I saw light again. Real light, not the dull throb of red that lined the seemingly unending tunnel. I had almost given up hope of ever seeing the clouds again, the long stretch of faceless dirt consuming my world. I had ended up carrying Emily for some of the journey, her legs giving way beneath exhaustion. When she had asked to be picked up

.e request came from a place of shame, a declaration that I extinguished
ıickly as I scooped her up in my arms. She was walking again now, though,
:r face as unreadable and drawn as my own. But when she saw the light, the
ay patch at the end of the tunnel, she began to come alive again.

"Is that the end?" she dared to ask.

"I think so," I said, feeling something like relief overwhelm me. The
nell of dirt slowly began to give way to open air and rain as we quickened
ır pace, the path rising upward toward the surface.

But as we did so, something shifted beneath our feet. It was enough to
op us, the shock wave jolting through my limbs, causing Emily to cry out
ıd stumble. I steadied her and waited for the moment to pass, my pulse
ıickening.

"The hell was that?" I muttered, taking Emily's hand.

"Was that an earthquake?" she asked cautiously, her face scrunched up.

"I don't know, sweetie, but we better get out of this tunnel just in case. I
ɔn't want it caving in on us."

She grimaced at that before the two of us jogged up the incline, climb-
g the slope toward the circle of open air above. As we neared the exit, I
gan to feel the first splatters of rain wash over me. Grunting, I pushed
mily ahead of me and out of the wide hole, then climbed up after her. I
lled onto my back for a moment, allowing myself a second of relief, the
in falling across my dirty clothes.

Where did we come out?

I sat up and absorbed our surroundings, suddenly aware of how careful
ıeeded to be now that we were back in dangerous territory.

We were in an open field—the side of the island that housed the Barn
ıere the Pig used to dwell. The forest was at our backs, a line of green
neath gray sky. I looked ahead of us and scanned the rolling hills. Rain
:kled down my face as I took in our situation. I felt Emily's hand suddenly
p my own.

She didn't need to say anything. I saw it.

The Pig loomed ahead of us, its massive form towering across the sky-
:. It stood before the Barn, a wary couple miles in the distance. Its long
ly swayed beneath its new evolution, the wriggling hooves lining its cen-
de abdomen. Its eyes smoked orange and its lips were twisted in a snarl.

Scattered around it were hundreds of Pig Born. They stared up at their ma
ter in silent awe, still and unsure as it gazed down upon them, as if they w
awaiting orders.

"Nick, I'm scared," Emily whispered.

I interlaced my fingers with hers and together we stood. I kept my e
glued on the Pig, bile staining the back of my throat. Rain and wind b
against the massive tower of flesh and fur. The Pig's mouth slowly open
and dripped black sludge over cinder-block teeth.

"We need to get to the woods," I said carefully. "I don't know wha
about to happen, but I don't think we're going to want to be around wh
it happens."

The Pig growled from the horizon, a sound like rolling thunder. T
Pig Born shifted where they stood and continued to stare up at it, the mo
turning.

Emily tugged at my hand, her voice thin. "Look at the water."

I swung my head toward the ocean, heart beating faster. When I s
what Emily was pointing at, I felt my jaw lock.

It was Berserker. The colossal Keeper's frame was outlined agains
growing darkness, sharp forks of lightning sparking over its cross-shap
head. Its giant limbs churned the water as it strode toward the shore with
the confidence of a god. The red glyphs lining its stone body flared brillian
in the gloom, like warnings of a coming storm.

"Oh no," I hissed, pulse flaring now. "Emily, we need to go. Now."

As I pulled her with me—headed for the woods, Berserker let ou
bellowing roar of fury and crunching stone. I threw a look over my shoul
and saw that it was coming faster now, headed straight for the Pig. Its sho
ders were lowered and its cross-head shoveled forward beneath the clou
gaining speed with each stride.

"Faster, Emily, faster!" I cried, sensing the coming violence. We bol
over the soaked earth, lightning sparking the heavens like flashes of a came

The Pig turned toward the approaching challenger, a guttural gro
forming in its chest, a noise like grating iron. The Pig Born quickly b
gan to back away from the coming conflict, cries of fear rising from th
throats. They retreated behind the Barn, a shield against whatever was ab
to happen.

Mud splashed beneath my boots and I begged Emily to hurry, the wall f woodland growing across my field of sight as we sprinted closer.

The Pig began to walk toward Berserker, its teeth exposed beneath an nraged snarl. Orange wafted from its eye sockets as it gazed upon the fast pproaching challenger, its hooves coming together like fists to form a clack-ng detonation.

The earth shook beneath our feet as we neared the woods, Emily pant-ng at my side. I could see a handful of wary Suicidals peeking through the rees, emerging to see what was happening.

Berserker made landfall at a full sprint. The Pig, only a couple miles way, planted its feet and braced for the assault, its hooves sinking into the oft ground.

God help us.

The beasts met and the collision sent a shock wave blasting across the vorld. The Pig grunted heavily in pain as Berserker plowed into it, wrapping s colossal arms around its body to pick it up, only to slam it back down into he earth, hard enough to crack stone.

The blast toppled me over, my hands outstretched to cushion the fall. mily somersaulted over me, the breath knocked from her lungs. One of er limbs caught me across the nose and judging from the pain it brought, I uessed it was her knee.

Skidding in the mud, I shook stars from my eyes and looked out across he field. Berserker was on top of the Pig, one long arm poised over its head. t delivered a blow a moment later, straight into the Pig's face with all the ower of a freight train behind it. The Pig roared and I saw teeth the size f bodies eject from its mouth in an explosion of blood. Dazed, it tried its est to buck the Keeper off itself, its hooves clacking against its attacker's one body.

Berserker stood without much encouragement, its head scraping the eavenly roof. But before the Pig could roll up and onto its feet, the stone tan took a step back and then kicked the demigod across the face. The blow ounded like a bomb had gone off, the force of the impact sending the Pig irborne, its massive body soaring high overhead, only to come crashing own into the Barn, obliterating it, along with a dozen or so Pig Born, in an xplosion of blood and wood.

I climbed to my feet, watching it all, and helped Emily stand. A fres cut ran along her cheek and she scrubbed a tongue of blood away, her fa bunched in pain.

“Why are they fighting?” she asked, out of breath and scared.

I watched as Berserker marched toward the downed Pig, my voice n quite steady. “Because they have to.”

The Pig snorted, exhaling a bloody mist. It pulled itself out of t wreckage, but instead of retreating to recover like I expected, it turned ar faced the approaching titan. Its lips pulled back into a snarl and the oran of its eyes began to drip down its face, smoke turning to liquid.

Berserker circled its injured prey, smacking its arms together like a pa of clubs, taunting the Pig. The sound of it was enough to make my ea throb, and I saw Emily cover her own.

The Pig growled, a building rage that echoed across the sky. It turned the Keeper continued to circle it, both of the entities waiting for a chance, opening in which to strike. Then, without any indication, Berserker charg once more. This time, though, the Pig caught the blow with its raised hoov using the Keeper’s own momentum to spin and throw the stone giant ov its shoulder and then straight into the ground. The crunch and explosion rock showered the two creatures, clods of dirt following the impact like plane crash. The Pig roared and then raised a hoof, stomping down on t Keeper’s body. The stone behemoth groaned as a shudder ran through i torso, a massive crack splintering across its chest. The Pig raised its hoof f another strike, but Berserker rolled away a second before it came down, rig where its head had been.

In one motion, the mountainous titan stood and swung both of its arn The duel blows caught the Pig in the back of its head, driving it to the ear like it had been struck with a colossal baseball bat. Lightning flashed acro the sky, forks of white spider web, and the Keeper roared into the storm, rai ing a giant arm up into the clouds. The lightning came again, and this tin it seemed to wrap itself around Berserker’s clubbed hand, dancing down t length of its arm.

The Pig pulled itself heavily to its feet, blood streaming from its sno From its knees, it looked over its shoulder at Berserker, orange drippi from its eyes.

The stone giant plowed its electric fist straight into the Pig's face, bringing with it a crack of light and sound so bright I had to turn away. The air screamed and popped around the blow, and a rush of heat blew past me, carrying with it the smell of cooked flesh.

When the stars faded from my eyes, I saw the Pig lying face-down a couple hundred yards away from the point of impact, its body half-buried at the end of a long dirt trench that had been carved from its beaten body. Berserker roared again, snapping its arm at its side to rid itself of the remaining electricity still licking its limb. Thunder boomed overhead and the Pig remained motionless where it lay.

Berserker approached it slowing, its body alive with red glyphs, all blinking rapidly as it closed in for the final blow. It was like watching an executioner climb the hangman's scaffolding, the inevitable only moments away. I bent down and picked up Emily, wanting to get as far away from the violence as possible. I sprinted the final distance to the trees and set her back down on her feet once we were safely hidden by the greenery. Panting and out of breath, I knelt down next to downed log and peered out at the rainy field, the earthquake footsteps of the Keeper shaking the ground beneath me. Emily slithered under my arm and shivered miserably at my side, her face pale and dirty. I could sense other Suicidals around me, watching the spectacle with morbid caution.

By the time Berserker reached it, the Pig's snout was almost completely covered in the orange ooze leaking from its eyes. It moved its head slightly to one side, exhaling a shuddering breath. It rolled its shoulders and painfully planted its hooves beneath itself, struggling to push itself up and onto its feet.

Berserker watched without interfering, its foe broken and bleeding profusely. A bolt of lightning snaked overhead, followed shortly by rolling thunder. When the sound faded, the Pig had reached its feet, its massive hooves spread far apart as it stood on two legs. It faced the Keeper, panting heavily, orange dripping from its face along with streams of black that leaked from between its teeth.

The stone Keeper brought its arms together, once, twice, each connection cracking the sky and echoing across the hills. Its massive cross-head towered over the Pig, staring down at it as if it were trying to decide the best way to finish it. Slowly, it began to circle its prey once more, its limbs grinding to form a growling crunch. The Pig tracked it, panting heavily, its face dripping, its shoulders slouched, the hooves lining its long middle wriggling painfully.

A second later, Berserker struck. Its enormous fist soared toward the Pig's head with terrifying speed, bringing with it a rush of wind. But instead of connecting, the Pig ducked at the last second and stepped up and under the strike so that its face was directly in front of the Keeper.

Roaring with sudden life, the Pig opened its maw and vomited a torrential current of orange vomit directly onto Berserker's cross-head. The stream was thick and explosive, like a burst pipe, the neon puke blasting and soaking the Keeper's entire upper half.

Berserker's reaction was immediate and terrible. It jerked away from the firehose of slime, screaming and clawing at its head. Its back arched as if it were in pain, its glyphs flaring urgently. It stumbled down to one knee as the Pig advanced, still spewing its foul poisons, the forceful orange waterfall pouring over the screeching Keeper. Mouth agape, the Pig cocked back one of its hooves and then slammed it over Berserker, smashing the titan to the ground. It went down in a splash of orange, the slime beginning to form a small pond around the Keeper, the Pig gushing torrents over the length of its body.

As I watched the Pig deliver another blow, I realized something. Berserker's figure was beginning to soften and drip like it was dissolving. Gray mixed with the orange and the Keeper continued to writhe and scream beneath the slime, driven back to the ground as a massive hoof connected with its back.

The Keeper outstretched its arms and swung wildly, trying to trip the Pig, but its movements were sluggish and pained and had no effect. Another giant hoof slammed down on the arm, pinning it where it lay, coating it in more of the dangerous orange vomit.

The Pig, towering over its opponent, suddenly shivered and the flow of puke stopped in an instant. Great drooling tendrils hung from its lips as it snarled and stared down at the melting stone form trapped beneath its hooves. The Keeper groaned and wriggled weakly, craning its head back to stare up at the Pig.

Like a bear trap snapping shut, the Pig leaned down and bit Berserker's
ead and gripped it violently between its massive teeth. Roaring, the Pig
rked its neck back, tearing the cross off the Keeper's shoulders in an erup-
on of fragmenting stone and spraying orange ooze.

The Pig, squealing loud enough to deafen the world, spit the severed
ead away and loomed over its fallen enemy. Its eyes burned intensely as
ey swept across the landscape, daring anything to move. It paused as it
ok in the ruined Barn, now a pile of splinters and leaning smokestacks.
rowling, it slowly turned away and began to walk toward the rubble. As it
d so, Pig Born began to emerge from their shelter. They stared up at their
d in awe and a rising, growling cry of elation filled the sky.

Their master had returned.

I looked to my left and saw a cluster of Suicidals peering out at the
rnage from between the trees. Our eyes met and they frowned, turning
vay. One of the three held my gaze, something like recognition fluttering
ross her face. Then she too was gone, joining the others in the safety of
e dense forest. Rain dripped down from the canopy overhead and sent a
ill through me. I looked down at Emily and saw that she was scrubbing
r eyes, her bottom lip quivering. The clash had left her shaking, her hands
embling as they grasped my arm.

"I don't want to be here anymore," she whimpered. "Everything is so
ud and scary and always wants to hurt me. I want to go home." She looked
at me, her eyes brimming with tears. "Please take me home. Help me get
my mom. I want to see my mommy."

I felt myself soften. "I know you do, sweetie. I want to go home too. I
nk we're getting close. I just need to figure a couple more things out. Can
u hang on until then?"

She nodded miserably. "Yeah, but I'm still going to be scared…"

"I'll protect you, Emily," I assured, staring out at Berserker's corpse. I
ldn't believe what I had just seen. The scale of violence, the eruption of
wer...I let my eyes travel back to the Pig as it thundered toward its sub-
ts, its fur coated in blood and slime.

What a horrible fucking place this is.

I suddenly became aware that someone was directly behind me. It was
alarming realization and I felt my heart surge up my throat as I spun

around, confused and frantic. A trio of shadows loomed over me and befo
I could speak or act, I was punched in the head, bringing a detonation
stars. I grunted and slumped backwards, feeling rough hands grab me a
jerk me across the forest floor. Somewhere in the chaos, I heard Emily cryi
in fear, calling my name, screaming my name.

Another fist plowed into my ear, all knuckles. My vision swam anc
scrambled to stay conscious. My mind reeled with pained, confused fear.

What the hell is happening!?

I was kicked in the ribs and then pressed down onto my back, rainw
ter trickling from the greenery overhead. I struggled to breath, flailing
hands wildly as I tried to fend off the attackers, their forms blurring befo
my beaten vision.

As I blinked focus back into the world, a face appeared and leered do
at me. It hosted a wicked, excited smile of white teeth and blue eyes.

"I've been looking for you," the man said, his voice thick with anticipati

When I recognized who I was staring at, I felt my body flood with te
ror. My eyes went wide and my breath froze in my throat.

"Peter?" I croaked, staring up at the face I had betrayed long ago.

Peter leaned down over me, his voice as sinister as the cult he had or
belonged to."We have a lot of catching up to do, Nick, don't we?"

And then I was kicked in the face, bringing a wall of darkness with i

Chapter 15

I knew I was in trouble before I even opened my eyes. My skull throbbed painfully from where I had been kicked and I groaned in the darkness. wirls of muddy color danced behind my eyelids, and noise slowly drained nto the swamp that filled my head.

"I think he's waking up," someone said thickly.

"It's about time." I recognized that voice. It was Peter. And he sounded xcited.

I forced my eyes open and the world gradually swam into focus. Green nd gray melded like colored ink, taking shape and forming my grim situa- on. It didn't take long to realize I was bound, my arms stretched overhead nd held by rope. Rough bark scraped against my back and I realized that I vas completely naked. Rain coated my skin, turning it blue with cold. I was linking lazily, trying to get a sense of what was happening. We were in the orest, in a large clearing with dozens of men filling the circular space, all urned my way, toward the tree to which I was bound.

I coughed violently, bringing stars. When the fit passed, I looked up to ee Peter standing directly in front of me, backed by fifty-odd angry faces. hey looked hungry, furious, each piercing gaze knifing into my own.

"Good to have you back with us," Peter said stepping forward, his face renched with rain that drilled us from overhead. "I was worried I might ave kicked your brain loose." He chuckled at that.

Pain ran down my arms and I craned my head back to see the rop
binding me was knotted to a branch high overhead, leaving my torso completely exposed and defenseless. I didn't like the implications.

"Don't worry, you're not going anywhere," Peter grinned, watching me
He turned to the crowd at his back. "He's not going anywhere, is he?!"

A chorus of "no!" echoed around me, half washed out in the rain.
shivered again, head throbbing. My bare feet brushed the ground, the rop
pulling me up so that I was forced to stand on my toes against the tree.

"I honestly wasn't sure if I would get a chance to see you again," Pete
said, returning his attention back to me, "and God knows I've been trying
Do you remember what I told you? Way back when you weaseled yoursel
into our good graces? Back when I—*we*—took you under our wing and al
lowed you access to our Temple?"

I kept my mouth shut, twisting my wrists into the biting fibers. I stoppe
suddenly, eyes going wide.

Emily. Where the hell is Emily?

Peter stepped toward me again, his nose almost touching mine now
"Do you remember killing me? Do you remember what I said to you righ
before you buried that axe in me?" His voice dropped dangerously. "I swor
that I would never stop hunting you." He smiled then. "And here we are
Here we are, Nick. Amazing, huh? I mean, what are the odds?"

"Where's Emily?" I finally rasped, vocal cords strained. "What have yo
done with her?"

Peter ignored me and turned to face the crowd of hollow faces. "Thi
is the man we've been searching for! This is the one who robbed us o
our Temple!"

A rumble of low growls swept through the mob. I saw a number o
clenched fists and murderous snarls. Peter nodded to them, as if assurin
them their anger was righteous.

"This is the man that murdered Ryder and burned our home!" Pete
continued, directing a finger at me. "Because of him, the Pig detonated th
dead sun and wiped out our land!"

The crowd began to bark threats at me, brows knitted together in fur
spit and rocks peppering the tree in which I was bound. I winced awa
from the projectiles as best I could, heart racing and wincing as one of ther

hudded into my shoulder. Peter raised his hands and stopped the commo-ion, silencing the ex-cultists with a wave of his hand.

"Now, I know you hate this man as much as I do!" Peter continued, his oice rising, "and rightly so! He is a snake and a bastard!" He stepped toward he crowd, bringing his hands together. "And he deserves pain." He slowly urned to look at me, his eyes dark. "Doesn't he?"

A cry rose up once again, a host of fists in the air. I watched it all with rowing trepidation, my body shivering helplessly in the rain. Peter faced his ollowers, his finger returning to point at me.

"We could beat this man, cut him, bleed him, fuck him raw until his ocal cords rupture," Peter tapped his chin, "but if he's to atone for all the amage and shit he's done, then I think a more proper punishment is in rder, don't you?" A call of agreement swept through the congregation and hen Peter continued. "Physical violence is a terrible thing," he turned and tared at me, a twisted smile rising, "but it's so much worse if you're watching happen to someone you care about."

The crowd roared and thunder cracked overhead, the rain coming down n great sheets as if to wash away the horror unfolding.

I felt my throat close up with fear and my stomach rolled in terror. I hook against the ropes holding me, my heart beating in my ears.

No, god, please no no not this...

A shrill scream cut through the chaos, a high, piercing exclamation of ear. It was a scream I knew all too well.

"Emily!" I cried, struggling, fighting, begging.

Peter folded his hands behind his back and watched as the crowd part-d. I shook freezing water from my eyes and clenched my chattering teeth. mily was dragged forward on a leash, her legs trailing behind her in the nud. Her big watery eyes stood out from the filth on her face, wildly rolling nd searching for someone to save her. She was crying and whimpering as he rope around her neck dug into her skin, cutting off her pleas with jerk-ng gasps.

"Let her go! She has nothing to do with this!" I screamed, leaning for-ard so hard that the rope drew blood from my wrists.

Peter faced me, his voice malicious and excited, as Emily continue to be dragged forward. "Of course she has nothing to do with this. That the point."

The man dragging Emily finally came to a stop at a large tree besi mine. Emily lay gasping and clawing at the rope around her neck, snifflir and crying weakly. She looked up at me and our eyes met.

Her voice shook with raw terror. "Help me, Nick."

Peter walked over to her and squatted down, tilting her chin back with gentle hand. He stared down at her and wiped a trickle of blood away fro her lip.

He smiled, his voice calm and soothing. "He can't help you, little one. I fact, he's the one who told us to do this to you."

Emily's eyes went wide a second before Peter grabbed her by the thro and lifted her off her feet. She gurgled around his iron grip, her legs thrash ing wildly as she tried to breathe. In one horrible motion, Peter ripped th clothes from her body and then tossed her, now naked, back down into th mud.

"STOP IT!" I screamed, eyes bloodshot. "DON'T HURT HE PLEASE!"

Emily curled into herself, shivering, weeping. She turned her head aw from me, lost in pain and humiliation. The crowd roared their approv pressing in tightly around the spectacle. They began to whistle and jeer her, a grotesque string of profanity pouring down around her.

"Look at her! She's got no tits! Hey little girl, where are your tits!?"

"Bet her pussy's sweeter than honey, though!"

"She'll bleed like a fuckin' hose!

"She better not, or I'll make her drink it!"

"I'm going to get her to suck me off!"

"Going to have to teach her how to first!"

"I just want to rip her open!"

"Me too!"

"God, does she ever stop crying?!"

"She will once I shove my cock down her throat!"

"You better get in line!"

"She's ugly when she's crying, look at her!"

"What a stupid bitch!"

"Cry, bitch, cry!"

Tears ran down my face, my voice a cracking plea as I watched the ;htmare continue to escalate. "SHUT UP! LEAVE HER ALONE, YOU ONSTERS!" I cocked my head to Peter, vision blurred. "Look at me! ddammit, look at me! I'm the one you want! Let her go and punish me!"

Peter's lips curled into a sneer. "Don't you see that I already am?"

Emily had her hands over her face as the crowd pressed in tightly und her. They continued to taunt her, the air filled with her heavy sob- g. She had no clue what was going on, who these people were, or why y were raining down such cruelty. Her small naked body shivered and ok beneath the rain, her cries drowned out in the mob. A few of them de mud balls and threw them at her, each one bringing a whimper as it acked wetly against her skin.

Finally, Peter raised his hands and voice. "All right, that's enough, every- ! Back off a little, let her breathe!" The crowd did as they were told and as allowed a glimpse at Emily's mud-soaked body. She looked terribly all from where she lay, her tiny shoulders trembling in the filth.

Peter went to her and gently stood her up, using his shirt sleeve to wipe ne of the mud from her face.

"There, there, little one," he cooed, drying her eyes. "I know this is hard. 're doing great."

Emily stared at the ground, bottom lip quivering, her arms wrapped und herself. She shot a look at me and I saw pain and confusion radi- from her eyes. They were asking me to save her, to shelter her from this niliation. I gritted my teeth and felt myself tear up, the rope biting into wrists.

Peter tapped Emily on the cheek to get her attention. "Hey. Do you w why this is happening? Why these men are being so mean to you?"

She shook her head, a lone tear escaping down her muddy cheek. "I n't do anything..."

Peter smiled kindly and nodded. "I know, you're absolutely right. You en't done anything." He pointed at me. "But he has. He's done a lot of re- bad things. He hurt me a long time ago and took something away from

all these men. He's not a very nice person." Peter looked hard at her. "But y
already know that, don't you?"

Emily said nothing and just stared at me with wet, vacant eyes.

Peter brought his lips close to her ear. "He told us to do this to you."

I felt a panicked rage explode up my throat, vicious and burning. "Th
not true! Emily, I would never tell anyone to hurt you! He's lying, don't lis
to him!"

Peter shook his head sadly and continued to speak into Emily's
"Do you hear him? How could he lie to you like that? I thought you t
were friends."

Peter shot me a look and I saw the corner of his mouth wrap int
sneer. "He told us to do terrible things to you. That you deserve it. T
you've been a bad girl."

Emily looked at him, eyes wide and full of fear. "I'm a good girl! I m
lots of friends!"

Peter exhaled dramatically, the eyes of the crowd on him. "Ahhh, th
not what I heard. Nick told me you've been pretty naughty. He told me y
don't listen to him and that you're horribly annoying."

"SHUT THE FUCK UP!" I screamed, spittle flying from my li
"Emily, cover your ears, don't listen to this bad man!"

Peter bit his lip and tried to hide a laugh. He stood and placed a ha
on Emily's head, raising his voice so everyone could hear him.

"We're here to punish the actions of the past," he boomed, running
hands through Emily's hair, "and what better way to deliver this punishm
than in the tradition of this godless island?"

From the back, the crowd began to part as something was brought f
ward. Rain lashed against my face and poured across my trembling body.
heart wanted to crawl out of my throat as I watched the scene develop, dr
rising like a shadow.

"Please," I sputtered, pleading now. "Please don't hurt her."

Peter continued to stroke Emily's hair, his eyes boring into my o
"Tell me, Nick...have you ever witnessed a Breaking?"

The blood drained from my face, memory rushing back in a dizzy
wave. I opened my mouth, but as I did so the crowd split and a massive m
strode forward holding a sledgehammer.

Peter, still staring at me, slowly curled his fingers into Emily's hair so tightly that she began to cry all over again.

"You destroyed our place in this hellish world," Peter said beneath the rain. "Now I'm going to make you watch as we destroy something of yours."

The giant man holding the sledgehammer walked forward, the crowd's excitement rising in volume. He tossed the hammer to Peter, who caught it with one hand and stepped away from Emily's quivering form. He began to roll and flex his shoulders in preparation.

"Emily," I gasped, tears forming in my eyes. "Emily, please look at me."

The massive man went and stood behind her, placing a pair of meaty hands on her bare shoulders.

"Emily, sweetie, please," I cried, feeling like I was going to throw up. Thunder boomed overhead.

She lifted her bloodshot eyes to meet mine.

"I didn't want any of this to happen," I choked. "You have to know that."

"I want to go home," she sobbed weakly, hugging herself, her face raw with sorrow.

"I know," I cried. "I know you do. Close your eyes, sweetie. I want you to close your eyes. When you open them again, this will all be over."

"Take me home, Nick," she wept, chest hitching. "I want to go home."

A rattling sob escaped my throat. "I'm sorry. I'm so fucking *sorry*."

And that's when the big man behind Emily grabbed her by the back of her neck and lifted her off her feet. The mob immediately roared their approval and jostled closer to get the best view. Emily began to cry harder, arms windmilling as the big man flipped her upside down and held her out in front of him by the ankle like a human piñata.

"Don't do this!" I wept, blood now running down my wrists. "Peter, I BEG YOU!"

Peter stepped in front of Emily's suspended form. Slowly, he raised the sledgehammer. The throat of the crowd surged with murderous lust as he did so. The rain drilled down upon the frozen scene, forever preserving it in my memory.

And then he swung the hammer with all his might. Emily's cries were immediately cut short as the iron head thundered into her soft, naked stomach. Her mouth ripped open in a silent scream, blood spurting from her lips as her insides ruptured. Her chest hitched as she tried to breathe and when she finally did, she let out a scream so loud I thought it would crack my skull.

I screamed with her, tears running down my face, my eyes horribly meeting hers. I could see every ounce of her agony in that look, feel every injury and pain.

Peter brought the hammer up over his shoulder again. The crowd raised their fists in the air, cheering. Emily, upside down and naked, drooled blood into the dirt as she gasped and howled.

I heard the child's ribs break as the hammer plowed into them. The force of the swing was so hard that the man holding Emily lost his grip and she went flying through the air, landing roughly in front of me. When Emily regained the ability to breathe, her screams brought mouthfuls of blood pouring from her lips. I could see a massive bruise already starting to form around split skin along her left side.

In wailing misery, she looked up at me.

"Be brave," I choked, vision blurred. "Be brave, sweetie. It's almost over."

Peter slowly walked over to us, pulling the crowd with him. Emily tried to crawl away, her tiny hands gripping for purchase in the thick mud. The air wheezed from her lungs in horrible hitches as she struggled to escape. Peter came to a stop directly over her, mere feet from where I was tied to the tree. He planted a foot on Emily's back, halting her where she lay. He gripped the hammer and looked up at me.

"I'm going to rip your goddamn throat out," I cried hoarsely. "I swear to god, I will find a way to make you pay for this."

Peter raised the hammer high overhead, the roar of the crowd escalating into a crescendo of raw noise.

Emily looked up at me one last time, her eyes so sad and hurt I felt my heart break. Her bloody lips parted like she was about to say something.

And then the hammer fell. It struck her in the back of the head, crushing her skull. Blood and bits of gray exploded outward from the impact and I screamed until I couldn't anymore. My howling was lost beneath the roar of approval emanating from the mob. Peter jerked the hammer out of Emily's head and handed it off to another. He wiped his hands and stared down at the ruined body like its presence annoyed him.

"You fucking animal," I snarled through the tears. "You miserable *bastard*.

Peter glanced at me. "Oh, don't worry, Nick. She'll be reborn from the clouds. Maybe we'll find her and bring her back here to start all over. You think you'd be up for that? No...no, something tells me you won't last that long because I'm about to start working you over. And I'm not going to be gentle. I think that tough-guy exterior is going to come crashing down once you take one or two hits from this bitch." Peter hefted the sledgehammer, spinning it slowly in his hands. A pair of ex-cultists came forward and dragged Emily's corpse away and out of sight, giving Peter more room to work.

I could feel my sorrow beginning to turn to anger, my cries to snarls. "I swear when I'm dead and done I'm going to find you and make you *hurt* for what you did to that little girl."

Peter shrugged casually. "Who knows, maybe you will? After all, that's the same thing I threatened to do to you and here we are. But look around. I have dozens of men ready to die for me. Hell, these are the same men who traded you to the Pig Born for my freedom. So even if you do come back, hackles raised, what are the chances you'll even get to me?"

I spat at him, blood starting to boil, sadness bleeding into rage.

Peter sidestepped and shook his head. "When I kill you in a couple minutes, do yourself a favor—go find a dark hole and bury yourself inside it."

"You're the only thing I'll be burying," I growled as thunder rolled overhead.

Peter smiled and raised the hammer, planting his feet. The crowd stepped back to give him more room, my naked body stretched and horribly defenseless.

"Here it comes," Peter grinned.

"Fuck yourself," I hissed, bracing myself, heart drumming.

Peter swung the hammer and I felt it collide into my side like an iron fist. I gasped and my eyes shot open, pain exploding across my torso. I heard the air leave my lungs in a horrible rush, and I slammed my teeth together so hard I heard my jaw pop. Blood ran down my arms as I squirmed against the ropes, refusing to give Peter the satisfaction of a scream.

"That...the best...you got?" I panted after a moment, wheezing, feeling pain pump through me with every heartbeat.

Peter spit into his hands and grinned. "Oh, a tough guy, huh? This will be fun; maybe I'll take bets on how many swings it'll take before you're begging me to just kill you."

"Do...your worst..."

"I plan to."

I watched as he raised the hammer once again, bracing myself for the pain. I knew this one would break my ribs. He wasn't going to hold back.

A second before he swung, someone from the back of the crowd yelled loudly, freezing Peter's hammer mid-air. It was a single word, bellowed in anger and authority.

"STOP!"

Peter turned around, his expression incredulous. The crowd turned with him, curious to see who dared to halt the execution.

When the source was spotted, I saw the fire in Peter's eyes fade a little.

"Ah, shit."

Danny stood at the edge of the clearing, backed by hundreds of Pig Born. They filled the woods with snarls and hungry snorts. They eyed the Suicidals with furious contempt, each one marked for annihilation at the drop of a hat.

"You FUCKERS," Danny yelled, stepping forward, "have been a MASSIVE pain in my ass ever since the Pig disappeared!"

The ex-cultists retreated a little, now watching the Pig Born with nervous unease. They emerged with Danny, hooves sinking into the mud, fur matted by the rain.

"But the Pig is back!" Danny yelled, sweeping his eyes across the mob. "And so am I! I've been thinking about you assholes for a long time now! I told myself that if I ever got back in the good graces of the Pig and resumed my role on the Farm that I'd hunt you down and wipe you out! Well, guess what? Dinner came early and we're all fucking *starving*!" He spread his hands and the Pig Born growled. They sounded like a pack of wild wolves seconds before feasting on their prey.

Peter raised a hand, trying to halt the escalation. "What is all this? We have no problem with you! Leave us alone, and we'll leave you alone! You don't have to do this!"

Danny smiled beneath dark eyes. "Oh, yes I do. You fucks didn't even try free me from the Pits. And don't act like you didn't know I was there. You ew damn well and good I was."

Peter pointed to the Pig Born, his voice rising an octave. "But they were e ones who held you prisoner, not us!"

Danny placed a hand over his chest. "I got a lot more room in my heart r these ugly bastards because now they gotta do what I say. Didn't you hear e? The Pig is back. First thing I did after it downed that mad Keeper was go to it and offer it my services once more. After all, now that it's been aled, we're back in business. The Black Farm is going to slowly tip back the way it was. That means you revolutionaries have to be taken care of fore you start giving us too much trouble." He flashed his teeth. "At least, at's what I told the Pig. For me, it's a little more personal, but it doesn't re just so long you're taken care of. And after we slaughter you here, don't en think about banding together again. Take your punishment and fuck f. As of right now, this little club is finished."

Peter clenched his fists, fear and anger rolling across his face in waves. ou don't get to decide how we live here."

Danny stepped forward with all the confidence of the army at his back. nd you don't get to talk to me like that." He shot his hand forward, his ice a commanding bark. "GET EM!"

The Pig Born screeched with excited bloodlust, rushing forward and o the ranks of the ex-cultists. It was like watching bodies being thrown o a shredder. Blood sprayed in every direction as the attackers cut a path m back to front. Screams filled the air as flesh was parted by razor-sharp oves and torn to pieces by snapping jaws. As the wave of bloody violence ssed toward Peter, I saw him step back, suddenly unsure and terrified. He pped the sledgehammer and then dropped it without warning. He spun his heels to flee and our eyes clashed, a brief spark of terror, anger, and stration all boiled down into a single look.

And then he was gone, crashing through the underbrush as the Pig rn continued their gory pillage. I watched it all through blood-red vision, throb in my side a constant knot of terrible pain. But through it all, I felt nething rising, a hot coal of rage that worked its way from my stomach l up into my throat.

The scene before me continued to unfurl in a flurry of bloody ribbo Some of the mob took Peter's example and tried to run into the woo followed quickly by howling Pig Born, happy at the chance to hunt. Lim were snapped, bones were shattered, skin was gouged and gutted, and so the violence began to slide into low tide, the last gurgling cries silenc beneath a swift hoof.

I sagged in my restraints, waiting for someone to notice me, that ra burning through the pain and grief.

Emily. Jesus Christ...

I curled my hands into fists, now slick with blood from the chafi ropes. The rain poured across the slaughtering ground, washing the last human life away. The Pig Born snorted and poked around at the corps hoping to find someone still clinging to life.

"I leave you for a couple hours and look what happens."

I turned and saw Danny standing next to me, knife in hand. The bla was red with blood.

"Cut me free," I said, my voice in the gutter.

"What happened here?" Danny asked, reaching for the ropes.

"Bad blood and old grudges," I muttered, feeling a murderous headac press against my skull.

"Christ, Nick," Danny muttered, finally cutting me down. I fell to knees and let out a cry, a lance of pain striking my side.

"Peter," I growled hoarsely. "Got to get Peter."

Danny helped me to my feet, legs shaking. "Don't know if you're qu up to the task. Your ribs look like they took a fastball."

I glared at him from over the dark bags clinging to my eyes. "They kil her, Danny. They killed her slowly."

Danny's face went taut, his jaw locking. "Goddamn it. I'm sorry."

"They fucking broke her into pieces," I hissed. "If you could have he her...the way she screamed...the way she *looked* at me...she didn't dese this. She didn't deserve any of this."

"I'm sorry you had to see that," Danny said quietly, watching as the Born looted through the scattered remains.

I bent down and picked up the sledgehammer, my heart pounding almost as loud as the hatred inside it. "I'm going to find that *motherfucker* and I'm going to *kill* him."

"He doesn't have much of a head start," Danny observed, looking me over, "but why don't you put on some clothes before your dick catches pneumonia?"

I shivered in the rain and realized just how cold I was. I quickly shed a corpse of its clothing and donned it with urgency. When I was finished, I gripped the sledgehammer and turned to where Peter had fled.

"Thanks, Danny," I muttered. "Seems like I owe you. Again."

Danny surprised me by placing a hand on my shoulder. "We'll be right behind you. Go get that bastard."

I nodded once and then I was off. The forest blurred past me, my feet hurling me forward like I had the hounds of hell at my heels. My side screamed in protest, but I ignored its warnings, instead using the pain as fuel to shoot me toward my prey.

Jesus, the way she looked at me.

Rain lashed across my face as it dripped from the trees. My breath hissed from between my lips like steam, and I felt everything but the anger melt away. I had come so far and promised so much. What had been the point of all of it? What had I really accomplished? Set the Farm back in order? At what cost? How much pain had I caused by coming back here?

They stripped her and broke her.

"Goddamn it," I growled, feeling tears form and streak down my face, "when is this going to end?" I leaped over a log, crashing through a cluster of bushes.

Remember why you came back. Remember the loved ones you left behind. You're doing this for them. Nothing else matters. Jess and Theo are waiting for you. Stop hunting, stop fighting, stop killing. It's time to go home, Nick. You did what you came to do.

I blew through a small grove and dodged around a massive tree, never slowing. As I did so, a singular thought rocketed through my skull, silencing all others.

You'll never be happy if you leave her behind, alone.

I ran and ran until my breath blew sour and my lungs burned. I began to see movement up ahead, flashes of color darting between the trees, away from me. I dumped my energy reserves into my legs and sped up, grinding my teeth together so hard I thought they would break.

It was Peter.

The forest began to thin, and gray light filtered in through the foliage. The chase was taking me out of the woods and back out into the open, back to where the Pig had killed Berserker.

When I burst through the treeline, I slowed for half a second, the skyline filling me with a jolt of fear. A stray Keeper was returning to the ocean, a distant skyscraper of glowing power, wading dutifully back to where it belonged. Across the island, the Pig filled the horizon, watching it with a commanding eye.

Along the beach were a handful of Pig Born with Suicidal captives. It looked like they were trying to offer the unlucky souls to the stone giant. I could hear their screams of terror over the rain.

Not my problem.

Still running, I turned my attention back to Peter. He was only a hundred yards ahead of me and slowing. I could tell fatigue was catching up to him. And so was I. Sweating, I hurled myself forward across the muddy ground. At fifty yards, he turned and saw me approaching. His eyes went wide and he almost tripped.

At ten yards, I hoisted the sledgehammer and let out a bellowing howl of sorrow and anger, catching up to him and slamming hard into his back. He let out a pained *oomf!* and went sprawling, mud splashing around us. I came down on top of him, feeling electricity burning through my nerves.

"You can't run from this," I snarled, rolling in the mud with him, catching an elbow in the side. I barely felt it.

"Get off me, psycho!" Peter yelled, rolling away from me and getting to his feet. I sprang up and began to circle him, spinning the hammer as I did

"You have a way of inciting that kind of behavior," I growled, distant Pig Born squealing in the wind.

"How many times are we going to do this?" Peter barked, panting heavily. He appeared to be completely spent, his face slack and pale, his eye haggard and pained.

"As many times as it takes," I spat back. "As many times as you keep tak-
ng people I care about." I braced myself to attack, shoulders tense. "What
rives you to be so heartless? How could you do something like that to an
nnocent child?! ANSWER ME!"

Peter shook his head, keeping his distance. "Of all the people I expected
o ask me that...you are not one of them. You know better than most how
his place can change someone. So quit the act and stop pretending you're
uch a saint. I remember what you've done and so does this place. I don't
now why the hell you came back—but this place? The Black Farm? It re-
nembers. It remembers every little sin you've committed. Who knows, Nick,
naybe I'm just a pawn being used to punish you. Maybe everything that's
appened to you here has just been a big cosmic game to make you suffer for
our actions. You ever think about that? Huh? No, of course not. You're too
usy pretending you're a good person. You kill and you kill and you kill and
nen you blame your shadow. What kind of man does that?"

"The kind that's going to kill you," I hissed.

I launched myself at him, spinning and swinging the hammer as I did.
t connected wetly, the iron head crunching into Peter's hip, breaking it in an
nstant. He screamed and went down like a pile of bricks, falling heavily and
lutching his shattered bone. I tossed the hammer aside and sprang on top
f him, snarling and swinging with all the might I could muster. Through his
gony, Peter managed to throw up his hands and block most of my punches.
sat up on him, allowing myself a quick breath, and immediately wished I
adn't as Peter counterattacked. With a grunt, he plowed a fistful of knuck-
es into my jaw with more force than I anticipated. I toppled off him, tasting
lood, but quickly got to my feet, the pain igniting fresh anger.

I faced him, rain lashing down around us, and saw he was struggling to
is feet but failing as his hip gave out. He barked a cry and rolled onto his
de, knowing he was beaten but unable to accept it. I bent down and picked
p the sledgehammer once more, slowing myself now that I knew Peter
vasn't going anywhere.

"I should break you as mercilessly as you broke Emily," I growled, ad-
ancing as he tried to slide himself away, "but after all the shit you've put me
nrough, I just don't have the patience." I stood over him, glaring down at

his rain-soaked form. "I swear to god, I wish I had the energy to enjoy this more." I raised the hammer over my head, preparing the killing blow.

Peter stared up at me, his eyes burning. "Don't think this is o—"

I caved his face in, the hammer shattering through his nose and mouth like they were made from cheap plastic. Blood and gore sprayed outward from the impact like visceral confetti.

Peter's body slumped over, his death coming quicker than he deserved. In an instant he became nothing more than a lifeless, bleeding shell. As his body fell away, it took the hammer with it. I let it go, content to leave it implanted in the bastard's face. Rain diluted the streams of blood now forming around the corpse, and I watched with half-lidded eyes. I knew Peter would be reborn, spit out from the clouds like everyone else that died here, but in the moment I didn't care. I had killed the son of a bitch and it felt good.

Really good.

Slowly I sat down. Exhaustion draped itself around my shoulders and I took a moment to wipe the grime from my face. The sky clothed me with freezing rain, dulling the fire in my head. My side was killing me, and I pressed a hand against it.

She's out there, alone again.

I scanned the world and spotted another Keeper finding its way back to the ocean. It was barely more than a smudge on the horizon, but it was another piece put back into place. The island was obeying. I turned to look in the opposite direction, back to where I had seen the Pig, but it was gone now—off aligning more pieces to its throne, its hold over this godless place.

She died thinking you wanted her dead.

I pulled my callused hands down my face. Somewhere, thunder rumbled and I felt empty.

How are you going to go back knowing she's here all by herself?

"Where are you, little one?" I muttered miserably, staring out at a cautious group of Suicidals making their way into the woods, a trio of figures who looked confused and terrified.

What the hell was the point of all this?

I squeezed my eyes shut, head draining. "Goddamn it, I miss you Jess." I pictured her holding Theo on her hip, staring down at the note I had left before killing myself.

You make everything worse, don't you? When are you going to stop hurting ryone around you?

"I did this for them," I said to no one. "To save them."

And who's going to save Emily? She shouldn't even be here.

"Just stop," I muttered, gripping my head.

She's out there somewhere, right now, confused and crying and begging some- to make sense of all this. It won't be long until someone or something finds her. n what? Will you find her back in some cave chained to a wall?

I pressed my fingers against my eyes so hard that I saw stars.

"Having a rough day?"

I snapped my head up, vision swimming from the pressure, and saw self staring at a familiar face.

"Ramiel," I said darkly, climbing to my feet.

The angel was standing in front of me, arms crossed, with a vaguely ised look on his face. He tilted his chin toward the ruined Barn and the d Keeper.

"Seems things came to a head here."

I glared at him, feeling a murderous concoction brewing in my gut. "You of a *bitch*."

Ramiel grunted, unfazed. "Relax. It seems things are settling down here. should too."

"Must have been quite the show from up there," I snarled, jabbing a ;er at the heavens. "Could have used an assist once or twice."

Ramiel sloped a smile down his lips. "You know I couldn't."

Rip that fucking grin off his face.

"Right," I said. "Can't have you overstepping your boundaries. Wouldn't t to upset the balance. Whatever the hell that means."

Ramiel nodded along. "I have to say, I'm impressed. I didn't think you'd ble to stay alive for so long. None of us did. There were a couple close s, but you managed to squeak by."

"None of us did?" I hissed. "What, were you taking bets up there?"

"Nothing so crude," Ramiel said, smoothing his face out, "but we did e our eyes on you. It appears the Pig has returned to reclaim its place :. It even managed to eliminate the mad Keeper." He looked at me ways. "The method in which it healed the sickness from its body was...

unfortunate, but we've concluded that the loss of the Mud Men is an accep
able exchange."

I stepped toward him, feeling the bottom of my sanity drop o
"Acceptable exchange? Is that what you're calling it? Do you people giv
shit about *anything* you create?"

"Of course," Ramiel said sternly, holding his ground. "Don't get arroga
with me. Don't act like you have the moral high ground here. It's nauseatin

I took another step toward him, hands curling into fists. "I spent t
better part of my time here looking after a little girl who had no busin
being on the Black Farm. What happened to her was an accident. She to
some pills and had no idea what she was doing. And your boss, the big *fu
ing* man, sent her *here*." I was nose-to-nose with him now, voice cracking
borderline hysteria. "As far as I'm concerned, you people are worse than t
monsters here."

Ramiel didn't back down, his voice even but hard. "Are you done w
the dramatics? You've always been one for theater, haven't you? Alwa
brooding and overthinking and gnashing your teeth at anything that mov
When did you grow such a bleeding heart? You're really this upset ove
little girl? Don't you have your own family to worry about?"

"My family is safe," I fumed. "The whole point of my return was to e
sure their safety. I did what I set out to do—but Emily? She's still here. S
doesn't get to go back like I do."

Ramiel cocked an eyebrow. "Who said anything about going back?"

I let the rain fill the deafening silence that swept between us, the ring
his words blaring through my head.

"What?" I finally asked, barely more than a furious whisper.

Ramiel smiled. "A little joke, Nick. Relax."

I suddenly grabbed him by the throat, snarling. "A joke? Are you k
ding me? We're talking about eternity here and you're cracking *jokes*? Is th
anything you people take seriously? Do you value *anything* that isn't flyi
around up in heaven?"

Ramiel roughly jerked himself away, all traces of humor leaving his fa
"I wouldn't advise doing that. My patience only runs so deep."

"You guys getting along?"

The two of us turned at the sound of the new voice to see Danny walking toward us across the field, backed by a handful of Pig Born. They eyed Ramiel with furious hatred, their mutated faces drooling and twisting as they approached.

"Stay out of this," I said as Danny reached us. "This is between me and him."

Danny looked Ramiel up and down. "Let me guess: This is the angel you were telling me about? The catalyst of your return?"

Ramiel coolly met his gaze. "Hello, Danny."

"Don't say my name like you know me," Danny spat, clearly not impressed.

"I know a lot of things about you, Danny. I've watched you traverse the island with Nick here. I don't think he would have gotten as far as he did without you."

"Blow me," Danny said, the Pig Born at his back growling aggressively.

Ramiel sniffed his disapproval. "Yes, always the crass one. I've noticed that, too."

Danny looked at me and then back to the angel. "What the hell are you doing here, anyway? Besides breathing my air?"

Ramiel cocked an eyebrow. "Breathing your—"

"Just shut up," Danny injected. "I know why you're here. The Pig is back in power, its sickness cured, and Berserker is dead. Which means Nick is in the clear and you're going to take him back, right?"

Ramiel cast a shadowed look my way. "Yes, I suppose so."

I planted my feet. "I'm not going anywhere."

It was Danny's turn to raise an eyebrow. "What now? What are you talking about? Hey, look, if you're giving up your ticket, I'll gladly take it."

I brought my teeth together. "I'm not going anywhere without Emily."

Ramiel's face grew sour. "What is this nonsense? What is it about this girl that makes you so insistent?"

"Because it's not right," I growled, "and that's enough for most."

"Ah, yes, I forgot I was talking to the pillar of morality here," Ramiel droned, "a shining example for the human race."

I flexed my fists, feeling my blood boil. "I'm getting real sick of you talking about me like I'm some kind of mass-murdering psycho. Coming back here, I've realized something. Everything I've done in this place, both past and present, I've done to survive and to get back home. I've suffered nightmares for it, but I'd do it all over again. And I'd do it not because I wanted to, but because I had to. Because people counted on me to do the violent, necessary things needed to get back to them. So if you're looking for some kind of remorse, then you're going to have to look somewhere else. My actions have caused me a lot of sleepless nights, but I've never felt *guilt.* For some reason that seems to piss you off. Get over it. Take your sanctimonious attitude and cram it up your ass. I've done some bad things, but I'm not a bad person. I just did them because I have more to live for than you. "

Ramiel looked down his nose at me. "Am I supposed to be impressed? All this hot air coming out of your mouth...what exactly do you expect me to do with it? If you're so worried about the purity of your intentions, I'm not the one you need to convince. I couldn't care less."

"If you think I would actually pray to your god—"

"Our God," Ramiel corrected. "You may not like it, but he's the one running all of this. He's the one who put life into your lungs and continues to do so. Just because you don't believe in him—"

"Oh I believe in him," I interrupted, "and I think he's a sadistic, self-involved fucking *cunt.*"

"Yeah, that makes two of us," Danny said, nodding.

"Watch how you speak of him," Ramiel said, his voice iron.

"I'm done being told what to do," I said aggressively. "If you don't like the way I'm talkin', then maybe you should get your hands dirty and do something about it for once."

"Don't tempt me," Ramiel said passively.

"For an angel, this guy is a real bitch," Danny said, casting a glance at me.

Ramiel forcibly calmed himself and brought his voice back to neutrality along with the conversation. "If we're done bickering like children, I'd very much like to get out of this rain."

"You really are taking him back," Danny said in mild disbelief.

"I told you," I said, standing my ground, "I'm not going anywhere without Emily."

"Well, that's not your decision to make!" Ramiel finally snapped. "Nor is it mine! So stop acting like a spoiled brat and take the gift you've been given!

Thunder rumbled behind my words. "If it's not your decision to make, hen whose is it? Who do I have to talk to?"

"Do you really have to ask?"

Darkness filled my head. "Then take me to him."

Ramiel blinked and then barked a laugh. "You have got to be kidding me."

Rain poured down my beaten face. "Does it look like I'm fuckng kidding?"

"You want me to take you up to heaven?" Ramiel asked, chuckling inredulously. "So that you can plead your case for Emily?"

"That about covers it."

Danny shifted next to me, his voice low. "Really rolling the dice here, Nick."

"Shut the fuck up."

Danny shrugged.

Ramiel ran a hand through his hair, a disbelieving smile plastered across is face. "You really don't know when to quit, do you?"

"Take me."

Ramiel's eyes grew fire. "No! No I will not *take* you! I'm not some puppet here to dance for you! So why don't you stop being such a stubborn fool nd accept the second chance you've been given before God decides to take away!"

"No?" I said slowly, feeling an unbelievable amount of rage rising in my hroat. "No is a word I'm really not in the mood to hear right now."

"Get over yourself," Ramiel growled, "and start behaving so I never have see you again. Take my hand and keep your mouth shut." He extended his and to me, a look of contempt bleeding through his expression.

Fuck this guy.

I punched him as hard as I could. His nose broke beneath my knuckles nd he cried out in shock, stumbling back and then falling to the ground.

"Oh, wow!" Danny cried in humorous disbelief. He held up his arms to op the Pig Born from interjecting and watched as I fell on Ramiel with vengeance.

"Have you lost your mind?!" the angel screamed as he tried to wiggle ut from under me.

I felt a burning throb in my skull like a hot poker, pushing the edges o tolerance to the limit. My eyes were bloodshot and my lips were pulled dow to reveal snarling teeth.

I'm so done with this shit.

I wrapped my hands around Ramiel's throat and choke-slammed hi face into my forehead, crunching his already broken nose into a pulp. Hi gasped and then screamed, unable to believe what I was doing.

"You're going to do what I fucking say," I hissed, keeping him pinne with one hand while the other plowed into his jaw. A tooth flew free like bloody shell ejecting from a gun.

"Get OFF!" Ramiel yelled, his voice rugged and wet.

"Are you going to take me to heaven?!"

"NO!"

Wrong answer.

I opened my mouth and filled it with the side of his neck, teeth sinkin and biting and then coming away in a bloody tear of flesh. Red warmth cov ered my chin and rushed across my nose as Ramiel's screams rose to a sum mit. I tasted copper on my tongue and the loose skin in my mouth squishe around my inner cheek. I spit the chunk of flesh away, and my thumbs foun the angel's eye sockets.

"It didn't have to get this nasty," I growled a second before plunging m thumbs down, popping his eyeballs like cherry tomatoes. Ramiel shrieke and his body convulsed, the pain overwhelming him. Yellow pus ran dow his cheeks like trails of snot filled with blood. I stood up slowly, allowing hi the freedom to feel what I had taken from him.

"I can't see! I CAN'T SEE!" he howled, weeping, shock gripping him.

I became aware of Danny at my side, his voice hushed. "Jesus…"

I stood over Ramiel and planted a foot on his chest, sweat and rain an blood dripping from the tip of my nose. "Once you're done screaming, you'r going to take me up so I can have that conversation. Is that crystal *fuckin* clear to you now? Or do I need to continue?"

Ramiel blindly held his hands up, his voice a hitching sob. "No more I'll take you! I'll take you right now! Just...no more!"

I exhaled heavily and got off him. I stepped back and let the sheets of n coat my body. I realized I was shaking, but it wasn't from the cold this ıe. I raised my eyes to the heavens.

I'm coming.

Ramiel climbed to his feet coughing and panting, his eye sockets like ıpty wells. His knees knocked together and a hoarse shudder escaped m his trembling lips.

"T-take my hand," he instructed, shoulders hunched like he expected to strike once more. "Just take my hand and we'll be gone. I promise."

"See how easy this could have been?" I muttered, reaching for him.

"Nick."

I paused and looked at Danny.

"What?"

Danny clapped me on the shoulder. "Tell the big guy to eat shit, uld ya?"

"Sure."

Ramiel hacked another cough, looking sightlessly at me. "A-are you dy?"

"Take us."

His fingers tightened around my own, and then we were gone.

Chapter 16

Cold wind rushed past us as the world went black. I felt the bottom of my stomach drop out, and I was overwhelmed with a sense of weightlessness. I gripped Ramiel's hand firmly in the void, unable to imagine what would happen if I let go. A roar filled my ears and I closed my eyes, feeling like I was being sucked down a massive air duct. Over the noise, I could hear Ramiel panting, the shock from our confrontation still wearing off. I wiggled my legs in the emptiness, my limbs streaming behind me like we were underwater.

After what seemed like far too long, the darkness began to give way. I sensed that we were slowing, and I pulled my eyes into focus. When I saw what lay around us, I instinctively grasped Ramiel tighter.

We were soaring high above an endless landscape, a stretch of rolling hills and dense forest. The sky was pitch-black and the only source of light came from an immense lake. The surface of the water sparkled like melted gold, the gentle ripples illuminating the world in a soft glow.

As we raced over it, I squinted and realized there were shapes floating on the lake. Human shapes. I focused on one of these shapes and realized that each figure was a person lying on their back as if asleep. Hovering a foot over them was a second person, parallel to the first, flipped so they were face-to-face. Reason and logic flew out of the window as I observed that the two people were exactly the same, twins from the same mold. The one floating on the water was connected to the one lying above it, a thick fleshy hose conjoining them at the mouth. This didn't seem to bother either of the mirrored bodies, their eyes closed, their faces serene and still.

What the hell am I looking at?

As we continued to fly over the immense lake, I noticed just how many of these odd twin duos there were. I swept my eyes over the golden waters, estimating millions if not hundreds of millions. They all seemed asleep, a conglomeration of every race, sex, and age just lying on the water with their strange twin above them.

My fascination was cut short as I was jerked downward. Ramiel was taking me lower, away from the lake and to our right, headed straight for a lone mountain. It was a titan of darkness, a singular peak that poked up into an equally inky sky. Still hundreds of feet above it, I scoured the earth below for some sign of life, movement, anything, but found nothing.

We dipped lower, swooping in toward the mountain. It stood like a watchman before the lake, the golden light casting a faint glow across the wooded slopes. Ramiel picked up speed and I felt the wind whip past me so fast my eyes began to tear. The mountainside rushed up around us and right as I thought we would crash, Ramiel pulled up, hovering feet above the treetops. Gently, we descended the final distance, the trees rising around us to block the lake from view.

I let out a breath as my feet touched the ground, grateful to be out of the sky. Ramiel let go of my hand as soon as we made landfall, turning his back to me, his voice laden with cautious contempt.

"I hope you're happy."

"Where are we?" I asked quietly, scanning the thick foliage around us. I noticed that we were standing on a path, a thin dusting of dirt that led up the mountainside.

Ramiel looked at me with his empty, bleeding eyes. "You got what you wanted."

I turned where I stood. "This? This is it?"

"Expecting something different?" Ramiel said thickly, gingerly touching his ruined face. "Perhaps a couple of fluffy clouds with fat, childish angel upon them?"

"Not exactly," I muttered, staring up the path. Was that light I saw?

Ramiel sat down in the dirt, sniffling. "You're a despicable man, Nick. A violent, impulsive fool that doesn't deserve any of the kindness he's been given. If I had any say in it, I would have left you on the Black Farm to rot."

"I bet you would have," I said, casting a glance at him. His face was covered in blood and he seemed to be struggling to decide whether to cry or scream. His hands kept traveling back to his empty eye sockets, each touch bringing with it a sharp intake of breath.

"What are you waiting for?" Ramiel asked, his voice a biting thing full of pain. "Go."

I looked up the path toward the summit. "Go? Up there?"

Ramiel just stared blindly at his hands. "That's where you'll find what you're looking for."

I caught a flicker of something high above. "What's up there?"

Ramiel's voice lowered. "A cabin. And something more than a man."

I hesitated, the world impossibly still and quiet. There were no traces of wildlife, no stir of the trees, not even the creak of wood. Just darkness and empty silence.

I turned back to Ramiel. "That lake we saw, those people floating on the surface—"

"Just go," Ramiel cut in. "I did what you wanted, I'll not be pushed into doing any more."

I looked up the slope, the path a straight slice up the center of the mountain. Taking a deep breath, I began to walk. Before I had gone two steps, Ramiel's voice stopped me.

"Nick?"

I looked over my shoulder.

"I sincerely hope you're denied every happiness for the rest of your life."

After a moment I looked away from him and began to hike up the mountain. My thoughts clouded with possibility and speculation as I left the bleeding angel behind. His words rang through my head, but I forced them out. I had bigger things to dwell on.

The climb was not a strenuous one. The path, while narrow, was devoid of rock or root, the firmly packed earth making for an easy ascent. The dark trees lining the path remained silent, but I couldn't shake the creeping sensation that I was being watched. I made myself focus on the path in front of me and not on the trees. Their eerie stillness made my blood run cold and goosebumps to rise along my arms.

I'm almost done, Jess. Just one more thing to do and then I'll be back with you and Theo.

I suddenly missed them, the thought of them bringing with it a terrible ache. It shuddered through my heart and across my chest, a need so strong that I almost sobbed. I pictured Theo sitting in his high chair, his face smeared with spaghetti, smiling up at me with all the innocence in the world. I could feel Jess's arms reach out from behind, her hands sliding across my stomach and up my chest, her cheek pressed lovingly against my back as she hugged me from behind. It was suddenly all I wanted, the rush of warmth grounding me back in the reality in which I belonged.

"I miss you both so much," I whispered to no one, feet plodding up the trail, each step feeling heavier than the last.

She would want you to save Emily. If she were here, she'd be right next to you without a doubt in her mind.

The thought gave me some comfort and I continued up the incline. After some time, I glanced ahead of me and saw that same flicker of light from above. It was closer now, much closer.

It's time this was over.

I mustered up a final draught of energy and climbed, the flickering growing nearer, now only a hundred yards away. As I grew closer, I realized that I could make out the dark outline of a cabin. It was nestled against the hillside and surrounded by towering trees, a wooden porch extending out from the front to meet the end of the path.

I kicked up dust as I huffed up the final distance, the cabin windows dancing with firelight from inside. As I approached the steps leading up to the front door, I slowed, the severity of the confrontation I was about to have slamming me full in the chest.

No time to back out, tough guy.

I took a deep breath and climbed the steps. They made no sound as I took them, the front door looming before me.

"Hey, Nick."

My heart leapt in my chest and I spun with a jerk toward the voice on the porch. A man sat at the far end in a rocking chair, his boots crossed and

ing on the railing. His face was clothed in shadow, but I saw he had a
e planted between his teeth.

I held myself against the front door, chest drumming as I tried to steady
nerves. The man on the porch rocked himself gently and I smelled to-
co waft across the open air.

"You've come a long way just to speak with me," the man said, his voice
less but shaded with a sense of assurance. In a way, I found that it calmed
. I pushed myself away from the door and took a tentative step across the
ch toward him.

"You didn't have to come all this way for that, you know," the man said,
I sensed he was smiling. "Could have just...talked to me. I know that
yer is a sensitive concept to you, but you don't have to think of it like that."

I finally found my voice, eyes glued to the man in the darkness. "I'm
re of a face-to-face kind of guy.'

The man chuckled and I heard his teeth clack against the stem of his
e. "That you are, that you are." He inhaled and a faint glow emanated
n the embers, casting a soft light across the man's face. I froze where I
od, catching a brief glance of the man's features. His skin was pale and
ooth, his lips white around the pipe. A mop of black hair tumbled down
ais shoulders, as dark as the night. An eye patch covered half his face,
one remaining eye staring into my eyes. As our eyes locked, I felt an
rwhelming surge jolt through me. It was as if I had been injected with
enaline and my veins strained to burst through my skin.

I gripped the porch railing and steadied myself, that insane buzz whip-
g down my spine and releasing with a shiver.

"Easy now, son," the man said, "you've had quite a journey. I don't want
conking out on me."

I licked my dry lips, fumbling to rid myself of that terrible feeling.
-what...are you?"

The man filled the air with pipe smoke. "You know what I am."

I forced myself to look away from the shadow in the rocking chair, my
crawling. I looked out past the porch railing and saw the distant lake, its
den rays sparkling across the empty horizon.

"Kinda pretty, isn't it?" the man said, still rocking.

"What is it?" I asked numbly, feeling as if my mind were leaking out the back of my head.

The man huffed his pipe, his words coming from around the st "That there is where all souls go when they die. 'Cept the Suicidals, but y know that."

I held onto the railing with both hands. "All those bodies floating on surface...there were two of each, one hovering just above the other."

"Mhmm," the man mused. "That's right. A design of my own maki You like it?" Before waiting for an answer, he pressed on. "It may look l twins, clones if you will, and in a way you'd be right for assuming so. see, the one floating on the surface is a person's soul. That vessel floats to surface as soon as someone is born. Over the course of one's life, they dec through their actions on Earth how that soul, that body on the lake, for How much buoyancy it retains. Once a person dies, they are connected b to their soul and if they lived a good life, they float and they stay here the weight of their sin is too much for the soul to bear? Well, I'm af they sink. They sink all the way down to the place I'd rather not talk abo I heard him pause and fumble for something in his pocket. "Once I g someone life, the rest is really in their hands. There's a lot of talk about h I'm a heartless S.O.B.," he paused and I felt him look at me. "But the rea of it is this—from the moment you're born, you decide where you'll di don't have anything to do with it. You wanna live a life full of sin? You w to hurt people? That's your choice, but don't call me unjust when you p away and your soul sinks. I gave you people free will for a reason." He pul a box of matches from his pocket and struck one, putting the tip to the p bowl, his words wrapped with smoke. "Everyone goes to heaven when t die. It's up to you if you stay."

I listened to all this, digesting it with careful precision. My eyes dan over the distant waters, the immense golden glow washing the skyline w warm color.

"You still with me, Nick?"

I nodded absently. "Yeah. Yeah, I hear you."

The man nodded from the shadows. "Good. Can you do me a mas favor, son?"

"What's that?"

He jabbed a thumb over his shoulder toward the corner of the porch. 'Can you scoop up a handful of tobacco and hand it to me? I'd do it myself, ut I just got comfortable."

Cautiously, I turned and faced him. I could see the dark outline of his humb, directing me behind him. I stepped forward and saw a massive pile f something at his back. I stepped around him, making sure not to come in ontact with the chair or the man, and I bent down. My fingers sunk into mass of something that felt like dry leaves and I pulled some out of the areless pile.

"Thank you kindly," the man said, holding out his palm to receive the obacco. I stood where I was, hand frozen in mid-air.

"Well, go on, hand it over, son, I'm not going to bite," the man said ently.

I dumped the tobacco into his waiting hand and stepped away, brushing ny fingers against my pants. I watched as the man crammed the substance nto his pipe bowl before bringing another match to life.

"Why do you do that?" I asked as I watched.

The man tossed the match aside. "What, this? The pipe thing?" he runted, like it was the most obvious question in the world. "This is how I eep all of you alive." He held up the pipe. "Once I'm out of tobacco, that's t, son. End of the line. Lights out."

My eyes went wide and I stared at the pile behind him. "You've got to e kidding me."

The man waved a hand at me dismissively. "Ah, relax, we still got a ways o go before it comes to that. Just so long I keep this thing lit, you and the est of humanity will keep breathing."

A sudden memory tickled the back of my mind, an obscure image that couldn't quite place. I stared at the pipe, my voice thin. "Have...have we net before?"

The embers flared and I could see the man was smiling, his one good ye twinkling. "Let's just say I've been watching you for a long time, son."

I looked away, feeling sick.

The man tapped his pipe against his teeth as if thinking. "Now, don't get ne wrong, I'm very much enjoying our conversation, but was there a reason ou came all this way to see me?"

I stared out at the bizarre world.

How the hell are you going to say this?

"Son?" the man prodded. "I would say we got all the time in the world but as we just discussed, time is not endless and you're wasting mine if you're just going to stand there and brood."

"You know what I want," I finally whispered, refusing to turn and look at him.

"Mmm, that I do, but here's the thing about how all this works. You have to ask me."

I felt my grip tighten along the railing "Do I now? And what purpose does that serve besides you getting to hear the sound of desperate people?"

I heard him suck on his pipe for a long moment before answering, his voice low, but calm. "Nick...tell me how I can help you."

I finally turned to him, an unexpected surge of anger rising dangerously in my throat. "I want to know why you send Suicidals to the Black Farm. All this talk about how fair you are, about how it's up to us to decide where we go..." I shook my head. "The first time I killed myself, I was at the lowest I had ever been. I was heartbroken, desperate, and couldn't take another day facing the despair that filled my head. I needed help, but there was *no one*. I even asked you, prayed for *once* in my life, begged you to tell me not to go through with it. But you didn't do anything except send me to the Farm to suffer for my sadness. So my question to you is why? Why would you do that to someone who just wanted a fucking *break*?"

The man was silent for a long moment before answering, his voice as gentle as the night air. "The world is a horrible place, son, and I'm sorry you experienced a life that brought you to that end. I truly am."

"That's not an answer," I growled.

"You're right, it was a condolence."

"How the hell does that help anyone?!"

"I gave you life," the man continued, his voice smooth as butter, "and I gave you a place to rest when it is over. How much more do you want?"

"I want you to admit you're not the saint everyone thinks you are," I stated aggressively. "I want to hear it from your own mouth, I want you to tell me that you made a mistake and that the Black Farm should never have been created. I want you to do something to fix it. Erase it. Take those poor people from that nightmare and give them the goddamn peace they deserve."

The man exhaled a waft of smoke before speaking. "You're a passionate man, Nick. That's always stuck out to me. You've always got fire burning up inside of you."

"Stop dodging the subject."

"And why must I sit here and explain myself to you?" The man asked.

I smiled grimly. "Ah. There it is."

The man sighed. "Son...I understand why you want me to sit here and affirm your belief in what I am, but I just can't do that. I am what I am. I am not something that conforms to whatever a person believes I am. You think I'm sadistic at heart for creating the Black Farm, right?"

"Yeah, that about sums it up," I said darkly.

The man shrugged. "Then to you, that is what I am. But it is not *who* I am."

"That's it? That's all you have to say?"

"There's nothing I could say that would satiate your desire to somehow punish me for the choices I've made. And there have been a *lot* of choices made, Nick. Some of those, I regret. Is the Black Farm one of them? I honestly don't know. It simply exists as part of the balance now in the trilogy of afterlives. It fits neatly between heaven and hell, a place where one can go and still hold onto their free will. It is the only place after death to do so, and that's because it is the only place a soul has not grown toward."

"And what about Emily!?" I finally yelled, slamming my fist down on the railing. "What about her? Her suicide was accidental! How can you send her to the Black Farm for something like that!?"

The man shook his head from the darkness. "Action has consequences, regardless of intent. That little girl did what she did and took action, knowingly or not, and there was a consequence for that. It may not seem fair to you, but again, that's not for me to rectify."

"Of course it is!" I yelled.

"Don't you understand?" the man pressed. "This is what everything here is all about. All of it. Action and consequence. That's it. heaven, hell, the Black Farm, it's all action and consequence."

"That doesn't make sense for someone like her!" I cried.

The man chewed on the end of his pipe, his voice patient. "Let's bring the spotlight back to you. Perhaps that'll help you understand the mindset we're working toward."

"What about me?"

"Why are you here, Nick?"

I paused. "What do you mean?"

"Your return to the Black Farm," the man continued. "Why did it happen? Why did you come back?"

I shook my head. "That's a stupid question considering you're the one who orchestrated the whole thing."

"And yet you didn't answer me."

"You know why I'm here. You forced my hand, threatened my family, and showed me the horrible things that would happen if I didn't come back."

"Sure," the man said slowly, "but *why* are you here?"

I furrowed my brow, not sure what kind of angle was being leveled at me. "Why? Because the Pig was sick and you needed me to come back and fix things."

"Wrong."

I stared at the shadow in the chair, heart pumping with adrenaline. "What did you just say?"

"That's not why you're here," the man said quietly.

I shook my head. "But Ramiel told me—"

"He told you exactly what he was supposed to."

I narrowed my eyes at the man. "What are you talking about? What kind of mind games are you playing?"

"Do you really think I needed you to come fix the Farm? To return the Pig back to its place of power? You saw how things played out—it wouldn't have taken long for it to restore its health without your help. Come on, Nick you're a smart guy. You should have figured this out by now."

I stared at the man, feeling ice crawl up my spine.

The man continued. "This was never about restoring the island. Don't get me wrong; you seriously messed things up the first time. That was a headache to deal with, absolutely, but that's not why you were sent back That's not why I sent Ramiel down there with those horrific visions."

"The hell is this all about, then?" I asked, my voice a disbelieving whisper

The man took a long pull from his pipe, the embers igniting his face. As he did so, he tapped his eye patch a single time.

"This."

I stared at him, cautious and confused. "Your...eye?"

"What did you call the lights on the mountain?"

My mind was plummeting. "The...lights on the mountain?"

"Yes, on the Farm during your first excursion here. The mountain. What did you call the lights on the summit before you climbed it looking for a way out?"

I felt my stomach sink to rot. "The Eyes of the World."

The man exhaled a cloud of thick smoke. "Yes, The Eyes of the World. Two beings, two telescopes into that horrible place. One that was mine and one that was not. And Nick...you took mine. You *ate* it."

I felt my mouth dry up. "No...no, it was an angel. I needed his flesh, I needed it so the Pig wouldn't send me to hell."

"Yes, very clever, that," the man said, leaning back, "but he was my creation. I molded him with a very specific purpose: to keep watch over the Farm and to provide insight into that place. I formed him from my own being, using my own abilities to form a living spyglass. He used my vision, seeing all there was to see. But his role was temporary." The man tapped the stem of his pipe against his eye patch. "And this blindness is eternal now."

I felt my stomach squirm and tighten, disbelief rattling me where I stood.

The man continued, his voice even and calm. "This was never about setting things right on the Farm, son. It was about making you atone for what you did to me."

I gripped the railing, my whole body buzzing with sensation. My mind reeled and spun and I felt sick. This whole time…

"Are you *fucking* kidding me?" I croaked. "You sent me back...to that endless place...because you were pissed at me?"

"Every man must face his sins," the man continued, voice smooth as glass. "Action and consequence."

I felt like my skull was cracking at the seams, my voice a hoarse exhale. "That's not good enough. That's just *not* going to cut it."

The man looked past me toward the golden lake, his tone passive. "When you took my sight away, I became...bitter...toward you."

"This is insane," I whispered thinly. "Do you really mean to tell me you forced me back to the Black Farm, NOT to save my family, but to fulfill a punishment over something I did the first time around?"

"Why is that so hard to understand?" the man said. "Do you think you are above punishment? Do you think you deserve some kind of pardon fo the sins you committed?"

"I did that to survive!" I yelled, trembling. "I did it to get out and ge my life back!"

"Action and consequence, son. There is no absolution from that."

"Shut the FUCK UP!" I screamed, slamming my hand down on th railing. "Stop trying to justify what you DID TO ME! I just went throug an unspeakable nightmare because I thought I was saving my family, but turns out I only did it because some ASSHOLE didn't like how I cheate the system!"

"Bold words," the man said, seemingly unaffected. "Passionate words. would expect nothing less from you. Your inability to see the bigger pictu is disappointing, but not surprising. What you did needed rectifying. Yo tipped the scales, you took away one of my eyes, and then you returned ba to your home like nothing happened. What kind of being would I be if I l that slide without consequence?"

I leaned toward him, hissing between my teeth. "Why are you so he bent on looking like the good guy here? You formed a vendetta and carri it out by threatening my family and forcing me to return to the one pla you knew I would suffer, that I COULD suffer without a reflection of t soul. Couldn't just wait and send me to hell, could you? No, because we bo know, deep down, I'm not a bad person. I wouldn't go to hell. And that dr you crazy, knowing what I took from you. So you started pushing pie around, moving your pawns into place, setting up this elaborate plot, and for what? Because I took something from you when I wasn't supposed to don't know if you're aware of this, but if you spent five minutes on the Bl Farm you'd realize in that time that you'd do anything to get out. Anyth at all." I leaned in even closer. "And I did."

"And here were are," the man said casually. "Your punishment has been carried out and you're still breathing. You're taking this the wrong way, son. I hold no malice over you. Not anymore at least. The scales have been leveled; you did your time just as I intended."

"How long were you going to let me suffer down there?" I asked suddenly.

"I believe Ramiel had come to take you home," the man said. "At least, that was before you beat him to a pulp. I figured once the Pig inevitably regained its hold over the Farm, it would be time to send you back and the narrative would have been upheld." The man shook his head. "I didn't expect you to find your way to my doorstep and demand answers, but I am happy to give them nonetheless."

"You're a sadist," I said lowly, "and I don't think you have any idea what you're doing anymore."

"Like I stated earlier, that is your interpretation of what I am. But it is not who I am."

"Keep telling yourself that," I snarled. "I'll just keep on believing what's right in front of me."

The man sighed as if he were suddenly very tired. "We've spent a great deal of time arguing about things that really don't matter. You've received all the answers I can provide and yet still you seem very upset. I can't make you understand things you aren't willing to grasp, but that's OK. Human beings tend to be like that, it's how I made you—for better or worse. But there is one thing I would like to uphold."

"I bet there is."

The man continued on like I had said nothing. "Like I stated, I hold no malice over you. You took something from me, you were punished for it, and now I extend my offer to you one last time. Would you like to return your family?"

"Now that my slate has been wiped clean?" I spat. "Are you sure I've suffered enough? Or maybe you'll send me back for a couple years because you don't like my attitude."

"That fire in your heart is both your greatest and weakest trait, son," the man said, "but it is not something I have the energy to combat anymore. Now, would you like to go back?"

My hands curled into fists. "Not without that little girl. Not without Emily."

"Such stubbornness," the man said wearily. "Such unbelievable stubbornness." He packed his pipe and struck another match before continuing. "What is it about that girl that you cling to so desperately?"

"She's innocent," I spat. "I shouldn't have to keep spelling it out for you."

"Innocent," the man mused quietly. "Is that really it? Or do you see her as some kind of affirmation for something you desire? A pardon from the nightmares that plague you?"

"You don't know what you're talking about."

"You can't take something out of darkness and expect it to heal your own," the man muttered.

"I'm not here to argue with you," I said, standing my ground. "I'm here to tell you she's gotta go back with me."

The man sighed. "Listen, son. Such requests can't just be thrown around like they are nothing. There is serious weight to what you ask."

"Figure it out, then," I retorted, "but that girl has her whole life ahead of her and she deserves a shot at it. She made a mistake without evening knowing. So make it right."

"Action and consequence, Nick. I can't just do something like that."

"You can and you will," I said, advancing, "if you're half of what you say you are, then you'll do it. Not for me, but for what you're supposed to stand for."

The man sucked his pipe slowly. "There are scales that need to remain balanced. You don't know what you're asking."

"It seems to me that I do," I growled. "Return her back to her life Anything is better than the Farm. Give her a chance to actually live. You know this isn't where she belongs. Have some goddamn compassion."

"And what about you, Nick?" the man asked.

"What about me?"

"You maimed one of my angels."

"Ramiel?" I asked incredulously. "He had it coming. He'll be fine. He's alive, isn't he?"

The man rocked in his chair. "Such a glaring double standard. Such hurt Someone has to atone for that hurt."

"Are you going to do what I ask, or what?" I said, glazing him over.

The man continued to rock for a moment before answering, his voice quiet. "I suppose I could...arrange something."

"For Emily?"

I could feel him staring directly at me with his one good eye. "Yes... for Emily."

I paused, realizing we were nearing the end of our conversation. "Then we have a deal? You'll send us both back?"

"Yes, son. I'll send you both back. On one condition."

"And what would that be?"

The man stood up, surprising me, his form taller than I had first thought. He leaned toward me, his pipe jutting from between his lips.

"Action has *consequences.*"

I kept my face neutral, his looming figure sparking the air with unseen energy.

"Whatever you say," I answered quietly.

"Are you ready to return, then?" the man asked, extending a hand.

I reached out for it. "I've been gone too long as it is."

The man nodded and his tone turned somber and ominous. "You have indeed."

And then our hands met and something jolted through me, a pain so intense I thought I would erupt. It felt as if fire were crawling through my veins, evaporating and charring me from the inside out. I opened my mouth to scream but found that I couldn't, the intense heat fracturing my face and splitting it apart. Pieces of myself fell away, exposing burnt, scarred darkness underneath, the flesh cracking like a dehydrated wasteland.

A voice filled my head seconds before everything went dark.

"Hell is never far off, Nick."

And then I was gone.

Chapter 17

elt as if I were falling through a river of molten lava, the world a suffocat-ng vortex of empty darkness. I gasped as I flew, panting, sweating, feeling skin flake off my arms like sheets of burnt paper. Wind roared past my s, deafening me and I was overwhelmed with a nauseating sense of ver-. With no clue as to what was happening, I could only pray for the pain top, everything flowing past me like a midnight tunnel.

My head thundered and my chest blazed with each beat of my heart. uldn't see my body, but I felt it sloughing away from my bones and the een image was so horrific I wished for the strength to scream and never .

My shoulder slammed into something hard, and stars exploded before eyes. The rest of my body came next and I felt as if every bone in my ly shattered in that moment. My back arched in agony and a shuddering finally escaped my lips, my vision swimming. I could hear voices, noises, ething mechanical grinding in the background. I tried to blink away pain, but my eyelids blew away to ash as the inferno continued to rage de of me.

And then it was gone. All of it, vanishing in a second. It was so sudden t I cried out, the shift catching me by surprise, racing out of me like a ease. The pain was gone, the fire dissipated, and all sound faded and bled the gentle chirp of night crickets.

I reached hesitantly for sensation and found it innocently waiting
me. I inhaled through my nose and breathed in earth and air instead of
and ash. I gingerly extended my tongue and ran it across my lips, find
them intact. I took another couple of deep breaths to center myself, realiz
that I was lying on my back. Grass tickled my neck and prickled along
arms.

Finally, I opened my eyes. A canvas of stars painted the roof of the
twinkling down at me with all the beauty of the cosmos behind them
gasped then, a long shuddering release that came without warning.

Did I make it back?

The crickets answered me and a breeze swept through the grass, fill
my head with life and hope. Slowly, I sat up and was surprised when I
no pain. I was overcome with dizziness and for a second I feared that all
was nothing more than a mirage, daring me to believe in it. But my h
cleared and everything remained.

I looked around and saw that I was sitting in a grassy field with a r
cutting through the center and winding into a distant grove of trees. Th
were no cars, no lights, nothing but the calm wind and the chuckling gr
As the darkness softened and my eyes adjusted, I spotted something ah
of me, forming out of the shadows.

It was my house.

My chest hitched as familiarity swept through me, a disbelieving bu
of joy bubbling up in my chest as my eyes settled on the dark windo
Everything I had fought to return to was waiting for me right there.

I scrambled to my feet, a needful urgency filling my lungs. I ran acr
the grassy field and crossed the road, each step bringing with it painful des

Can this be real?

I stumbled up the driveway and climbed the front steps, feeling lik
had been a lifetime since I had last done so. I tried the doorknob and fou
it was locked. Where was Jess? I craned my head back and absorbed
night sky. What time was it? How long had I been out? Questions floo
my mind, too many to answer. I raised my fist and hammered on the do
An energetic desperation took hold of me as I waited. The wind trave
across my face carrying with it the sweetest scents I had ever breathed.

I knocked again, harder, and this time a light came on from inside.

"It's me!" I yelled, voice cracking. "It's Nick! I'm back! Open the door, please!"

Suddenly, my whole body bent over double as pain coursed through me so intensely that I could only gasp and clutch my chest. It was as if a pillar of fire had been crammed down my throat, splitting me in two. My skin ignited with unseen flame, like I had been doused in gasoline and set ablaze. My eyes watered from the horrible sensation, but the feeling evaporated a split second before I released a scream. I stood on the front stoop with my hands on my knees, panting, trying to calm myself from the unexpected onslaught. I could feel my heart beating against my ribs, and a hot sweat stood out on my forehead.

What the hell was that?

Before I could even comprehend what had happened, I heard someone turn the deadbolt from inside. I stood up straight, wiping my face, fingers tingling.

The door was pulled open and a very tired man stood before me. He was about my age, wearing boxers and a T-shirt, his hair matted on one side and sticking up in the back. He addressed me with the tone of a man who had little patience to spare.

"What is it? Who are you? What do you want? And what the *hell* are you doing pounding on my door this late at night?" he asked, rubbing the sleep from his eyes.

I just stared at him, openly confused, a horrible sinking feeling sweeping through me. I cleared my throat, the burning sensation clinging to me like a shadow.

"W-what are you doing in my house?" I stuttered.

The man seemed to wake up quickly, sensing that maybe he shouldn't have been so quick to open the door.

"Your house? I've lived here my whole life, I don't know what you're talking about. And I don't appreciate you waking me and my wife up. Do you even know what time it is?"

"No, this is some kind of mistake," I stuttered, feeling more and more desperate.

The man shook his head. "I'm not really the cop-calling type, but I won't hesitate if you start getting crazy on me, OK?" He squinted at me in the darkness. "Say, are you all right?"

I took a step away from him, my heart sinking all the way down into the pit of my soul. "Something...something's not right..."

The man pulled the door open a little more and I saw his expression change as something overcame him. Brow furrowed, he turned and flicked the outside light on, blinding me for a second. I lowered my hand to the glare and when our eyes met again, I saw his face go white.

He stepped out toward me, his voice suddenly hoarse and trembling and overflowing with emotion. "Oh my god...Dad?"

The word exploded over me like a bomb, the detonation taking me full in the chest, the debris falling all around me. The air left my lungs and my throat tightened, one hand fumbling for the railing so I wouldn't fall to my knees.

The man stepped out onto the stoop with me and the light washed over his face, his features so much older and sharper than when I had left him.

"Theo?" I croaked, tears budding in my eyes. "Jesus Christ...is that you?"

The man nodded slowly, his eyes wide with disbelief, shock rolling over him in waves. "W-what...how..." He took a step toward me, hand outstretched toward my face. "H-how? How are you?"

A sob escaped me, mind reeling, but I plowed through the confusion and embraced my son in a hug that could never last long enough. I buried my face in his shoulder, feeling him tense and then relax, his arms slowly wrapping around me in a cautious hug.

When I pulled away, I found that I was crying and I quickly wiped the tears away. I stared into Theo's face, now decades older than when I had left him. I could see the little boy still in there, twinkling behind his eyes.

"Where's your mom?" I asked weakly, feeling like I might pass out at any moment. "Where's Jess?"

Theo continued to look at me with absolute disbelief, his face torn between confusion and unease. He cleared his throat and ran his tongue along his bottom lip.

"How are you here?" he finally asked when he found his voice. "How the
ell are you here? What is going on?"

I shook my head, releasing a gasp of air that acknowledged how insane
his all was. I felt my eyes water up again and tried my best to blink it away.

"I don't know how to explain this," I said, the wind whipping between
s. "I don't know how much time has passed since I left or why it's passed
t all...but...but I'm back now and we'll figure it out, OK? We'll figure it
ut together."

"Dad," Theo said, and I could see the madness of the situation written
cross his face.

"I'll explain everything as best I can," I assured him, half-choking, half-
miling. "I promise I will. But I need to see Mom, OK? She'll understand,
he'll help make sense of all this."

Theo's face twisted with something that horrified me, and then he
pened his mouth and said the words I never wished to hear. "Mom's dead."

The night seemed to close in around me and fill my head. A feeling so
errible rose up in my chest that I thought I would evaporate from existence
n that very moment. It was worse than any physical injury I had ever en-
ured, more painful than every nightmare I had ever suffered. It was a pain
o big and so real and so present that I completely forgot everything in the
ntire world and sank to my knees.

Theo placed a hand on my shoulder, eyes sorrowful. "I'm so sorry, Dad.
he passed away three years ago."

"How?" I whispered so silently I was surprised the wind didn't snatch
he word away.

"The doctors don't really know...she just...they told me that she just
idn't have anything left," Theo said softly. "It broke my heart."

I stared off into the distance, my vision blurred and unseeing. I felt like
couldn't breathe. It felt as if the earth would open up and pull me down
nto the darkness where I belonged, left for eternity to grasp this emptiness.

"I'm sorry, Dad," Theo said, "and I'd love to give you more time to digest
his, but I really need to know what is going on and how you're here. I need
o know how we look the same age and where you've been."

The questions seemed impossible for me to answer, the mountain o loss avalanching down over me, crushing my heart with all the weight of th world behind it.

Gone...my sweet Jess...

I clenched my teeth and let out a long, rattling sob, pressing my hand against my eyes as I released a river of sorrow. I felt Theo hold me awkwardl as my shoulders shook, wave after wave hitting me, the agony of loss takin over.

You left her and now she's gone.

I cried and wept until I didn't have the energy to release another rattlin sob. My face was wet as I wiped my nose, still kneeling in the night. I fel Theo above me, my body half-leaning against his legs, his hands a comfort ing weight on my shoulders.

"I'm really sorry," he said, more to fill the silence than to ease my pair "She was a good woman."

I pulled myself to my feet, feeling dizzy and sick and tremendously nau seous. I ran my arm over my eyes and forced myself to take a long, steady ing breath. I was suddenly more exhausted than I had ever been before, fatigue taking me so swiftly that I almost collapsed where I stood. The quickly reached out and steadied me before I could fall, his face a novel o uncertainty.

"Why don't we get you inside?" he said gently. "I have no idea how an of this is possible, but if there's one thing Mom drilled into my head...it wa you. Everything about you. Pictures, stories, the whole bit. So come on, let get you indoors."

I let myself be led through the front door, legs feeling like taffy. The put an arm around my shoulders and together we went into the living roon where I slumped down onto the couch. I felt like I was dreaming, like m body was floating high above the world, waiting to plummet back down.

Theo grabbed a blanket and pulled it over me, busying himself so that h wouldn't have to confront the paradox sitting in his living room. I watche as he went to the kitchen to get me a glass of water, hurrying back like m life depended on it. I took the glass numbly and took an obligatory sip befor setting it down on the coffee table. Theo just stood to the side, watching m as if he were waiting for me to disappear in a poof of confetti.

"Theo? What's going on?"

Both of us turned toward the hallway, the voice announcing the new-comer with the same sleepiness that Theo had greeted me with. A woman came around the corner, rubbing her eyes to stare at the stranger on her couch.

"Oh, hon, um...this man—" Theo stumbled going to her, but stopped when he saw her face. "What's wrong, babe?"

My eyes met the woman's and I saw her face ripple with terror so real I thought she would scream. She clutched her husband's arm, knuckles white, her lips coming together so tightly her mouth almost vanished.

"How?" she whispered, her eyes still locked with mine.

And then I saw.

"Emily?" I whispered, the blood draining from my cheeks.

She took a slow step back, shaking her head, horror rising in her eyes. "No...no, you're not real. You don't exist. You can't exist. None of that was real."

Theo looked helplessly between us. "Do you two...know each other? Have you met? What on earth is going on?!"

I stood slowly, fresh tears springing from my eyes as I took Emily in, now twenty years older than when I had last seen her on the Farm.

"You made it...oh my god, you made it back," I choked after fighting for my voice, unable to stop myself from crying once again.

Emily clutched her head like she was in pain, her face melting with distress. "It was a nightmare...none of it was real...you're not real...YOU'RE NOT REAL!" she screamed suddenly, huddling into herself. Theo grabbed her and hugged her to himself, desperately trying to hang on to his own sanity.

I stood helplessly in my son's living room, tears pouring down my face. "I'm so sorry, little one. I'm so *so* sorry." I wiped my eyes with the back of my hand, sniffling.

"Get out of my house! GET OUT AND NEVER COME BACK!" Emily shrieked, thrashing in Theo's arms.

I looked at Theo, frozen in place and unsure what to do. My heart was racing and my mind thundered with the impossibilities before me. Emily was staring at me like I was something that had walked out of her nightmares, her eyes huge and full of things long forgotten.

"GET OUT!" she screamed again, lurching in Theo's arms.

"I'm sorry," I stuttered again, stumbling toward the door, feeling like the floor was disintegrating. I reached the front door and realized that I was panicking, my breath coming in harsh pulls. I looked back at Theo. "I-I didn't mean to upset her...I just—"

"OUTTTTT!"

I tripped out the door and almost fell down the stairs, catching mysel a moment before face-planting. Tears stained my cheeks and blurred my vi sion as I raced down the driveway, teeth clenched to contain a sob.

This is wrong, everything is wrong, it wasn't supposed to be like this.

I reached the edge of the driveway and suddenly gasped, hand clutch ing my chest as a bolt of fire ignited inside of me. I let out an agonized his and dropped to my knees as every nerve in my body roared with the unsee inferno. My vision blurred and I felt a scream crawl up my throat as the hea ate me alive from the inside.

I heard Theo calling to me from somewhere, but I couldn't seem to fo cus on anything but the darkness in the corners of my eyes.

Just when I thought I couldn't take the pain another moment, ever thing vanished and I slumped to the ground, blacking out.

* * *

Something cool spread across my forehead. I wasn't aware of it at fir my mind slowly wading back from the dark tide that had swept it away. B as the sensation grew, so did my consciousness. The relief the damp cc offered me was overwhelmingly welcome, the embers of the heat hidd behind my last memory.

I became aware that I was lying on my back and that someone v touching my shoulder. The coolness was removed for a moment, only return with renewed vigor. I sighed from the void and tried to pull mys from the emptiness behind my eyes.

"Dad?"

The word was like a life raft, one that I grabbed onto with desperati feeling it zip me away from the inky waters of my pain and pull me back consciousness.

I opened my eyes and saw that I was back in the living room, resting on the couch with Theo kneeling next to me. He pulled a damp rag off my forehead and stared down at me, his face filled with cautious concern.

"You back with us?" he asked.

I touched my head and winced, nodding. "Yeah. I think I'm OK now."

"You sure? I thought you were having a heart attack."

I looked around the room. "Where's Emily?"

Theo bit his lip. "In the bedroom."

"Is she—"

"She's fine. She's calmed down, some. She just needs some space."

I saw through the big bay window that the sky was starting to bruise. "What time is it? How long was I out?"

"It's almost dawn. You were out for a couple hours. I wasn't sure if I should call an ambulance or not, but after I saw you were breathing, I figured you just needed some rest. You look exhausted."

I closed my eyes and ran a rugged hand down my face, exhaling heavily. "Look, Theo…"

"You don't have to talk about it right now if you don't want to. In fact, maybe it's better if you don't. I think you should sleep, at least for a little while longer. You really don't look so hot."

I shook my head stubbornly, forcing myself to sit up. Theo's hands went out to help steady me and in that moment, I loved him more than I ever had. I took his hands in mine and looked him in the eye.

"I can't thank you enough for your kindness, son. I know you must be going mad with questions right now, and I want to answer some of them for you. As many as I can. But I need you to know right up front, that I won't be able to answer all of them. Do you understand?"

He nodded, his eyes floating in his head. "All right...just...answer one for me, first."

"What is it?"

"You're really here right now...right?"

I smiled sadly and squeezed his hands. "I'm here. I know you probably don't remember much about me—"

"I remember a little. Just images mostly," Theo said. "I'm not quite sure if they're my actual memories or if they're something I constructed over the years from all the pictures Mom used to show me of you. And the stories. God, she loved to tell stories."

"What kind of stories?" I asked, feeling my heart soften.

Theo shrugged. "I don't know. Good stories. Stories about you two laughing."

I felt my chest swell and had to fight against a sudden rise of sorrow. "That's good," I said quietly. "That's good she told you about that."

"She really loved you, you know."

I turned away and had to clench my teeth, fighting as best as I could.

"Dad?"

I squashed moisture from my eyes, my voice a whisper. "*Goddamn*it…"

It was Theo's turn to squeeze my hands. "What *happened* to you? Where did you go?"

I looked back at my son and for a second I was overwhelmed with the urge to tell him everything. Absolutely everything. From the first suicide all the way to the present day. I wanted to tell him about the Black Farm, the Pig, about Danny and the Suicidals. But as I looked into his eyes, I knew that I could never.

"That's...that's one of the questions I don't think I can answer," I finally said softly. "But...I can tell you this. I left all those years ago to protect you and your Mom. I went off and did something for someone so that you and her wouldn't be hurt. I didn't do it because I wanted to, I did it to keep you two safe, because there is nothing in the world more important to me than that. Nothing at all. I know you don't really know me, but son...I have gone to hell and back for you and Jess—for Mom. And I would do it again if I had to. I need you to believe that, I really really need you to—" I trailed off, my voice shaking and my vision blurring.

Theo let go of my hand and touched my arm. "OK, Dad. I believe you it's OK. I believe you."

I just stared into his eyes, tears running down my cheeks. He looked so *goddamn* grown up and I felt myself hitch a sob.

"I'm sorry I had to leave you," I finally cried, covering my face with my hands. "I'm so fucking sorry, son." My shoulders were shaking now. "I wasn't supposed to be gone for so *long*."

Theo shifted and sat down next to me and slid his arm around my shoulders, his voice gentle."It's OK, Dad. I'm not mad at you. I was never mad at you. I knew something happened back when I was a baby, something terrible. I had questions back then about where and who you were, but Mom was always extremely quick to assure me you were a good, honest man. She never spoke poorly of you and that kind of rubbed off on me. You were like this mysterious icon in my life. And it's stupid, but I kind of always guessed that one day you'd come back and I'd get to meet you. That I'd get to see who this guy was that Mom looked up to so much."

I looked at him with open innocence, a weak smile trembling on my lips. "Sorry to disappoint you."

Theo grinned and for a moment I saw the little kid in the high chair with spaghetti on his face.

"Well, unless you're planning on leaving again, I would say we have some time to figure each other out."

"I'm not going anywhere," I assured. "Never again. I promise. I did what I had to do and it's over now. It's done."

Theo slid his arm away and shifted on the couch, his face turning somber all of a sudden. "There is something I need to ask you," he chewed his lip for a moment before continuing, "and I need you to actually answer it."

"What is it?"

He pointed out of the room and down the hall. "It's about Emily. We've only been married for a year now and I love that woman with everything I got. Seeing her in such a state of distress really put me off to you for a second, but once she calmed down she told me to come in here and talk to you. You'll get your chance to talk to her as well, but right now I need to know something." He paused and collected himself before continuing. "Have the two of you met before and did you do something to hurt her in the past? Because to me it seems like...like somehow there's a history there, though I don't see how that's possible considering you don't look a day older than me."

I held his eyes for a long time, fighting for an answer to offer. I gripped the fabric of the couch as I struggled to construct the words. After a couple drawn-out seconds, I took a deep breath.

"We've met," I said quietly, "but she was much younger. It's been a long, long time for her. Has she ever talked to you about...I don't know...about nightmares she used to have as a kid or something like that?"

Theo was watching me very carefully. "Yeah. She told me when she was little that she used to have this recurring dream that really messed her up. At least she thought it was a dream. But it was so vivid that she had to get help, therapy and medication, later in life. Her mom was a single parent and not a very good one at that. She's dead now and I don't think Emily misses her much. When I met Emily two years ago, she was much better than she used to be. At least, that's what she told me. She still has dreams every now and again, but she's OK. She's moved on and dealt with whatever those bad memories or nightmares were." Theo stared hard at me. "But I think seeing you somehow brought all that back up again. I think that's why she freaked out when she saw you and I need to ask you something that is going to determine how we deal with all of this going forward." His voice turned hard, but not cruel. "Did you do something to her?"

I shook my head, feeling my thoughts cloud "No...no I would never do something to hurt that girl."

"Then what the hell happened?" Theo pressed. "You gotta give me something."

She woke up from the Black Farm as if she had fed the Pig and returned to herself back here. I bargained for her innocence and in exchange, I think I lost a whole lot of years.

I twisted where I sat, knowing I could never say those words. I closed my eyes and tried to gather my thoughts, each one fraying out in a different direction. There was so much I couldn't explain, so much I couldn't say. It had only been a couple hours since I had stood on that mountain over the golden lake, and yet time here had marched on without me.

Action and consequence.

Yes, but Emily was returned and able to live out her life. You did what you set out to do. She's safe and your family was saved from that horrific future. They lived a life without you, but at least they lived.

I opened my eyes and stared out the window, up at the sky.

Bastard. Fucking bastard.

"Hey, you still here?"

I turned away from the window and back to my son. "I died, Theo. I died for a long time and somehow I'm back as if I had never died at all. I know that sounds like lunacy, but you deserve the same honesty you've given me. I don't expect you to understand it—hell, I barely do—but it's the truth. It's why I look like this, why we appear to be the same age. When I left all those ears ago," I slowed, careful now, "I saved Emily from something terrible. I von't speak of it out of respect for your wife, but I understand why my presnce would upset her. I don't want to stir any of that up, especially since she's ought so hard to forget it." I looked down at my hands, choosing my words arefully. "After I...saved her...I died for a long time. And somehow I'm back. ack like no time has passed at all." I looked at him, praying to see some rm of acceptance. "Look, Theo..."

He stopped me, one hand raised. "Are you telling the truth?"

I blinked. "What?"

"Are you telling me the absolute truth?"

I nodded, helplessly. "Yes."

His face softened. "Then I believe you."

My eyes watered suddenly. "How?"

Theo stood up. "Because Mom believed in you."

Tears filled my sight and I fought to keep control of myself. "You're a tter son than I deserve, Theo." I looked up at him, wiping my eyes. "I really sh I could have been here to see you grow up. I wish I could have been here raise you with Mom. There's so much I missed out on...so much I wish I uld have shared with you..."

Theo squatted down and took my hands in his once more, his voice ntle. "But Dad...you saved Emily for me, right?"

I looked up at him, crying, my face helplessly desperate. "W-what?"

"You saved Emily and kept us safe from something bad, right?"

I just nodded, miserably, choking down a sob.

Theo smiled warmly. "Then don't you see? You've already given everything."

I hugged him then and cried for everything I had lost.

Chapter 18

I sat in the back seat of Theo's car, watching the world blur past the windows. It had moved on without me, an advancement that would take time to understand, but none of that concerned me now.

Emily sat up front with Theo, her eyes strategically avoiding mine. She hadn't said a word to me yet, but I knew there was a conversation to be had there. I wasn't in any rush to have it.

After talking to Theo, I had rested the remainder of the day. Theo had taken me into the guest bedroom where I had slept all the way through the night. When I had woken up, I had smelled breakfast cooking. I got up and ate at the table with my son, speaking gingerly and carefully to him. It wasn't just me who had been drained from the day before. As we ate, Emily had silently busied herself around the kitchen. I could tell she had spoken in depth to Theo and some kind of peace had been made, but even so, she avoided looking at me.

When we were finished with breakfast, Theo gently came to my side.

"Would you like to see where Mom is buried?"

And now I sat in the back seat, staring out the window, wrestling with memories and regret and longing. Emily had surprised me by coming along, sliding silently into the front seat next to her husband.

None of us spoke as we made the short journey to the graveyard, the sun spilling morning light across the windows. I stared up at it, closing my eyes and absorbing the warmth, forehead pressed against the glass. There were so many things to figure out still, so many questions that needed answering, but in that moment, all I could focus on was the way the sun felt on my face.

When we reached the cemetery, we got out and Theo pointed across the manicured grass toward a distance gravestone.

"She's right over there," he informed me quietly. "Do you need some time alone with her?"

I felt a bubbling in my chest, a rise of sorrow that I couldn't handle alone. I looked at my son, my voice thin.

"Come with me?"

He smiled and nodded and Emily watched us from where she remained by the car. Her face was tight and pale, but she no longer looked frightened. That was good.

Theo crossed the distance with me and when we reached my wife's gravestone, I felt the inevitable tears begin to form. Theo held my arm and allowed me to cry in silence, an understanding passing between us that I didn't have the words to appreciate.

As I stared down at where Jess had been laid to rest, my eyes shifted over to the gravestone next to hers.

It was my own.

Theo squeezed my arm when he saw me take notice. "I figured it was only right that you two lay next to one another."

The sight of my name written across the gravestone burned itself into my head, a horrible, confusing reality that I couldn't comprehend.

"Mom used to take me here all the time when I was little," Theo continued. "This is where she'd tell me most of the stories about you." He smiled and glanced at me. "She cried, too."

I smiled back, but it was twisted with sadness.

She believed in you until the bitter end.

Theo reached into his pocket and handed me something then. "Here She wanted you to have this."

It was a sealed envelope.

I took it, heart burning. "What is this?"

Theo shrugged. "I don't know, I didn't open it. She gave it to me on he deathbed. She told me that if you ever came back that I was to give it t you. I didn't really know what she was talking about, or how that was eve possible, but I took it just the same." He paused. "I never thought I'd actually get the chance to give it to you." He stared down at my gravestone, his face impassive.

My eyes were glued to the envelope in my hand and I felt my heart racing. Theo looked at me and then touched a hand to the center of my back.

"I'll give you some privacy."

I heard him retreat, the world fading with him.

Without warning, my chest erupted in pain. I let out a surprised gasp and gritted my teeth against a sudden pillar of fire that rocketed through me. I slammed teeth together, trying to contain a scream. It felt as if I were being cooked, my skin roaring with invisible flame. I bent over double, feeling as if I might pass out, my vision shaking.

It vanished almost as quickly as it had come, allowing me a shuddering pull of air as I righted myself, sweat standing out on my brow. Before I had any longer to recover, I felt a hand touch my arm and was surprised to see Emily looking at me with concern.

"You all right?"

I swallowed hard and nodded. "It's nothing. I'm OK, thank you."

She continued to stare at me, her eyes familiar behind her age. "You sure, Nick?"

The way she said my name made me pause. I looked at her and saw a gentleness that I didn't expect.

"I'll live," I said, wiping a trickle of sweat from my forehead.

She kept her hand on my arm, speaking quietly. "That pain...what is it? What's it from?"

Consequence.

I chanced a glance at her. "I don't exactly know." I looked at the gravestones around us. "I think I'm being punished for something."

She surveyed the cemetery with me. "Does that something have to do with me?"

I said nothing, keeping my face as neutral as I could.

"I remember you, Nick."

This time I did look at her, studying her face.

Her hands knotted together. "I don't want to...but I remember. Most of it, anyway."

"Does Theo—"

"I haven't told him anything. How could I?"

I nodded.

"He's a good man, Nick," she said softly. "It was easy to fall in love with him. He's a wonderful husband, better than I deserve most of the time."

I smiled at that, but it hurt. "Emily…"

She cleared her throat, struggling. "That pain that you feel...it comes from that place, doesn't it?"

Slowly, I nodded.

"Does it mean you're going back one day?"

"No," I said gently. "I'm done with that place. What I carry with me now...I think it's a scar, a punishment for what I did right before I left."

"What did you do?"

I looked down at Jess's gravestone. "I hurt someone. Badly."

"Did they deserve it?"

"I don't know," I said distantly, "but I had to do it in order to save you. To get you out of there. To get some answers."

"Who were they?"

The memory blew through me like a stale breeze. "His name was Ramiel. I don't know how much he was to blame in all of it, but he was the only way to you. To pardon you from that place."

Emily's hand found my arm again. "Nick…"

I faced her and found her eyes were soft.

"Thank you. For what you did."

I offered her a weak smile and looked away, back down at the pair of gravestones. She followed my gaze.

"Do you think you're buried down there somewhere?" she asked after a moment.

"I honestly don't want to know."

She simply nodded and then patted my arm. "I'm going to go find my husband. Take as much time as you need, Nick. We'll be here."

She walked away, leaving me in silence. I felt a weight in my chest as looked down and realized I was still holding the unopened envelope.

I turned it over in my hands and found they were shaking. Slowly, I tore t open and pulled out a very old and crumpled piece of paper. When I realzed what it was, I felt myself melt.

It was the note I had left Jess before I killed myself. She had kept it all hese years, holding it close like a final memory. The thought was almost too nuch to bear, and I felt sorrow crawl up my throat and fill my head. I wiped ny eyes and stared down at it, the words all too familiar.

My sweet Jess,

I have to leave you and Theo for a while. I don't have time to explain it all you and even if I did, I don't know if I could bear the way you'd look at me. omething bad is going to happen if I don't go back to that place. The place we've orked so hard to forget. I love you to the moon and back, baby. Please don't cry. lease. Just wait for me. I'll be back soon, I promise. Give Theo a kiss for me. And hile you're at it, keep one for yourself. See you soon.

I was openly crying by the time I finished it, my heart breaking. As I ared down at the note, feeling more alone than I ever had before, I saw at something was scribbled at the bottom. I wiped my eyes and brought e paper back up, heart beating so fast I thought it would explode from my est. I knew the handwriting all too well. Jess.

Wherever you are, I hope you'll find me again, my love. And know that wherer I am, my heart remains with you.

I read it three times before I finally sank to my knees and covered my e with my hands. My shoulders rocked with grief, and tears rolled down cheeks.

I took a long, shuddering breath and turned my face to the sun.

I missed my wife.

THE END

ELIAS WITHEROW lives in New England and can usually be found mu tering to himself and staring blankly out a window. Having written ov sixty short stories and five novels, Elias hopes to continue to provide ho rific entertainment to his readers.

Twitter: @EliasWitherow
facebook.com/FeedThePig
www.reddit.com/r/feedthepig

THOUGHT
CATALOG
Books

Thought Catalog Books is a publishing imprint of Thought Catalog, a digital magazine for thoughtful storytelling. Thought Catalog is owned by The Thought & Expression Company, an independent media group based in Brooklyn, NY which also owns and operates Shop Catalog, a curated shopping experience featuring our best-selling books and one-of-a-kind products, and Collective World, a global creative community network. Founded in 2010, we are committed to helping people become better communicators and listeners to engender a more exciting, attentive, and imaginative world. As a publisher and media platform, we help creatives all over the world realize their artistic vision and share it in print and digital form with audiences across the globe.

MORE FROM THOUGHT CATALOG BOOKS

The Black Farm
—Elias Witherow

The Worst In Us
—Elias Witherow

The Third Parent
—Elias Witherow

Before The Farmhouse Burned Down
—Holly Riordan

THOUGHTCATALOG.COM
NEW YORK • LOS ANGELES

Made in the USA
Las Vegas, NV
05 February 2025